IN NEED OF SOME PERSUASION

Bone looked up at me and sneered. The man appeared absolutely certain of his position. "Well, you'll have to kill me in cold blood, boy, 'cause I ain't about to fight you."

Shot him in the left elbow. Must've hurt like the dickens. He fell out of his chair, and flopped around on the porch like a beached fish. Squalled and bellowed so loud, I was afraid some of them cowboys out on the range might hear him. Got tired of listening, after a minute or two. Grabbed him by the collar, stood him next to a porch pillar, and stuffed his pistol back into its holster. Backed off about four steps and let him know how the cow ate the cabbage.

"Here's how this dance works, Bone. You'll draw that pistol, and I'll kill you. Or, you can stand there, all weepy and red-eyed, not do anything to protect yourself, and I'll kill you. However you want to do the deed's fine with me . . ."

A BAD DAY
TO DIE

THE ADVENTURES OF LUCIUS
"BY GOD" DODGE, TEXAS RANGER

J. LEE BUTTS

BERKLEY BOOKS, NEW YORK

THE BERKLEY PUBLISHING GROUP
Published by the Penguin Group
Penguin Group (USA) Inc.
375 Hudson Street, New York, New York 10014, USA
Penguin Group (Canada), 10 Alcorn Avenue, Toronto, Ontario M4V 3B2, Canada
(a division of Pearson Penguin Canada Inc.)
Penguin Books Ltd., 80 Strand, London WC2R 0RL, England
Penguin Group Ireland, 25 St. Stephen's Green, Dublin 2, Ireland (a division of Penguin Books Ltd.)
Penguin Group (Australia), 250 Camberwell Road, Camberwell, Victoria 3124, Australia
(a division of Pearson Australia Group Pty. Ltd.)
Penguin Books India Pvt. Ltd., 11 Community Centre, Panchsheel Park, New Delhi—110 017, India
Penguin Group (NZ), Cnr. Airborne and Rosedale Roads, Albany, Auckland 1310, New Zealand
(a division of Pearson New Zealand Ltd.)
Penguin Books (South Africa) (Pty.) Ltd., 24 Sturdee Avenue, Rosebank, Johannesburg 2196,
South Africa

Penguin Books Ltd., Registered Offices: 80 Strand, London WC2R 0RL, England

This is a work of fiction. Names, characters, places, and incidents either are the product of the author's imagination or are used fictitiously, and any resemblance to actual persons, living or dead, business establishments, events, or locales is entirely coincidental.

A BAD DAY TO DIE

A Berkley Book / published by arrangement with the author

PRINTING HISTORY
Berkley edition / November 2004

ISBN: 0-425-19915-0

BERKLEY®
Berkley Books are published by The Berkley Publishing Group,
a division of Penguin Group (USA) Inc.,
375 Hudson Street, New York, New York 10014.
BERKLEY is a registered trademark of Penguin Group (USA) Inc.
The "B" design is a trademark belonging to Penguin Group (USA) Inc.

PRINTED IN THE UNITED STATES OF AMERICA

10 9 8 7 6 5 4 3 2 1

For Carol
She's still with me this deep into the game.

AND

Ole Texas Cowboy Neil Ross
He personally handed me the basic ideas used
in the story you're about to read.

ACKNOWLEDGMENTS

Continued thanks and appreciation to Michael and Barbara Rosenberg for their efforts on my behalf. Special expressions of gratitude, once again, to Kimberly Lionetti for her invaluable help and understanding. A big tip of the sombrero, and deep bow from the waist, goes to the membership of the DFW Writer's Workshop for a weekly dose of reality. And finally, a number-10 washtub of appreciation wings its way to Roxanne Blackwell Bosserman in Shreveport, Louisiana—a cheerleader the likes of whom every writer should have.

Vengeance is mine: I will repay, saith the Lord

—Romans 12:19

All existing civilized communities appear to have gone through a stage in which it was impossible to say where private vengeance for injuries ended and public retribution for offenses began. . . .

—SIR FREDERICK POLLOCK,
from *The King's Peace in
the Middle Ages*

The country around the hamlet of Sweetwater is under a perfect rein of terror from a family of desperate characters and thieves, named Nightshade, who infest the entire area. It is a sparsely settled region, and the opportunity for unlawful behavior is presently unfettered. I believe Boz Tatum and Lucius Dodge should easily remedy the wicked state of affairs.

—CAPTAIN WAG CULPEPPER,
in dispatches to his
Austin-based superiors

PROLOGUE

*Lucius Dodge's Sulphur River ranch
near Domino, Texas, October 1948*

Little over a week ago my old friend Hayden Tilden hoisted his ancient bones aboard the Texas Flyer and rode her down from Little Rock for a visit. He'd been out here in the mosquito and tick-infested boonies a couple of days, slapping and scratching, when—late one cool damp evening—we wallowed out individual spots in the overstuffed chairs I keep on my back porch. Stoked up the tin stove till she glowed, cracked the seal on a jug of mighty fine Kentucky sour mash, and us two decrepit, broke-down, old lawdogs spent the rest of the night slinging massive amounts of fully aged, manly bullshit around.

Whole jawbone session and square dance concerned evil men we'd chased, fought, or killed, and the occasional beautiful woman left behind, who waved good-bye and wept with regret. And, being as how there weren't no women in attendance that evening, our spur-of-the-moment prayer meeting turned out about the way you'd expect. Don't know 'bout you, but it's been my experience that when unsupervised old running buddies, who can chew off each other's plug anytime the urge hits them, sit down for a snort or three, well, Katie bar the door. The rough and ready profanity that escaped our whiskey-soaked mouths would have put plenty of snap in a spinster schoolmarm's garters.

Hell, we recollected a boatload of windy whizzers about our respective gunfights, fistfights, knife fights, ax fights, and horse fights. Spent damn near an hour just comparing bullet holes, knife wounds, and scars. Had a ton of fun going over the time the two of us blew the hell out of Martin Luther Big Eagle with Cletis Broadbent's Civil War-vintage cannon, *Beulah,* up in Red Rock Canyon.

'Bout halfway through our free-wheeling shindig, I managed to curry an oft-repeated tale from my nearly fossilized brain concerning a couple of drunken fellers, from over in the vicinity of Mineral Wells, who went at each other with red-hot horseshoe tongs. Worm-brained ignoramuses ended up setting one another on fire. We got a damned fine laugh out of that one. But Good Lord Almighty, I had a hell of a time cleaning that smoldering mess up. Swear before Jesus, there ain't much of anything worse than folks that have been burnt crispier than a piece of well-charred beefsteak.

Then, Tilden recounted my favorite chestnut about his best friend, wild-man Carlton J. Cecil. All about the time that hot-tempered rowdy whomped the hell out of a killer he'd just shot to death. Used the day-old corpse of a dog. Cain't beat memories like those, my friends.

Couple of times, we laughed so hard I thought my moth-eaten socks might pop right out of my mouth. Messed around, and got the old-man croup going once. My sidekick had to roust himself out of his lumpy lair and thump me on the back for almost a minute. Tilden slapped me a-twixt the shoulder blades about twenty times and kept yelping, "Come on, Dodge. Spit 'er up. Ain't gonna let you choke to death on memories."

Long about my fourth or fifth dipperful of hundred-and-ninety-proof spider killer, something my friend recalled brought home to me as how maybe some events might not have transpired exactly the way I always remembered. Or told them, when the golden opportunity presented me with an appreciative audience.

Gave the question about five seconds worth of serious thought. Then Hayden shook a jelly tumbler full of scamper juice my direction and said, "By God, even if things didn't happen the way we remember 'em, they should've. And think on this, Lucius. It don't really matter how anything we ever did actually came to pass anyway. All that matters is the way we tell it now. All them other folks are dead—good and bad. We're the living, by-God authorities on this stuff. We can say whatever in the blue-eyed hell we want. Besides, once you get as old as we are, people will believe anything you tell them. Amazing how gullible young folks are these days. Write it down, put it in a book, and, by God, they'll believe every word."

He lost the string on his thoughts there, for a bit, I guess. Scrunched up his eyebrows, sifted it all around in his brain again, then spit the end of a maduro panatela on the floor. Man looked like he'd been hit by lightning when he said, "Can you call to mind the time we met out on the Red River over near Coffee's Bend? You, me, Daniel Old Bear Westbrook, and my big yeller dog, Caesar, started out from there looking for Rufus Bloodsworth and Blackie Daggett."

Soon as the question passed his cracked purple lips, I realized my antique friend just might have retained about a handful more active brain cells than me. Ever so often, these days, I spend considerable time puzzling over things scattered amongst the cankered cogs of my rusted-up thinker mechanism. It's even got to the point where I might have to consider keeping my spectacles on a piece of string. Sometimes go a day, or two, wearing one boot because I can't find both of them.

Tried to put him off till the foggy past came hoofing back my way with, "Sweet Jesus, Hayden, that had to have been sometime back in the eighties. Good God Almighty, that's more'n sixty year ago. We was just a couple of hen-wrangling kids them days, and too damned green-assed stupid to know it." Scratched one of the three remaining hairs on my head and added, "Am I anywhere close on this thing, pardner?"

"Yeah, fall of '85, or maybe '86. She's a mite hard for me to summon up exactly which myself. Was somewhere in that general vicinity, though. Don't matter if the year's exactly dead-on. We're close enough for government work."

Sucked down another tongue-singing swallow of tonsil paint, and gandered at the sun's dying reflection in the river. Hesitated for about a minute before I offered up anything that resembled an honest-to-God, for-certain answer. Absolute truth be told, I wouldn't have known either one of those maggots he'd mentioned if they had popped up next to my red-hot stove and asked for a drag on our bottle.

"Blackie Bloodsworth and Rufus Daggett, huh?"

Tilden's head snapped back. He blew a gunmetal-colored smoke ring from the stump-black stogie he'd bought at my friend Cooley Churchpew's general mercantile, a few miles up the road, and huffed, "No, Lucius. *Rufus* Bloodsworth and *Blackie* Dagget. Hell's bells, surely you remember that pair of murderin' skunks. Don't you? Ain't no way you could have forgotten the trouble we had with that brace of night-crawling, three-tailed rattlers. You especially. Running gunfight, you boys ended it all with, turned me into nothing more'n an awe-struck spectator."

Well, friends, he didn't help me out a whole bunch. I fought so many horseback pistol duels in them days, I still couldn't sort that particular one out. Waved at him with my own see-gar like a sideshow magician, trying to make doves appear out of the tobacco-laden cloud hovering over the stove, and with the greatest of confidence said, "Oh, hell, yes. Remember them boys well. Rufus was that cold-eyed killer who robbed the Kay-Tee Flyer just outside McAlester, and killed a couple of freight handlers and a woman bystander in the process. Weren't he?"

Considerably more irritable when he snapped, "No, no, hell, no." He leaned over, and decorated my glowing wood burner with a gob of spit that sizzled and danced, then thumped ashes in the general direction of the coffee tin, next to his chair. Most of them landed on the floor beside the bit-off tip of his cigar.

He snatched at the collar of his jacket, and jerked himself around in the chair. "Jesus H. Christ on a crutch, Dodge. Don't tell me you're getting as forgetful as all the rest of my own personal crew of hundred-year-old gomers still gumming their lime Jell-o at the Rolling Hills Home for the Aged. Most of those walking corpses can't be trusted to remember whether they're sporting any underwear these days."

I let his cantankerous slur lie there for about a minute, but couldn't pass the opportunity to offer up something like a defense. "Well, by God, Tilden, I can damn sure tell you, with little fear of contradiction, that I am not wearing any underwear myself, and never have." Mumbled off into my favorite grape-jelly glass with, "Personally ain't never had any use for the damned things."

Then, it hit me like a frozen steer had dropped from Heaven's Pearly Gates, right through the roof, into my lap. "Now I've got it." A golden spark suddenly appeared in my brain and led me in something like the general direction Tilden wanted. "They're the pair of evil bastards who killed that horse-tradin' Jameson feller, over near Choska, in the Creek Nation. Did him in for a long-legged bay gelding and a bag of cash. Am I closer this time?"

A curtain of rum-saturated haze rose between us. He grinned again and propped his booted foot on a piece of split firewood. "Knew you'd find 'em, if you scratched around long enough in that rat's nest you call a brain, old man. Yeah, they're the ones, sure as long-horned steers in Texas. Them bad boys wore out saddle leather headin' for the Red River, but stopped long enough to attempt a robbery at Charlie Youngblood's Store, on the Canadian, in the Chickasaw Nation."

"Right. Right. And Youngblood didn't take kindly to folks trying to steal from him. You told me he put up a noggin-knotter of a fight. So, Blackie Daggett just naturally chopped him up with a double-bit ax from a barrel of 'em sittin' at the end of the crude store's counter."

"There you go, Dodge. While Daggett was killing Charlie, Rufus murdered Mrs. Youngblood, after he'd gone and raped the hell out of her. Thank God Almighty, a terrified Chickasaw gal, working as a clerk, witnessed the whole mess while hiding behind a rack of newly arrived women's clothing. Killers stole a five-pound sack of pork cracklin's, and all the sugar tits in the place. Damned poor showing for the lives of two mighty good Christian folk."

Entire account came a-pouring out of my old trail mate with the same kind of passion I'd known him for when it all happened. Appeared residence at Rolling Hills hadn't affected his ability to recall the past. Shamed me into trying to respond in kind.

"Well, now the fog has lifted, Tilden. Don't know how I managed to forget scum as murderous as them ole boys. Remember as how I got your wire, and rode like yellow-eyed demons chased me to meet you at Coffee's Bend. Claimed you wanted an o-ficial lawman type from Texas along for the hunt, in case those killers crossed the Red, and ended up trying to hide out with relatives, or some other such horse manure."

He chuckled, grabbed hold of the yarn, and started

running with it. "Old Bear, Caesar, and me had been on their trail for about three weeks before the Jameson and Youngblood slaughters. You surely remember now as how them bloody fellers had actually started the ball rolling by sending a Fort Smith prostitute, everyone called Sweet Sweet Sally, to meet the Good Lord by beating her to death with a hoe handle."

"Oh, my God, yes. They're the ones who nailed that sad girl's nude broken body to an outhouse door behind one of the dance halls, down on the Arkansas River."

"Yep. Liquor-crazed churnheads thought no one cared what happened to whores. Next day, they bragged about the killing to anyone willing to listen. Fort Smith policeman named Rufus Crossley tried to arrest 'em. They shot the hell out of him. Man lived, but never worked again. Turned him into a twenty-two-year-old shuffling cripple who lived another fifty years."

Tilden blew about half-a-dozen smoke rings at the ceiling, spit a chunk of errant tobacco toward the stove, and went to hacking at the tale again. "They ran from Crossley's leaking body to a cock fight over near Tuskahoma. Got into an argument with the owner of a well-known fighting bird named Bloody Bill. Heard tell he was a beautiful piece of poultry. Had a head the color of fire. Blackie and Rufus ended up killing the rooster, and its owner. Afterward, my friend Billy Bird always noted as how it takes some pretty sorry fellers to pull a pistol on a defenseless pullet. Two-man plague left bodies everywhere they stopped long enough. So I wired you, and we met up at Coffee's."

"We damned sure did. Chased that pair of murdering slugs out of the mountains, through the grasslands, to windswept nothingness, all the way to the Mulberry River, and then some. Almost three weeks on their trail. One of the roughest runs I ever made. Hard to believe I'd managed to forget it."

A blanket of good feelings dropped over me, and brought

the entire chase back in a flash of electric energy that snapped through my brain like ball lightning flying along telegraph wires. Glad the memory finally made an appearance. But what happened out west of the Mulberry didn't turn out to be much fun—leastways not for me. Closed my eyes, and could finally see them ole boys' ugly, perambulating swath of death and destruction as if it all happened yesterday.

Murdering scum turned north from Coffee's, and made for the Wildhorse River. Then, hoofed it for the Salt Fork of the Red, where they met up with two other hymn-singing pilgrims who were equally famed for piety and love of their fellowman. Nevada Nate Billingly and a renegade Comanche called Wolf Tail were as bad, maybe worse than either of the fugitives we started out looking to catch. The four of them together resembled a living pestilence, sweeping across the land in front of us. We couldn't ride fast enough to stop them, once the killing started.

Thinking back on it, I can't even begin to imagine how such a massacre could slip through the cracks in my calcified ability to recollect such things. But friends, once you've accumulated as many war marks against your leathery hides as I have, we can have a heart-to-heart about fading memory.

Added my own series of smoke signals to the cloud hovering above us and said, "You know, I watched that semi-Indian tracker of yours through my long glass as we rode into the valley of the hoodoos, out on the Caprock. His waist-length gray hair flyin' 'round his head like a battle flag. Sun was on the way to setting. Lit up all that red dirt like liquid fire poured over burnished gold. Big yeller dog running ahead of him stood out like a palomino pony."

The glowing tip of Tilden's smoke exposed crinkled eyes and a toothy grin. "Daniel Old Bear and Caesar surely loved the hunt. Soon as I set them on Bloodsworth's and Daggett's trail, those boys were nothing more than dead men riding horses. Thought we'd lost their sign in that near-endless pile of rocks someone named the Wichita Mountains. Took a couple of extra days, but Bear proved he could track sucker-toed tree lizards over a ten-thousand-year-old gravel bed."

Pushed myself deeper into the mangled chair cushion, and sipped at my drink. "Still think the place he picked to camp was haunted. You remember the site, Tilden?"

"Up under a giant hoodoo?"

"That's the one. Had some terrible dreams while we camped there."

"Only because you paid too much attention to all those stories Old Bear told."

Tilden was right. Can still see Westbrook sitting by the fire, running his damned near foot-long bowie knife around on a spit-wetted Arkansas stone. He could have easily passed for some prehistoric hunter, getting ready for the next day's kill. Overhead a gigantic moon played hide-and-seek with the occasional cloud that turned it as red as an open chest wound—fine night for murderers and grave robbers, according to my grandmother.

He tested the edge on his blade with a calloused thumb, and glanced at the inky sky. Reflected flames danced in his eyes when he said, "This place haunted by many spirits. Used to come here with some Cheyenne folk back when they first captured me. Still more white than Indian then. Years later, visited again with my Kiowa family. Both groups told similar stories."

He sliced through the night with his knife. Dancing light glinted off the steel. "Buffalo covered the land like a trade blanket. Beasts so large, it's hard to believe. But I've seen their bones. Usually find those of men mingled amongst them. Humbling to know such creatures once existed." He stopped, smiled, and with great respect in his voice added, "And there lived men brave enough to hunt and kill them. Many died trying to stay alive. Right time of year, on night of the killing moon, you can see them wandering the Llano like lost souls."

Before I dropped off to sleep, heard him say, "We'll catch Daggett and his friends in the morning, Tilden. They know we're coming. If this moon is a true hint of things to come, tomorrow looks to be a bloody day."

Don't know if his wide-eyed ramblings caused my nightmares, or if, maybe, Tilden's version of son-of-a-bitch stew hit my persnickety stomach the wrong way. Whatever the root, my blanket-roll reveries raged with men fighting animals I'd never seen in this life, or even thought of before. Shaggy brutish beasts brought horrifying scenes of death and destruction with them.

'Bout two hours before the sun got straight up, the following morning, we ran those heartless murders to ground, a few miles east of the confluence of the Tule and the Prairie Dog Town fork of the Red. Crimson rivers looked like gory arteries sitting on the world's blistered hide. We pulled up after a rump-burner of a ride that turned into a seven-man horse race.

Tilden jumped off Gunpowder's back, and jerked that massive Winchester .45–70 hunting rifle of his. Flipped up the back peep sight, dropped one of the reins, and tossed the other over his shoulder. Whispered something in the animal's ear. It went spraddle-legged and as rigid as a piece of Italian marble. Tilden rested the barrel on his saddle, and sent one of those big chunks of lead nearly a quarter of a mile.

Horse didn't even flinch. Damnedest rifle shot I've seen, before or since. Not even Moses Hand came close years later. Sure as hell caught Nevada Nate unawares. Hit him right between the shoulder blades. Massive four-hundred-and-five-grain slug knocked him clean out of one boot, and set his sorry carcass to flying between his mount's ears. Killed that child-murdering son of Beelzebub deader than a six-card poker hand.

Tilden's piece of showboat marksmanship uncorked a hellish bottle. Them sons of bitches turned and charged us. Poor stupid jackasses didn't have enough brains, between the three of them, to spit downwind. I'd been fighting Comanches, from horseback, since the age of eleven. Them ole boys wanted to do my favorite kind of dance.

Jerked my Colt's dragoon pommel guns, wrapped the reins around my saddle horn, and put the spur to Hateful. Stringy mustang jumped like she'd been hit in the rump with a flaming bullwhip, and set out for the fight eyes a-blazing. Daniel Old Bear Westbrook, and that yeller dog, trailed.

Tilden yelled, "Go get 'em, Lucius," but kept his place. He tried to perform another miracle by hitting targets thundering our direction. If he'd managed to bring a horse down, I'd be bragging about that shot today too. Swirling dust turned an azure sky the color of copper, and the bitter smell of black powder filled my nostrils.

Three remaining killers started firing from several hundred yards away. Weren't doing themselves a damned bit of good. Glanced to my left. Old Bear leaned into his animal's neck, and the pair seemed to become a single sinewy being.

As we raced toward our prey, blue whistlers chewed holes in the air all around me. One notched my ear and another punched through the edge of my hat brim. Fired my first shot when the five of us had closed to about sixty yards. Ball hit Wolf Tail dead center, punched a massive hole through his bone breastplate, and snatched him backward like he'd been roped and staked to the ground.

I snapped off several more, before we passed each other. Lots of dust and confusion, but did see sunlight bouncing off sharpened steel. Rufus Bloodsworth grabbed at his neck, and hit the ground harder than a sack of railroad spikes. Tilden's dog jumped him so quick he didn't have time to recover. Trust me, it was a gruesome sight to behold.

Hateful twirled around in time to have Blackie Daggett put one down her side. The bullet cut my cinch strap sure as a hot knife slices through butter. Saddle, and me, flew through the air. Thought I'd grown wings. Landed in the only bed of cactus within a mile of that Pecos promenade. Turned me into a living, breathing pincushion, in less than ten seconds. Then, I suppose, the lucky son of a bitch charged back with the intent of running me down. On my third attempt, a .44 ball in his brain box put an abrupt end to that idea.

Good God Almighty, but I was a mess. Had more cactus spines sticking out of me than a Kentucky bluetick hound that had just discovered his first porcupine. Painfully, stumbled over to check on Bloodsworth. Don't know to this day what kept the man's head attached to his body. Old Bear had damn near decapitated the poor luckless bastard. Dog almost ripped off what was left. Hell of a bloody mess where he fell. Learned a healthy amount of respect for Old Bear's skill with his knife that morning. Watched Caesar out of the corner of my eye from then on too.

Well, friends, Tilden and me kept the drinking, story-telling, and general roof-raising going almost all night. Best time I'd had in twenty years. Tilden stayed till the end of the week. We had a grand time every night on the porch with our whiskey, cigars, and tall tales.

Yesterday, under what had to be the bluest Texas sky since God created it, I loaded my old friend's raggedy cardboard suitcase into my antiquated rattletrap of a truck, and drove him back to the depot in Texarkana. Hugged his wrinkled neck like a long-lost brother. More than one person on the loading platform looked mighty surprised to see a pair of ancient geezers blubbering like babies. Course, weren't no way for them ignorant whippersnappers to have known they'd just witnessed the final goodbyes of a pair of trail-hardened former man-killers. We wept, and sensed we'd never see each other again. Time and what that soul-stealing, night-running bastard Tilden likes to call "the ole boney-fingered dude" will certainly catch up with us first.

Helped my arthritic trail mate cane a hobbling path through the crowd, and up the Pullman car's metal steps. Shook the weathered claw he offered, and waved him good-bye as the Texas Star, heading for Arkansas, set to chugging, gathered speed, and finally vanished from sight.

Last words I heard from Tilden before he climbed aboard and left my life forever were, "Ain't many of us ole boys left, Lucius. In spite of what the ignorant and ill-informed might think, our lives had weight and importance. When called on, we were the ones what stepped up, toed a brutal line, and did the right thing. The likes of us saved an untold number of people's lives, and, when necessary, we punished the wicked. My friend Barnes Reed called it the grim work of good men. No one will remember any of that when we're gone. Folks are just too busy with the world these days to care even the least." Then, with tears streaming down his leathery cheeks, he finished by saying, "Write everything down you can bring to mind. I'll talk with my biographer in Little Rock. He might be able to get it published. You never know. Take care of yourself, amigo. We'll meet again in glory, on the other side."

The keeper of Tilden's literary flame is a young newspaper writing feller name of Lightfoot. He's done gone and made ole Hayden famous, again. Seems they've collaborated on a bunch of the former marshal's bold recollections, concerning his days chasing bad men out in the Indian Nations for Judge Isaac C. Parker. Surely you remember Parker. Everyone used to call him "The Hanging Judge" 'cause of all the men he sent to executioner George Maledon's grim gallows in the little holler down the hill from the courthouse in Fort Smith. Parker snuffed the lamp on eighty-eight of them altogether, if memory serves.

Hayden and me felt about the same when it came to

the subject of hanging. He said he'd once told his friend Lightfoot, "Don't ever let nobody tell you different, Junior. Hanging is a hell of an awful way to go out of this life. Even for those pitiful sons of bitches that were guilty as Judas and, most assuredly, destined for the everlasting tortures of Satan's fiery pit. But someone had to catch them, and, for almost twenty years, Judge Parker walked a blood-soaked line others before him, and after, simply found impossible to come to grips with." Yep, my friend saw it all, and truth be told, I witnessed more than my share too.

So, on the way back to my Sulphur River digs from Texarkana, I stopped at Churchpew's Grocery that afternoon and bought me a stack of Big Chief tablets, a fistful of No. 2 pencils, and a big ole gum eraser.

Cooley said, "What you gonna do with all this stuff, Lucius? You done gone and found yourself a female pen pal?"

Stopped in his doorway as I was leaving, turned, and held those tablets up. "Gonna bring the past back to life, Cooley. Probably be some folks ain't gonna like it, but it's gotta be done."

I heard told as how some writer feller once said there's only two things of any real consequence in this life—love and death. Never believed that ole adage until Nance Nightshade and me met up. Guess I've hidden the story of our short, violent relationship, and the gory consequences of her family's destruction, long enough.

Sat down at the kitchen table the other day. Whipped out my Barlow and sharpened six or seven of those pencils. Poured myself a big mug of double-strength stump juice, and started scribbling. At first, I found it hard to bring it all back to the front burners of my age-dulled memory. But, just like my talks with Tilden, eventually the entire sad tale laid itself out in front of me like my checkered tablecloth. Faces from the past swam to the surface of my memory like minnows in a bucket, and them little red blocks under my tablet reminded me of all the blood. If you're interested, what follows is the story I wrote. You're gonna have to cinch her up tight, though. 'Cause this ain't no fairy tale. It's a wrenching confession of love, hatred, betrayal, and death that no one but you will know about—a dark and evil secret I expect you to keep.

1

"WE'LL SETTLE OUR DIFFERENCES RIGHT HERE, RIGHT NOW."

SUPPOSE THE MURDEROUS tale I have to tell started on a steamy afternoon back in 1867. Seven years old, almost eight, at the time, but I remember as how my pa and oldest brother came thundering up to the house, and jumped off their sweaty mounts. They stormed inside with me in pursuit. I barefooted it behind them as fast as my bony legs would allow.

Stood behind my mother. Clung to the hem of her dress as Pa grabbed her by the shoulders and said, "We're gonna have to leave this place, Mattie." My mother's given name was Matilda, but he'd always called her Mattie when there weren't nothing but family about. Company caused him to use the more formal Mrs. Dodge. No matter the situation, she referred to him as Mr. Dodge. Didn't know until my twelfth birthday his name was Hudson. Always got a laugh out of that, and, for obvious reasons, it's even funnier today. Hudson Dodge.

She said, "What can you possibly be about, Mr. Dodge.

Louisiana has been our home since the year young Lucius came into this world. We can't just jump up and leave."

"That carpetbaggin' son of a bitch down at the Elk Horn Bank stole the farm, Mattie. Called it 'foreclosure due to nonpayment.' So, Denton and me pulled our pistols, and took every dime in the place. Need to get as far from Shreveport as we can by tomorrow morning. Figure it'll take about that long to break the door on his big ole safe open and let him out. Goin' to Texas, Mother. We should be out of harm's way there."

"My Sweet Lord, Mr. Dodge. You didn't kill anyone, did you?"

"No, Mattie. Not yet. Throw a few essentials, and some food, in a gunnysack. We've got to be on the other side of the Red as fast as possible."

Pa owned some of the best Tennessee horseflesh any of them Cajuns had ever seen. The four of us headed for the cane breaks, and before night fell we'd crossed over into the wilds of Texas. Spent a lot of days in the saddle. Didn't stop running till we got to a primitive burg called Lampasas. Never forget the look on my mother's face when my father opened up that bag of ill-gotten loot for the first time. He took enough to impress a feller what had some land for sale, and bought us a nice-sized ranch about ten miles west of town.

When people asked where we'd come from, all my pa ever said was, "Well, neighbor, I woke up one morning, turned to my Mattie, and said, 'Darlin', I cain't stand these Louisiana swamps for another minute. Let's move to God's country.' "

Usually satisfied those curious enough to inquire. But you know, most folks never asked, because many of them had arrived in Texas under similar circumstances. The end of what Mother referred to as the Unpleasantness, and the almost endless hell of Reconstruction, made refugees out of just about every other family in the South.

Things went along right well for around a dozen years. Never heard from anyone over Shreveport way. But like the old philosopher always said, nothing good lasts forever.

As I recollect, it were mid-August when the real trouble hit. My God, but it was hotter than a stoked-up depot stove in January. Hadn't rained in more than a month. Every flat surface available to the eye was decorated with a layer of fine dust, getting deeper by the minute. Mother hated the powdery grime. Spent most of her waking hours locked in a deadly struggle for supremacy over the powdered haze she accused of "assaulting" her most precious family heirlooms. Course them "heirlooms" had only been there a short time, but she acted like we'd inherited them from her family back in Virginia.

The Colorado River skirted one end of our property. Had some mighty fine grass because of it. Fat cattle and sleek horses nourished the Dodge family's reputation all over that part of the state. Truth be told, Las Tres Colinas had grown into the best by-God rancho in the county. At the time, weren't any reason in the whole wide world for me to believe I'd soon take part in an infamous murder inquiry, or that it would be hushed up, and almost forgotten, for more than fifty years. But that piece of my story's gonna have to wait 'cause, hell, I'd be getting a shade ahead of myself unless I started at the real beginning.

Us Dodges arrived in the Great Lone Star State near on to the end of the worst Comanche raiding and killing. We fought them horse-riding imps a time or two, though. About all anyone in his right mind would want. Lost a fair number of neighbors to the bloodthirsty devils over the years. Mostly men and women caught too far away from civilization. Their pitiful corpses usually ended up looking like naked, hairless targets for arrows.

The Dodge clan had so much hard bark clinging to our calloused rumps, we managed to keep our scalps, and stay put on the land, in spite of some pretty hot efforts from those savages to dislodge us. Had to kill off more than a few of them, but you do what you have to.

By the time my eighteenth birthday rolled around, my own skills with rifles, pistols, knives, and horses rivaled any full-grown man's. Youthful exuberance sometimes led me to believe I was bullet-proof, tomahawk-proof, and knife-proof. And, after consuming enough of brother Denton's homemade coffin paint, I occasionally even thought myself invisible.

We spent better than ten years getting situated the way Pa wanted. Dug a damned fine well, lined it with smooth stones from the river. Built a comfortable dog-run house with a deep porch all the way around. Put it on a hill covered in live oaks. Had us a big ole barn, corral, and outbuildings where the hired help slept. Vaqueros called them bunkhouses. Ours appeared a sight nicer than any others I ever saw. Pa kept as many of them oaks as he could. When full-bore summer hit in Texas, you needed all the shade you could muster.

He always said, "Lucius, cover from anything between you and heaven can make a fifteen-degree difference in the sun's power to bore a hole in your head."

Just about the time everything seemed on the way to being so good you couldn't hardly beat it with a stick, feller named Slayton Bone stormed up, one day, heading a pack of gun-totin' animals known for scaring the hell out of everybody in the county. Their reputation preceded them sure as the smell wafting off a week-dead animal—mighty unpleasant bunch. Sported a well-earned reputation for killing folks without having anything like a good reason.

Whole damned gang rode into our grassless yard stomping chickens and scaring hell out of the dogs. Forced everybody inside, or onto a porch. I stood next to my pa, and heard every word ole Slayton said. Arrogant son of a bitch wanted our ranch, and had got right blunt about his desires several times before. He'd made generous offers. Pa forthrightly turned all of them down.

"Dodge, how're you and the missus doing this hot, summer morning?" he asked. Swept his palm-leaf sombrero off, and wiped at a dripping shiny pate with a red bandanna the size of a saddle blanket. Smell of horse manure, people sweat, chicken droppings, whiskey, and every other kind of nose-twisting odor imaginable stirred in the barely moving air. Made my mother cover her face with an apron, and back deeper into the doorway.

Everyone on our side of the question had managed to get pretty well armed by the time all them lathered-up animals finally came to a hoof-stamping stop. Ain't no way Bone and his bunch couldn't see it. Pa cradled an iron-framed Henry in the crook of his left arm. I had a couple of Colt's pistols cocked and ready behind my back. My brother Denton slouched in a strap rocker with a long-barreled shotgun across his lap. Burl, my other brother, who'd arrived five years after we vacated Louisiana, favored a Spenser's carbine he'd carried at a place named Gettysburg. He stood with several of the hired men, who lurked in the noonday shadows and scratched at their cartridge belts with nervous trigger fingers.

Once the flying dust settled some, sweet smell of baking bread from my mother's oven pushed all them other odors aside, and tickled my nose. Pa smiled, and glanced over the faces of Bone's iniquitous gang of cutthroats. The six heavily armed men stayed on horses that twitched under the assault of an army of flies bedeviling their legs and rumps.

I could feel the trouble oozing off those ole boys. Most of them shuddered and shook like chute-crazed cattle. You'd a-had to have been carrying a pretty full load of stupid not to recognize the whole festering state of affairs was about to pimple its way to a nasty head. All us Dodge boys tried to motion our mother inside. But she refused, kept to the door, and listened.

When he finally had the situation pretty well reasoned out, Pa eyeballed Bone and said, "Well, Slayton, if life was any better I couldn't stand it. And the county sheriff, if'n he was worth a tinker's damn, wouldn't allow it. Probably arrest me. Tell the judge I was just too happy to be sober. Must be bootleggin' on top of my other life endeavors. But I don't think none of that means much more'n a gob of spit today. Way I've got it figured, you didn't ride this far, and scare hell out of my chickens, just to inquire as to my health and welfare. Guess you've come to talk about buying our land again."

A ferretlike look crept across Bone's face as he mopped the inside of his hat and said, "That I have, Dodge. Recently discovered a neglected account in Grady Sims's First State Bank. More money than I realized. And, turns out, the perfect amount for a little land speculation. Thought a sweeter offer might get you to reconsider your last rejection."

A blind schoolteacher could have seen Bone's fuse was getting pretty short with answers Pa sent his direction during previous meetings. He stuffed the sweat-stained hat back on his glistening head, and smiled like a greedy rattlesnake that'd just discovered a fat mouse under a woodpile.

Pa tried to maintain a friendly front, but twisted at the waist just enough to bring the Henry's muzzle in line with One-eyed Whitey Krebbs. Krebbs sat at attention on a dappled gray to Bone's immediate right. Story that got told, most often, said a bear took Whitey's left eye back when he made a meager living as a trapper up in the Rockies, around Jackson Hole, Wyoming. Some even said the ragged slash on his face made the man mean, and he'd come to realize his real calling lay in killing people for money, rather than unarmed bears.

However he'd managed to get tumblebug ugly and outright vicious, ole Whitey screwed his head so far around, you could barely see the greasy, crust-covered leather patch over his mangled eye. Whole of Lampasas County knew Slayton Bone for a liar, thief, and scoundrel. But One-Eyed Whitey Krebbs enjoyed the hard-earned reputation as a widely feared man-killer that wouldn't hesitate if encouraged to do murder by his soulless, land-coveting boss.

I noticed Whitey had removed the thumb and forefinger of his right-hand glove and, with a ragged fingernail, kept tapping the butt of the Colt lying across his belly. A hand-tooled, double-loop Mexican holster cradled the weapon. His crooked grin revealed tobacco-stained teeth, and, more than once, he sent spittle flying between his horse's ears. Juicy wads landed in the dirt before they reached the steps of our porch—and my father's feet. Whitey often missed his mark, and he'd decorated that big gray's head so many times, the poor animal's ears were stained brown.

No invitation, or friendliness, left in Pa's voice when he said, "You can't make an offer sweet enough to get this land, Slayton. We traveled hundreds of miles, found it, paid for it in our own blood, and ain't about to sell. Why don't you give up on the effort; write it down in your ledger as one of your failures."

Bone dragged the bandanna over his face again, scrubbed at his neck, and leaned forward as if to emphasize his words. "Well, now, I cain't oblige you with giving up on the proposition, Dodge. You know, well as I do, this here land is mighty important to me." He leaned back in the saddle, and waved majestically at the heavens. "Only plot left in these parts keeping me from owning sunrise to sundown. Gonna have to turn the place loose sooner or later, ole pard. Just ain't no two ways about it." Last couple of sentences came across like a threat—brutal, obvious, and mean.

Krebbs spit another stringy gob of tobacco juice and mumbled, "Ain't no two ways about it. You Dodges gonna have to give 'er up."

Denton, who'd always been something of a hothead and openly hated Krebbs, caressed the polished stock of his 12-gauge Greener and snapped, "Well, it ain't gonna be today, or anytime in your foreseeable future, Bone. So why don't you take this pack of egg-sucking dogs, along with your mealymouthed hired killer, and get back across the river to that snake pit you call a ranch."

Jesus Christ, I thought Krebbs's one good eye was gonna pop right out of his claw-scarred face. "Come down off 'n that porch, Denton, and we'll settle our differences right here, right now. Nothing would give me more pleasure than leavin' your sorry carcass a-twitchin' amidst the mud, blood, and chicken shit."

My brother chuckled, pulled the hammers back on his shotgun, and snorted, "Keep hearing all kinds of rumors 'bout how fast you are with that fancy slick-barreled pistol, Whitey. Know some of our friends have watched you murder members of their families. But I'd be willing to bet, no matter how fast you are, or claim to be, you can't match my shotgun from this distance. Make the wrong move today, you goggle-eyed son of a bitch, and I'll splatter you, and that ugly gray horse, all over this part of Lampasas County."

If all the big talk from Brother Denton threw a scare into Slayton Bone's one-eyed gunman, he sure as hell didn't let on like it bothered him much. Several of his friends moved their animals a few steps away from him, though, and Bone kind of sidled off with them. Most folks knew us Dodges could be a handful, if things didn't go our way. Them boys must have figured there was less chance of getting hit when some of ours came flying back in their general direction, once Whitey finally decided to put hot lead in the air.

By and by, I got to thinking they'd left ole Whitey kind of hanging out there in the wind alone. At least it seemed that way at the time. Looking back on the thing, from the safety of the present, I can say with damned little or no equivocation Brother Denton seriously misjudged his competition. We all did. No one could have figured on what happened next.

Shamed by the bold-as-brass challenge to his pistoleering manhood, Whitey tilted a scarlet face even further back in an effort to get a better view of his opposition through that one good window to the murderous workings of a lethal brain. Rolled the milky-blue thing around in its socket a time or two. His odd, bug-eyed countenance had a somewhat spellbinding effect on all of us, I think. For certain sure, I couldn't stop looking at that lonely eyeball twirling around in his ugly, bear-scratched skull.

But Good Lord Almighty, I still don't know, to this day, how he managed to get his pistol out, and shoot my father, quicker than God could get there to stop it. Whitey was so close to Pa when he fired, the concussion from his .45 almost knocked me down too. Pa died before his knees hit the porch planks.

In a flash, Denton had the Greener up, but he'd spent too much time worrying about Whitey, and not enough watching another shooter off to his right. Erasmus Delaquoix popped my brother with shots from a long-barreled Schofield. Whole damnable bunch contributed to some general spraying of lead that riddled the front of the house. Then, the bloodletting scum spurred terrified animals away from the scene of their most recent killings.

Blue whistlers cut holes around the murderers' ears as they fled. Fired all twelve of mine as fast as I could thumb them off. Know for a fact, at least one of those found a home, but somehow he stayed horsed. Heard later, his friends had to take him straight to Lampasas for some real, honest-to-God doctoring. Story was he almost died. Shame he didn't.

Burl unsaddled two of them cowardly son of bitches with his Spenser. Some of their gamer friends turned back, and snatched them boys up. Didn't kill them, but I'm pretty sure the wounded duo carried Burl's lead to their graves a few years later.

It was all too little, and way too late. My father, and older brother, lay deader than the withered flowers decorating the altar of last week's Sunday service, over at Reverend Castleberry's Baptist church. Someone's stray lead had shattered Ma's arm too, and for a spell afterward, we feared the mangled limb might have to come off. All because a greed-driven murderer like Slayton Bone wanted land he couldn't have.

The following day we committed our dead to eternal slumber on a hill behind the house set off especially for family burials. My two-year-old brother Grady rested inside the iron fence up there. He died of the diphtheria some years after our arrival in Texas. We placed our most recently departed next to him, so they could all spend time without end together.

My mother, a woman of uncommon strength, wept enough to refloat Noah's boat. Her bitter tears seared a blazing path through my heart, and hardened me for what I knew must come to pass. Stood by those freshly covered graves, held her close, and whispered, "They'll pay for what they did, Mother. If it takes the rest of my life, they'll pay. Slayton Bone's gonna be first. With God as my witness, I swear it."

Being as Burl was the only other one of us boys left, I made him stay at home. He wanted to go along. Did some mighty fancy talking to make him understand he had to take care of Ma and the land. Hell of a responsibility to put on him, but I knew he could carry the freight. Pa always said a man never finds his destiny—it finds him. Think he might have been right about that one.

Got myself loaded for bear, kissed everyone good-bye, and headed for Bone's scorpion's lair of a ranch. His main house sat on a nice piece of grass about twenty miles north of us, on the west side of the Colorado. I fully anticipated drenching every blade of it with blood.

2

"... DO HAVE MY PRIORITIES. GOT TO KILL YOU FIRST."

HELL, I KNEW Bone and his bunch of murdering scum expected me. Sweet Weeping Jesus, you just don't kill a man's father, and brother, then shoot his mother right in front of his face, and not expect some serious vengeance to drop upon your head. About the only real law a man could depend on, out in the wild places, rested in the rifle he slept with and the pistol on his hip. Anyone bold enough to think they could murder several members of the same family, and get away unpunished, had to have been sticking his finger in too deep when he picked his nose.

Figured on at least eight, maybe ten, of those boys who doubled as gunmen and ranch hands. So, I took my time. Spent most of three days watching them through my long glass from the bushes and brambles around a ranch house ole Slayton called The Devil's Roost. Hard to keep from being spotted. But by the third day, my opposition had re-laxed its guard considerable. Suppose they figured, seeing as nothing wayward had occurred since their latest killings, the Dodge family hadn't been able to gut up and do what was required. To this very moment, I think they felt like we'd been buffaloed, didn't have the *huevos grandes* necessary to punish their transgressions. Course, they'd made a serious error in judgment. Damned deadly one, as a matter of fact. They'd pissed in their own well, as my pa used to say.

In spite of all my spyglass work, never did locate them murdering bastards Whitey or Erasmus. Bone stuck to the house, always kept at least a pair, sometimes three, of his hired thugs with him, day and night.

But, sure as flames flick around the edges of Hell's front door, everyone has a weakness or a blind spot. Didn't take me long to find Bone's. See, he spent at least ten minutes every morning out on his porch, giving instructions to the ranch help. Then, he took breakfast with two bodyguards there, once them cowboys had all headed out for the day's work. Soon as I got his habits lined up in my mind, his death was an absolute certainty. Little piece of advice to all those who might be contemplating an act of Biblical retribution—when it comes to cold-blooded murder, *mis amigos,* patience is always your best friend.

Somewheres around midnight of the fourth day, I tied my blue roan, Grizz, to a stand of stumpy trees, 'bout half a mile from The Roost's main house. Left a nose bag to keep him happy and quiet. Strapped Pa's Henry to my back, and spent most of a moonless night crawling for the barn. Made the hayloft 'bout the time a rooster got everyone up and moving around. Covered myself with straw, and waited. Heard the help ride out for the day's work just after daylight. Climbed down, and snaked my way around the house to the breakfast porch.

Sons of bitches didn't see me till I'd walked right up on them. With no kind of effort at all, I could have spit on the top of Johnson Keeler's head after I stopped directly behind his chair. Across the table, Bone looked up from his breakfast and spotted me. His fork hovered over the plate, circling between eggs and bacon like a confused buzzard.

"I'll just be goddamned if it ain't Lucius By-God Dodge," he snorted like a man dismissing a bothersome insect.

Enrique Esparza, the third man in the group, dropped his eating utensils and mumbled, "Jesus Maria," made the sign of the cross over his chest, and went for his pistol.

Dumbest, and last, thing the stupid bastard ever did. We couldn't have been more than six feet apart at the time. He tried to hide the move with a napkin. Didn't work. I blasted him dead center. Big chunk of slow-moving lead punched through his breastbone, knocked a hole the size of my fist in his back, and lifted him out of the chair. Impact pitched him through the porch rail into a patch of water-starved wild-flowers, struggling to grow along the gravel walk from the hitching post. Just goes to show that if you're dumber than the head on a hammer, you shouldn't try to do two things at the same time. Especially if one of them might get you killed graveyard dead.

Poor ole Johnson Keeler's luck ran out, right in front of me. His boss hurried the only shot he managed to get off. Guess Bone must have thought he could shoot through Keeler, and hit me. That one didn't work for damned sure. He only managed to send one of his own bodyguards to hell in a heartbeat. Course it saved me the trouble. I kept my place behind Johnson, used his corpse as a shield, leaned over, and pushed the Henry's muzzle against Slayton's chest. He dropped the smoking pistol on the table, raised his hands, and mouthed off like he had me under the gun. I'm still amazed at the nervy display the man put on.

"Didn't think any of you leftover Dodges actually had sand enough to pull off a move as brazen as this here. Have all my boys looking for a military-style assault from your whole camp. Got a dozen men out watching. Cain't believe you snuck up on me all by your lonesome, boy. Damn sight bolder than I'd of ever believed possible, for any of your sorry clan."

Shoved the Henry's muzzle deeper into the slab of muscle across his chest. Venom came boiling out of me. "Well, looks like you mis-thought yourself again, Slayton. Like you did with my father. Now, you murdering polecat, is there anyone else in the house?"

He leaned back in his chair. Brutal lout's composure was nothing short of amazing. Dead men within a few feet of him, and he acted like we were just passing the time of day. "The cook. He's a Chinky feller. Don't speak much English. Makes a damned fine flapjack, though. Why don't you sit down, and enjoy one. Blood on these eggs, but he can fry me up some more. We can talk over this unfortunate situation. Maybe work somethin' out."

Couldn't believe the absolute effrontery of the son of a bitch. For about half a second, the vision of us having breakfast, within spitting distance of a pair of oozing corpses, flashed across my brain.

"Where's One-Eyed Whitey and Erasmus, you snake-bellied bastard?"

"Fired 'em. Wasn't supposed to be no shooting yesterday, Lucius. Not in my plans a'tall. Those boys took it upon theirselves to make some real poor decisions. Felt so bad 'bout your father I run 'em off. Heard Whitey say they was headed for Fort Worth. Bet you everything in my poke, they'll be in the Indian Nations soon as their drinking money runs out and they've gone through all the whores in Hell's Half Acre. You've probably got about another four or five days to catch 'em whilst they're still in town. Might want to get moving that direction. Already wasted almost a week. They could both be gone by now."

"Well, they're gonna have to wait a bit, Bone. I do have my priorities, you know. Got to kill you first."

"Now, now, now. You don't mean that, Lucius. You saw it all. I didn't have anything to do with shooting your kinfolk.

Never even fired my weapon, in spite of the fact that damned near all you Dodge boys poured plenty of lead my direction. If'n Denton had kept his mouth shut, nothing would've happened. Whole affair seems like an unavoidable altercation, between men who hated each other, that ended in the accidental departure of members of your family. Sad, sad event, I must admit. But not much I could've done to stop it."

"You shouldn't have been there to begin with, Bone. That thought ever cross your blood-saturated mind? Pa had already turned you down at least twice that I'm aware of. Fact is, you shouldn't have ever been born. Think maybe God made a mistake letting you come into this world, and I'm here today to rectify that heavenly error. You're just gonna have to consider the upcoming events as a matter of blessed intervention. 'Cause, you see, I'm about to send you back to hell where you belong."

He looked up at me and sneered. The man appeared absolutely certain of his position. "Well, you'll have to kill me in cold blood, boy, 'cause I ain't about to fight you."

Shot him in the left elbow. Must've hurt like the dickens. He fell out of his chair, and flopped around on the porch like a beached fish. Squalled and bellowed so loud, I was afraid some of them cowboys out on the range might hear him. Got tired of listening, after a minute or two. Grabbed him by the collar, stood him next to a porch pillar, and stuffed his pistol back into its holster. Backed off about four steps and let him know how the cow ate the cabbage.

"Here's how this dance works, Bone. You'll draw that pistol, and I'll kill you. Or, you can stand there, all weepy and red-eyed, not do anything to protect yourself, and I'll kill you. However you want to do the deed's fine with me. But the undeniable truth is, when I walk away from your porch this morning, anyone finding you boys will swear on his mother's grave you had every chance in the world to defend yourselves, and just couldn't manage it."

"Damned if I'll draw on a snot-nosed whelp like you," he squawked.

Shot him in the leg, that time. God Almighty, you'd have thought I chopped his foot off with a log-splitting maul. He yelped, and cussed me, my family, even my dogs, from the beginning of time, on into the distant future. Made spit-slinging, detailed allusions about the legitimacy of my birth, and cast ugly aspersions on the reputation of my mother. Course none of his slanderous behavior did a thing toward helping his situation.

He finally settled down a bit, but kept yammering at me. Guess he thought more bullshit might do him some good. "Dammit, Lucius, ain't no reason to do this. You cain't just kill a man a piece at a time."

"Pull that pistol, and I can guarantee all your earthly suffering will come to an abrupt, and much-desired, halt. Keep talking, and you're gonna end up praying for a Comanche war party to show up and save your sorry ass."

By that point, the wretched son of Satan must have figured he didn't have anything to lose, and, by God, he was right. Sent his hand diving for the Colt. My shot hit him under the eye, 'bout the time he cleared leather. Bullets sometimes do strange things when they strike bone. The one I put in ole Slayton ricocheted around in his skull a bit, shot out through the top of his head, along with a sizable chunk of brain matter, and lodged in the ceiling of his porch. He pitched over onto a plate piled with bacon, and blasted a hole in the table on his way down. Rolled onto his back and stared up at me with glassy eyes. Looked right surprised.

Pretty sure he was still in there when I bent over and said, "No doubt in my mind, Saint Peter's gonna turn you around at the Pearly Gates, so you and Satan can get to know each other better. Have fun shoveling coal from now till the Second Coming, you murdering son of a bitch."

'Bout then, Bone's Chinese cook came flying out of the

kitchen with a meat cleaver in his hand. Pulled up short when I pointed the rifle at him. He glanced around at the havoc I'd wrought, smiled, and said, "Very, very good. Very bad men, these ones. So happy them dead." He buried his cleaver in the top of the table, snatched off a greasy apron, waved, and vanished as suddenly as he'd shown up.

Got back to Grizz as soon as I could, and kicked for Fort Worth. Wanted to put them other murderers on the path to perdition. Offered up hourly prayers I'd get the chance, before someone else messed around and beat me to it.

3

"TAKE YORE PICK—
GUNS, KNIVES, OR FISTS."

ME AND GRIZZ covered a hundred and twenty miles in record time. Hit the south end of Fort Worth, and that area known as Hell's Half Acre, just before noon the second day of the chase. Kinda snuck in behind a herd of bawling longhorns from San Antonio, and rode through a gauntlet of streetwalking whores. Been in town a time or two trailing cattle myself, so I knew the drill, but had no need of their services.

One right nice-looking but well-used gal grabbed onto my cinch strap and said, "How 'bout it, cowboy? I'll do anything you can think of fer a dollar. Got a crib not far from here. You can ride the tiger all night long for three. Stop this horse, and we'll do the big wiggle right here in the street, if'n you'd like. That'll only cost you fifty cents."

As I pulled away, she kept her pitch going till her pleas gradually bled into the general noise and hubbub of a street what looked like an anthill stomped on by a couple of mean-assed kids, with nothing much to amuse them. Last thing I heard from the aggressive girl was, "You'll regret it. You ain't never had any as good as mine, you stingy cow-wrangling son of a bitch."

A dance hall, or liquor emporium of some sort, occupied a treeless site on every block along Rusk Street. Whole parade of animals and men kept moving north toward the stockyards. Moved over to Main and the Uptown area. Found The White Elephant Saloon and Restaurant, W.H. Ward, Proprietor. Appeared to me the biggest, brassiest, busiest spot on the heaving thoroughfare. First place I stopped. Being a country boy, figured if a joint got my attention, probably had the same effect on Whitey and Erasmus. Seemed as good a place to look for the killers as any, to me.

Pulled Pa's Henry and stepped inside. Moved directly to the wall. Learned that trick from an old cowboy named Crow Foot Stickles. He'd worked for almost every well-known cattle operation in Texas, at one time or another. Claimed to have ridden with Chisholm, Charlie Goodnight, and once spent time chasing cows on the famed Frying Pan Ranch for several years, before he headed south and hired on with my father at Las Tres Colinas.

Studied staying alive at that old man's gimpy knee. I felt anyone who'd managed to live as long as he had must have something useful to offer on the subject. He would sit by our bunkhouse stove at night, cut off a chunk of plug to-bacco, stuff the wad into his mouth with the blade of his knife, and get right philosophical.

"If'n you don't wanna end it all belly-up with your toes in the air, boy, you gotta be smarter'n the dumb bastard wantin' to take yore life," he would say. Made right good sense to me.

Crow Foot could set a spittoon to ringing like a cathedral bell. He'd lean back, look thoughtful, and rattle off another pearl of wisdom like, "Whatever you do, don't let 'em git behind you, boy. Back-shooting bastards are a-hidin' be-hind every bush and tree, these days. Ain't been no honor amongst men since the great war of Yankee aggression. If you think any of these gun-totin' snakes will give you a chance in a fair fight, you've got another think a-coming. That ole horse shit 'bout meetin' yer enemy in the street, a-facin' him like a man, is nothin' but dime-novel bilge. There's scum-suckin' gun hounds out and about, what'll kill you for the coppers on a dead man's eyes."

He'd wipe dribbles off his mouth with the sleeve of a rough linsey-woolsey shirt, and do his grinning imitation of a possum in a melon patch. "Always shoot first. Go to court afterwards. Ain't no jury in Texas gonna convict a man fer defendin' hisself. And, hell, even if'n that other sumbitch is just a-scratchin' his nose, you can always claim he was a-reachin' and a-grabbin', and you didn't have no choice but to plug him afore he plugged you." A man could live a long time on Crow Foot's kind of advice.

I'd barely managed to get comfortable in the White Elephant when a disagreement at one of the tables caused everyone in the raucous establishment to tense up and get real quiet. Feller about the size of a Butterfield stagecoach, covered in hair and sweaty buckskins, grabbed a chair and flung the thing backward. I had to step out of the way to keep from getting knocked down.

He quaked like a man in the throws of malaria and yelped, "Stand up, Tatum. I'm gonna kick your sorry ass from here to sundown. Ain't no man in Texas got enough grit to be puttin' family members of mine in jail on trumped-up, bullshit charges, like them you Rangers done slapped on little brother Jacob, and not expect to suffer some fer it. Come on, Boz, get yer dead ass out'n that there chair."

Man at the table didn't move, except to thump ashes from a smoldering panatela into a brass spittoon snugged up against the leg of his chair. He pushed a Mexican palm-leaf hat to the back of his head and grinned. "You need to calm down, Peaches. Everyone in Posey, Texas, knows your jackass-stupid brother murdered Harvey Monday, then set out on a horse-stealing and stage-robbing rip the likes of which most folks hadn't seen since the days of Sam Bass and his bunch."

Near as I could figure, the whole country had heard of Ranger Randall Bozworth Tatum. He'd jerked many an evil man up by the roots. Had his share of enemies because of it. Got to admit he looked the part. Tall, lanky, 'bout thirty-five years old. Face covered with long mustaches and side-whiskers. Pistols and knives hung off each hip. Short-barreled gun across his back, and an under-the-arm hideout thing peeked from beneath a rough leather vest. Appeared way more than capable to me. Messing with a man like Tatum was the dimwitted equivalent of teasing a rattlesnake with your nose.

But, as is the case with many a drunken disagreement, the Ranger's reputation didn't seem to have any effect on his tormentor. "That's a pack of black damnable lies, Boz, and you know it. And don't call me Peaches, damn you. Only my friends is allowed to call me Peaches. Don't consider Texas Ranger Randall Bozworth Tatum one of my boon companions."

"Whatever you say, Peaches, but of your other names which do you prefer—Hubert or Gladstone?"

"Damn you, Tatum, don't change the subject. I come in here to cut you up, shoot holes in yer worthless hide, or kick hell out of you. Take yer pick—guns, knives, or fists. Tomahawks, axes, or fence posts. Don't matter a damn what you choose to me. Ain't nothing I can think of gonna give me more personal pleasure than tying your ears in a bow knot. 'Cept maybe pulling yer nose back across yer eyebrows, and attaching it to yer head with some of 'at 'ere strangy hair of yer'n. Bad-assed gunfighter reputation of yer'n don't mean spit to me."

Most of the drunken bystanders had drawn away from the noisy antagonists, and staked out spots against the walls all around the room. Easier to prop themselves up

that way. Got right crowded in front of my hidey-hole next
to the door. Didn't seem to me that many of the spectators
wanted to contribute to whatever bloodletting might occur,
but, at the same time, none of the giggling tipplers appeared ready to jump in and stop the squabble either. Near
as I could determine, no one had given up whatever he was
drinking when the dispute commenced, and some snigger-
ing, from behind the buckskinned, hairy gentleman, seemed
to add to his considerable agitation.

"You self-righteous badge-toters done be-smirched the
good name of McCabe, and I'm a-gonna put a stop to such
slanders," snorted the quaking, sweat-stained colossus.

The Ranger threw his head back, laughed out loud, reset-
tled his hat, and said, "Besmirched? Did I hear you right?
Did you say besmirched? Where in the hell did you learn a
three-dollar word like besmirched, Peaches? I know, for a
fact, you've never bothered with much in the way of formal
schooling. Hell, when you, Jacob, and I were still kids back
in Posey, took everything your poor sainted mother could
do to keep you McCabe boys out of jail. If memory serves,
you outlaws burned Ole Man Wattle's barn before either of
you managed to get past your tenth birthday. Been a down-
hill slide for Jacob ever since, and he bit off way too much
of the plug when he busted a cap on Harvey. Best school-
master Posey ever had. You can't shoot a man like him on
the front porch of the schoolhouse, while he's ringing the
bell for classes to commence, for God's sake."

Peaches McCabe slammed his ragged felt hat on the
floor, and kicked it. "Who done seen Jake do that? Show
me the lyin' stack of horseshit what says he seen my little
brother shoot Ole Man Monday."

Texas Ranger Randall Bozworth Tatum dropped his
friendly smile and tickled the grips of his Colt. "I saw it,
Peaches. And so did half the kids in Harvey's classes. De-
livered my younger brother for lessons that morning as
Jake rode up and shot Harvey deader than Davey Crockett.

Personally chased the murderin' skunk all the way to Tuskahoma in the Indian Nations. Found him in the company of other evil men, and brought him back to face the consequences of his deeds. He'll hang sure as death, taxes, and Texas. And if that's not the way of it, you can take a piss in your own hat."

"He won't swing if'n you cain't testify agin' him, Boz. If'n you're dead, that'll take care of the whole sit-chi-ation, won't it?"

"Well, Peaches, I don't intend on dying in your foreseeable, or my immediate, future."

Barely heard him when Tatum's surly antagonist hissed, "Guess I'll jest have to kill you today then, won't I, Boz? And right now seems like as good a time as any to start this fandango."

A greasy hand darted for the pistol jammed behind his thick leather belt. Before the slobbering creature touched those oiled walnut grips, Ranger Tatum had his weapon out and blasted a crater, the size of a summer squash, in the big man's right foot. Peaches McCabe made Slayton Bone sound like a deaf-mute. Never heard such hollering in my entire life. Man had feet like canoes, and I suppose having a cavern punched through one of them ugly boats must have really hurt.

Hell of a show followed. Peaches grabbed his mangled foot with one hand. A geyser of blood squirted between his fingers. He kinda half-fell, half-stumbled, and half-jumped at the seated lawman. Grabbed the collar of Tatum's bib-front shirt with his free hand, and pitched the startled man across the room like a little girl's raggedy corn-shuck doll. Screamed and hollered like a wounded bear the whole time. Tatum feller landed all crooked, and made a kind of sickening crunch of a sound when he ricocheted off the foot rail under the bar.

Heard one of the booze hounds next to me mutter, "Jest 'bout time fer ole Boz to get a serious comeuppance.

Smort sumbitch been needing a good ass-kickin' fer years. Glad I'm here to witness the deed. Hope it gets a sight bloodier 'fore it's over by God."

Bouncing off the bar didn't seem to have much negative effect on the object of everyone's attention, though. Tatum popped up like something on a piece of coiled steel spring and snapped off another shot that hit the big man in his good foot. God Almighty, I don't know how my mother, more than a hundred miles away, kept from hearing him holler. But, Sweet Jesus, it didn't even slow ole Peaches down. Foot-shot beast stumbled forward on unbending legs that seemed to be made from aged ivory. Massive arms out-stretched, he dropped on the Ranger with a resounding thump that rippled through the floor all the way over to where I stood.

They grappled around a bit, and somehow McCabe man-aged to slap the pistol out of Tatum's grip. Bone-handled Colt came sliding across the blood-drenched floor and spun to a stop right at my feet. I grabbed the .45 'fore anyone else could get hold of it. Mighty fine example of a custom-made firearm. Figured Tatum might want the handgun back when the fracas ended. Course that all depended on whether or not Peaches McCabe squished him as if he'd stepped on a south Texas dung beetle.

With both of the clawing cussing combatants down, folks in the crowd got considerable braver. They ganged up around the bone-crunching, spit-slinging, and bloodletting like it was a church social, or something, and Grandma's yellow cake was about to be served. Crowd kind of elbowed me aside, and I couldn't see much of anything except a lot of rolling around, grunting, and such, for a minute or so.

The twisting and screaming went on till the mob got rest-less, and started yelling the most scornful kinds of things at poor stupid Peaches for not being able to put an end to it. Then, after the bloody warriors had flopped around and de-stroyed a table and several chairs, the big man managed to get on top of the Ranger, and proceeded to pound the hell out of him. The mob heartily approved the possibility of a bare-knuckled killing. Didn't appear anyone intended on stopping it.

Got me to thinking as how the brutal murder of a Texas Ranger of Boz Tatum's well-known fame was beyond the pale. So, I stepped up and took the situation in hand. Pushed my way through the seething, drunken multitude. Laid the barrel of the Henry across Peaches McCabe's massive noggin like I was chopping wood. Crowd sucked back like waves on a beach, and let out a single shocked gasp as his scalp split open, sagged into his eyes, and exposed a sizable span of pale, grayish-white skull beneath.

His head bobbled around on his neck for a second. Then he looked up at me kind of skronkey-eyed and slobbered, "Who'n the hell 'er yew?" So I whacked him again. Blood and gobs of gory hair splattered everybody in the front row of gawkers. Sissy-looking feller—probably a drummer of some kind—got hit right in the middle of his vested chest with a sizable chunk of the stuff and went to puking in the manner of a two-year-old with the colic. Must have eaten some tamales and chili, because he christened about a dozen pairs of boots in every direction. His friends grabbed their noses and stumbled away. Been my experience over the years that grown men can watch fellers beat each other to death with railroaders' sledgehammers, and not even blink. But, Good God, you let someone go to puking and it'll clear out a slaughterhouse faster'n a family of skunks at a prayer meeting.

Grabbed Boz Tatum under the arm, and dragged him toward the door. Waved the rifle back and forth at the crowd to keep 'em at bay long enough for us to make our exit. Got him to a water trough, next to the boardwalk, and dropped him in headfirst. He came out coughing, spitting, and shaking water out of his hair. Handed him my bandanna so he could wipe his split lip, busted ear, crooked nose, and bloodstained face. Stuffed his pistol back in its holster.

Once he'd recovered a bit, the Ranger gave me a serious eyeballing and said, "Do I know you, son?"

"No, sir. Don't think we've had the pleasure. Name's Lucius Dodge. My family raises horses and cattle out west of Lampasas, over on the Colorado."

He brightened up a bit. "Your father Hudson Dodge?"

"Yessir."

"Well, then, I know your father. Damned fine feller."

"He's dead, Mr. Tatum."

"The hell you say."

"Murdered on his own front porch by a belly-slinking snake named Whitey Krebbs."

"Last I heard, that one-eyed son of a weasel had his gun rented out to a hard case named Slayton Bone. Rumor had it he was riding with Bone's bunch of cutthroats from over at The Roost. Neither of them men to be trifled with."

"Krebbs and Erasmus Delaquoix murdered Pa and my brother Denton. Bone rode at the head of the gang when they did the sorry deed."

"Well, by God, we'll just have to take care of them boys, won't we?"

"Already brought Bone to book myself. By now Saint Peter should have sent him on the way to his proper place in Hades."

Tatum hesitated as he squeezed water and blood from my ragged neckerchief. "You killed Slayton Bone, boy?"

"Yes, sir. I did indeed. Along with a couple of his bodyguards that couldn't get their pistols up fast enough. Would've done the same for Whitey and Delaquoix, if they had stayed around. Before ole Slayton caught a sunbeam for the Pearly Gates, he claimed those boys headed for Fort Worth and all the glories available here in Hell's Half Acre. Said he figured they'd strike out for the Nations after. Gonna find 'em and see to it they all meet back up at Perdition's front gate as soon as possible."

Tatum cupped some water down the back of his neck. He flipped his head from side to side. Could hear the bones crack. He chuckled, and threw me a quizzical look. "You're a hard one to be so young, Lucius Dodge."

"Eighteen, Mr. Tatum. Been fighting the Comanche since I was nine. Went out on my first horseback chase a few weeks after my eleventh birthday. My brothers and me made them savages pay heavy for the murder of one of our vaqueros. They'd slaughtered a fine feller named Alex Martinez and his entire family of seven. I've doled out my share of justice for a spell now. Slayton Bone was easy. Whitey and Erasumus won't be any different, as far as I'm concerned. They'll be dead within a few minutes of me finding them. Today, tomorrow, next week, next year, I'll find 'em sooner or later."

Texas Ranger Boz Tatum squinted, and looked pensive for a minute. "Well, son, what you need is the blessing of something in the way of law for such endeavors, and I'm just the man who can help you out. Ranger Company B has its base camp set up a bit northeast of here on the Trinity. Man in charge, Captain Horatio Waggoner Culpepper, and I go back more years than either of us would like to remember. We've been fighting wild Indians, and bad men, for so long we cain't do anything else. He tried to ranch a bit. I bought a farm once. As you can see, I'm not farmin' these days, and Wag ain't ranchin'."

It sounded like one hell of a good idea. Figured I might as well have the law on my side when I finally found Whitey and Raz. Far as I could see, Tatum's offer would make snuffing their lamps all legal and such.

"You can get me an appointment as a Ranger?" I said.

He stood, smiled, and put his arm around my shoulders. "My friend, ain't no appointment to it. All you gotta do is follow me to camp, sign an oath of allegiance to the state of Texas, and get sworn in. Think I can virtually guarantee you'll get accepted. Hell, figure I probably owe you my life. If'n ole Peaches could've had his way, family or friends would be identifying my corpse right now. Hard to believe you can shoot a man in both feet and still have him beat you to death. But, thank God, you stopped him. So, you come with me, and in a few hours from now Lucius By God Dodge will most assuredly be one of the Great Lone Star State's finest."

4

"...MEET...CAPTAIN HORATIO WAGGONER CULPEPPER."

MY NEWLY MADE friend and I retrieved our animals and headed north. Stayed on the heavily traveled cow path locals called Rusk Street. For the most part, the better-known *boardinghouses* in town fronted the dusty, wagon-rutted avenue. Don't think I saw a single tree in the entire hodgepodge of clapboard buildings.

Boz kept dabbing at his various wounds and bruises as he pointed out what appeared to be the only home in town that had something like grass growing in front of it. The verdant sod certainly drew your attention to the place. He said, "That there's Little Mary Golden's whorehouse. Her girls have worked like Mississippi field hands on their yard. Her lovelies have done themselves right proud. Spend just about every waking minute, 'cept when they ain't entertaining, pulling cockleburs out'n that patch of weeds. Them gals is the first folks to plant real grass around here, as I know of."

We crossed the Trinity River, and hoofed our way toward the cattle bedding grounds, but turned east after about half a mile, and hit the winding, sluggish stream again. Lots of trees hugged the edges of the slow-moving water—mostly cottonwood, elm, blackjack oak, and post oak. Shade provided sure made life some easier. Sun had got a little past straight up and felt like an auger boring a hole through my palm-leaf sombrero.

We ambled along for a piece, and finally came upon a sizable tent village situated under a sprawling stand of sycamores. Place swarmed with men and beasts. Thought to myself, must be nigh on to a hundred Rangers, twice that many horses, and three times that many dogs. Smell of tobacco in every available form hung in the air. Rough-looking men sat around open fires. Smoke, laden with the aroma of burning meat, wafted through their leafy retreat. Some fellers played their Jew's harps. Others cleaned weapons or laughed, and seemed mighty pleased with the situation.

Boz led me to an open-sided canvas pavilion under the sheltering limbs of an ancient live oak. Near half-a-dozen capable-looking men occupied seriously abused strap chairs situated around a cavalry officer's battered field table. And, while most seemed little older than me, the demanding lives they led had already etched hard lines around flinty eyes.

Those five Rangers must have been wearing, or carrying, twenty or thirty guns of just about every sort I'd ever laid eyes on. Looked like each pistol or rifle was matched by an equal number of bowie knives, Arkansas toothpicks, daggers, dirks, stilettos, or steel-headed tomahawks.

When a massive gentleman seated at the head of the group stood, the four others followed suit. The tall man's attire separated him from the rest of the Rangers by way of its heavy dependence on military-looking flourishes. Polished brass buttons decorated a navy-blue, double-breasted, swallow-tailed coat that looked like something an admiral of the British navy might wear. A carefully knotted ribbon tie at the neck of his frilly-fronted white shirt, along with brightly polished knee-high boots, branded him a dandy of the first order. Up to that point in my life, only place I'd ever seen such a gussied-up hombre was in books my mother made me read, as part of her gallant efforts at my spotty education concerning European history.

Tatum made a halfhearted effort at saluting, then shook hands with the dandy, and motioned for me to come forward. "Want you to meet a dear friend of mine, Wag. This here young feller is Lucius Dodge from down Lampasas way. He just got through saving me from the murderous wrath of Peaches McCabe. Ole Peaches tried to jerk me through a knothole backward for bringing his baby brother in for trial. Might have done the ugly deed, if not for Lucius. He'd like to sign on with us." He stopped, leaned ·closer, and almost whispered, "Told the boy you'd talk with him about the possibilities of becoming a genuine Texas Ranger." Then he turned, took me by the arm, and said, "Lucius, my boy, step up here and meet my good friend Captain Horatio Waggoner Culpepper. Toughest man in Texas, next to me, of course."

Culpepper didn't wait. He grabbed my hand with one the size of a camp skillet and almost reduced my knuckles to powder. Shook it so hard, I thought there for a second my arm might separate from the shoulder and end up a useless dangling appendage, for the rest of my natural life.

A voice that boomed like God Almighty speaking from the gates of Heaven rumbled from somewhere inside the man. Hadn't heard anything to match him since an itinerant evangelist named the Reverend Ellis P. Thunderation Jones stopped by the ranch and tried to "save" all us Dodges from the evils of sin and the likelihood of eternal damnation. Ole Thunderation possessed the undeniable vocal power to literally scare hell out of a person.

The captain's words came out as a leisurely, bearlike roar directed at me in particular, and the rest of the camp in general. "Most pleased to make your acquaintance, Mr. Dodge. As you probably already know, the Frontier Battalion of the Texas Rangers is in desperate need of redoubtable young men such as yourself."

He dropped my wrung-out hand, placed an arm the size of a tree trunk around my shoulders, and waved in an effort to intimately include the other men at the table in his remarks. "I'm sure you are aware, four years ago the Texas State Legislature changed our direction dramatically. We matured from a voluntary force, whose primary thrust involved the protection of Texas citizens from murderous assaults by the heathenous Comanche, to establishment as a statewide constabulary. All happened on April 10 of '74. Company B now serves at the pleasure of the governor, and possesses a wide range of civil police powers."

I got the impression Wag Culpepper could have given Thunderation Jones a run for his money in the pontificating business. He had all the mannerisms of a future politician. Figured him for governor someday, soon as I felt the typhoon from his chest battering the insides of my ears.

He fumbled with some official-looking documents for a moment, then blasted us with, "Before you can be admitted into the finest body of law enforcers in the United Sates, however, I have the crucial responsibility of determining your fitness to serve."

The statement startled me a bit, given the assurances from Boz that by showing up I faced a mere formality. I blurted out, "What does that mean, Cap'n?"

"Don't trouble your mind about this, young man. Just a few questions I'm going to let my second in command, Lieutenant Benjamin Franklin Beaumont, ask." He turned to the man on his right, and rattled the sheath of the papers his direction. "Go ahead, Beau. You're pretty good at this." He resumed his seat, and took on the all the aspects of an interested spectator.

Beaumont pushed himself to a somewhat more official-looking position. He crossed his legs, fingered the rowel on a Mexican spur, fixed me in a steely gaze, and said, "Do you own your own horse, Mr. Dodge?"

Seemed a stupid question to me, but when I glanced at Boz Tatum, he smiled and made a motion like he was pushing me forward.

"Yes. Possess a damned fine animal named Grizz. My father gave him to me five years ago."

Beaumont removed his faded beat-up hat and dropped the shapeless thing over the toe of a well-used boot. He fished out makings for a smoke and poured tobacco on paper. "Under indictment for any kind of criminal activity—including acts such as public lewdness?"

"No, sir, I am not and never have been." Now, my answer was correct so far as I knew. Figured there wasn't much point in saying anything about having recently sent Slayton Bone and his boys to meet Jesus. Besides, figured weeks would pass before anyone in Fort Worth, other than Boz, knew about them shuffling off their mortal coils. With no more law than could be had around Lampasas at the time, and Bone's well-earned reputation as a murdering skunk, I felt the whole episode might best come to light by whatever means fate offered.

Wag Culpepper's lieutenant didn't even blink at my answer. Just kept moving forward. "Any possibility you're a whiskey-swilling drunkard, or suffer from the need to indulge in the mind-robbing evils of opium?"

"Only drink on special occasions, Lieutenant Beaumont. Last one I had was almost two months ago at a celebration of my father's birthday. I've never touched an opium pipe or laudanum bottle, and have no use for those who do."

"Any known medical problems, or history of softhead-edness in your family? Got any melon-headed, big-eyed crazy folks under the front porch?" He welded me to the spot with his gritty gaze. A sly grin flitted behind a ragged growth of whiskers.

"Well, my only living brother isn't the brightest burning log on the fire, but he's not exactly a slobbering idiot either."

My inquisitor's smile broadened as he lit his hand-rolled cigarette. Soft blue swirls of smoke wafted from his lips and enveloped most of his head as he said, "Think he'll do just fine, Cap'n."

Culpepper's face lit up like a kid who'd just been handed an apple crate full of puppies. "By Godfrey, knew he would. The formidable Boz Tatum hasn't brought in a bad one yet."

He stopped for a moment, and worked pretty hard for several seconds clearing his throat. Then he said, "Private's pay is forty dollars, in gold coin, a month, Mr. Dodge. Corporals receive the same sum, but promotion to sergeant will get you an extra ten. The state of Texas has seen fit to provide you with a rifle and cartridges." He motioned at the Henry in my hand with his wad of papers. "Appears as how you have one of your own that is probably as good, or better than those at our disposal. You are required to supply your own pistol. If memory serves, you're the first man I've recruited, in the better part of a year, who came to us wearing three of Mr. Colt's Peacemaker guns. Horse, saddle, traps, and such are also your responsibility. State does, however, furnish provisions, and we have a damned fine cook right here in camp. He works out of a chuck wagon and kitchen not far from your new pardner's digs. Don't have an official badge for you. But Boz can introduce you to a feller who can make one. Carves a right fine Texas star out of anything silver. Some men wear 'em, majority don't. Most folks know us for Rangers when they see us. But if the choice was mine, I'd have a badge of some kind fashioned, or make a point of visiting Fort Worth to acquire one."

Then the Ranger captain twisted around in his chair,

pinched the bridge of his nose for a moment, and looked tired. "I'll be the first to admit the state's remuneration is a pretty paltry amount given the hazards of this work, Lucius. No mistaken beliefs here, son, this is a dangerous profession to make damned little in the way of money. Hopefully the legislature will rectify its shortcomings at some future date. Presently, however, those on the knife's edge have to do the best we can with what those who think themselves wiser than us are willing to provide."

Boz clapped me on the shoulder and said, "Captain has eight other new Rangers to be sworn, and will perform the ceremony tomorrow morning. Wants to do as many as he can at the same time."

Lieutenant Beaumont perked up again. "We'll get 'er done after breakfast. Probably about nine o'clock. Boz can take care of you till then. Get you a cot, and such. Bet he has plenty of room over in The Viper's Nest."

Culpepper hopped up and stabbed his massive hand my direction again. Treated my mangled fingers a bit gentler that time, but pulled me slightly forward as he spoke. "Only require two things from my company of lawmen, Mr. Dodge—loyalty and discipline. We are no longer a loose-knit band of citizen volunteers who come together at the whim of bloody necessity. Ours is now an organization of paid professionals, and I expect my men to conduct themselves as such. Rambunctious, drunken behavior, while on duty, will not be tolerated. During the past month I've drummed four men out of the state's service because of their intoxicated and dishonorable deeds. I have no doubt you will do your best to respect my desires for maintaining good order. Till tomorrow morning, Ranger Dodge."

Tatum pulled Culpepper aside. The two of them talked low and fast for several minutes. Once they'd finished, Boz grabbed my elbow, and ushered me back toward the hustle and bustle of the larger encampment. We strolled deeper into the flurry of activity.

By and by, he stopped at the flapped opening of a tent-and-log dwelling that appeared large enough to shelter four to six men. A wooden sign dangled from the leading pole. Scrawled red paint proclaimed the rustic lodging as THE VIPER'S NEST. Trinity River trickled along about twenty-five or thirty paces behind the heavy canvas structure. A stout corral, large enough for several horses, stood over to one side.

Boz blessed the coarse shelter and horse pen with a regal salute, as though his digs rivaled English castles in majesty. "Just turn ole Grizz out, and throw your saddle and such anywhere you like. Last feller who bunked with me got killed over on the Red 'bout a month ago. Wasn't paying attention, and let his poor stupid self fall into an ambush. Name was Jefferson Gates. Fine feller. Had a Mexican wife and about a dozen kids. Long as I knew the man, though, he tended toward dangerous lapses of judgment. Went out after Dexter Speaks and his bunch of cutthroats. Said he didn't need any help bringing back scum like them boys. Guess he figured wrong. They lured him into a little box canyon near Spanish Bend, and shot the hell out of him. Heard the body sported twenty-eight bullet holes when some folks traveling between Wichita Falls and the Indian Nations found it."

My new quarters, while spartan, appeared right cozy for such temporary accommodations. Two cots, one on either side of the entrance, a camp table at the rear, and several large chests in one corner made up the only furnishings.

Spent about half an hour getting situated. Don't think Tatum stopped talking the whole time. He had a way of filling a person's ears up. Followed Grizz and me to the corral, and yammered like someone who hadn't conversed with another living human being in years. Man loved the sound of his own voice. Seemed to me everything he said simply led to another gruesome tale of death and destruction. He'd fought in the Civil War all over Texas, and most of the Southwest. Near as I could tell, Boz had killed blue-bellied Yankees by the score, and slaughtered Comanches, Apaches, and the Kiowa, along with just about every other kind of "red devil" I'd ever heard anyone mention.

Soon as I dropped my saddle, he said, "Let's amble over to Alfonso Esparza's den fer a spell. Just a few steps further down the river."

"Who's Alfonso Esparza?"

"He's the feller what's gonna fix you up with a solid silver badge."

We picked our way through the huckleberry bushes and scrubby trees, for about fifty yards past The Viper's Nest, to a clearing around a neatly kept stick-and-grass hut. The shelter appeared to have been erected as near as possible to an anvil attached to a tree stump and a small forge nearby. A Mexican man, of indeterminate age and the color of baked red clay, sat in the doorway on a three-legged stool. Tobacco rolled in a corn shuck dangled from cracked lips. He made no effort to stand, slowly removed the homemade cigar from his mouth, and flashed a brilliant, toothy smile.

"Buenos dias, Señor Boz. Como está?"

"Muy bien, mi amigo." They shook hands, but Esparza still made no attempt to rise.

Tatum turned to me and said, "Need you to make my young friend a badge, Alfonso."

"Qué?"

Tatum struggled with the interpretation. Finally he pulled his vest back and pointed at the heavy star pinned to his own chest. *"Ah, una emblema. Una estrella plata. Exactamente. Comprende, amigo?"*

Esparza's face lit up. *"Sí, sí. Una estrella de plata. Necessito una moneda de ocho reales."*

Tatum made motions at me. "Give 'im two eight-real coins, Lucius. He'll turn one into a silver star for you. The other'n pays fer his efforts."

Glanced into the hut, as I handed the money over.

Reminded me of the bunkhouse at Las Tres Colinas. A well-worn hammock dangled from one corner, ready to be stretched out for an evening's siesta. A variety of tools lined the walls—everything from horseshoe tongs to heavy hammers. No additional clothing, or anything like personal amenities, in sight. Place was neat as a pin, and the packed dirt floor appeared swept.

Boz hooked a thumb over his concho-embellished belt. "Alfonso can fashion damned near whatever a man might possibly desire out of an eight-real coin. Made this here belt for me. He does right fine work with horses too. Hammers out shoes, mends saddles and bridles. Mighty handy with all other kinds of leatherwork as well." He placed his hand on the Mexican's shoulder. "His repair work on a broken pistol or rifle is, far and away, better than any of Colt's traveling gunsmiths. He can tune a pistol so's all you have to do is breath on the trigger. Man of many parts. Right, my friend?"

Alfonso puffed at his cigar and grinned. "Sí, amigo. Un hombre de muchos partes." Got the impression the aged peon could probably speak English about as well as he understood it. Just didn't want to, for one reason or another.

"Mañana, amigo?" Boz asked.

The old man squirmed on his stool and eyeballed the coins. "No Señor Boz. El dia siguiente. Muy ocupado hoy."

Tatum nodded. "Day after tomorrow's just dandy. Adios, my friend."

He turned away from the blacksmith's coarse throne and started back for our tent. I followed and said, "He didn't appear all that busy to me."

Boz shook his head and chuckled. "Well, Alfonso tends to work on Alfonso time. Think his clock, along with his notions on what he wants, or doesn't want, to do is a mite different from yours or mine." He laughed and slapped his leg. The man really enjoyed his own jokes. He said, "Let's take a siesta, amigo. Wanna put my poor ole bruised self down for an hour or so afore supper. Some of these knots Peaches put on me are beginning to hurt a bit. 'Specially the ones on back of my head. Bet he left some ugly marks on my ribs too."

I fully intended to spend the rest of the afternoon lazing in camp chairs out front of my new home. But Tatum went right to sleep and made noises that reminded me of a hibernating bear. Put me to walking the cooler areas around the riverbank, till I found a restful spot and settled in for a nap of my own.

Long 'bout sundown Boz came back to life, found my hiding place, and led me over to the kitchen for the evening meal. Cookhouse seemed closest to being the most permanent structure I'd seen that day. A pair of chuck wagons sat cheek by jowl to a canvas-roofed log building of about ten by twelve feet. Spotted a brick oven built into one end. A likely enough place to prepare a meal, but the victuals provided damned sure couldn't compare to my mother's cooking.

Hash slinger was a feller named Noah Biggerstaff. All visible evidence indicated he rarely missed a meal, and probably spent right smart of every day sampling his own efforts. Honest to God, the man had a belly the size of a flour barrel. Several Mexican helpers spooned a variety of good-smelling but highly suspicious-looking stuff for anyone holding a plate and with nerve enough to try some.

Boz pushed a wooden dish into my reluctant hands and said, "Don't worry, Lucius. Long as Noah's grub don't bite back, you can probably eat it. But if anything wiggles, or winks at you, just flip the offensive piece out on the ground. One of the dogs'll take care of it for you." He grinned like a man having the time of his life, and turned to the cook. "I'm hungry enough to eat a boiled armadillo, Noah."

Biggerstaff ran a greasy hand across the front of an apron that could stand alone, thumped at something clinging to the edge of the pot he stood behind, and snapped,

"Well, we ain't got no goddamned armerdillers tonight, Boz. Yer gonna have to settle fer a couple pounds of beef-steak, covered in chili made from yestiddy's beefsteak, a dozen or so tamales, big spoon of frijoles, and a handful of corn fritters doused in black-strap molasses."

Tatum elbowed me and winked. "Should keep me till to-morrow morning. Course I do get to hankering for a little something to smooth the edges off my appetite around mid-night. Got any of your world-famous sucamagrowl cooked up?"

Biggerstaff kept shoveling food and pointed to the end of the serving table without looking. "Swear to Jesus, Boz. You're worse than a kid about sweets. They's a bucketful of 'em down yonder. Don't take 'em all. Last time you et so many, rest of the company didn't hardly get none. No more'n six, you hear me."

Hated to show my countrified ignorance, but they'd left me in the dirt. Leaned over and whispered, "What the hell's sucamagrowl, Boz?"

"Ain't for certain sure. Kinda like biscuit dough fried in sugar, vinegar, and cinnamon, I think. Don't know exactly what he does to 'em. They's a bunch better'n sugar tits, though. Damned fine stuff. But if Noah Biggerstaff actu-ally believes I'm only gonna take six, then he's about half as smart as a wooden Indian."

Once we'd near'bouts filled ourselves to overflowing, Boz led me around camp and introduced me to most of a hundred other fellers. That's when I discovered each com-pany of Rangers consisted of seventy-five men, commanded by a captain and two lieutenants. Right difficult for my pea-sized brain to keep track of that many folks. Couldn't have told you one of their names ten minutes after we met.

Tatum near wore me out, roaming from fire to fire. Man nipped at the bottle of anyone who offered, and made sure I got some too. Swapped tall tales with those who'd listen. Even sang a couple of songs with some boys who had a fiddle, mouth organ, and tambourine. Learned, right away, that in spite of his reputation as an Indian fighter and Texas Ranger, Boz Tatum had the worst singing voice this side of the fiery pit. Didn't keep him from performing with a goodly amount of gusto, though.

When we got back to The Viper's Nest, Boz lit a lamp and said, "Sit down and write your mother a letter, son. Best she knows what you've done got yourself into so she won't be any more worried 'bout you than necessary."

Being as how we'd had a snort or three that evening, I can't recollect exactly what I said in my badly scribbled note. But I'm fairly certain I penned something like:

Dear Mother,

　　Am still in pursuit of Whitey and Erazmus. Have enlisted with Company B of the Texas Rangers. Will return to Las Tres Colinas, and real employment, once I've brought Pa's murderers to book, or killed the evil sons of bitches outright. Tell Burl to be strong. I will return as soon as I am able. I remain,

Your loving son,
Lucius

Boz read over my missive and said, "You done good, young feller. We'll post her first chance we get."

Guess we cashed in an hour or so before midnight. Slept right well, in spite of skeeters the size of frying pans buzzing outside my net. Woke up once. Boz sat on the edge of his cot slapping at the bugs and popping them sugary biscuits in his mouth like beer nuts in a Fort Worth saloon.

At exactly nine o'clock the next morning, according to my two-dollar silver-plated Ingersoll pocket watch, the entire company fell into military formation, and watched as me, and them other recruits, mounted up and formed a line in front of the officers' pavilion. The captain strutted out, dressed in a splendid red coat and black hat sporting a white feather that grew out of the top and hung over the brim.

Boz told me later, "Wag only wears that red thang when he's a-swearing new men, or going to a dance and wants to impress the ladies. Do declare the man suffers from the worst case of vanity I've ever run across."

The lieutenants brought everyone to something that approximated attention. Soon as all the attendees got quiet, Culpepper read the oath of allegiance to the state of Texas, and had us newcomers sign our names. Just as easy as that, we were proclaimed as officially enlisted for the next twelve months.

Quick as the fleeting ceremony ended, Boz and Ben Beaumont came over and shook my hand. Beaumont said, "We've decided to put you under the capable wing of your friend, Ranger Tatum, Lucius. Not a better man in Texas to learn from. Pay attention, what he has to teach you could very well keep you alive."

Boz did a toe-in-the-dirt, aw-shucks act, and said, "Well, I owe this boy my life, Ben. Hadn't been for him, ole Peaches McCabe would probably have turned me into little more'n a greasy spot on the floor in the White Elephant. Gonna be my pleasure to have young Mr. Dodge ride with me a spell. Oh, I have something for you, Lucius. Picked it up this morning."

He dipped into his vest pocket and came out with a spanking-new silver star. Pinned the shining symbol of my newly acquired authority to my vest and said, "Alfonso tends to work faster if you give him a bit more incentive. Wanted you to have this soon as you got sworn, and he agreed when I laid a few more reales on him. Now you're a Ranger, for damned sure."

I had not considered the burden of the work until Tatum pinned that badge on me. Felt the weight against my chest. Suddenly I realized just how much responsibility I'd taken on. Course I'd ridden with Rangers in the past when the Comanche got on a killing rip. But most of those red devils had been exiled to the Nations and the frontier situation from Fort Worth to the New Mexico border had civilized up dramatically.

By and by, the notion came to me that Ranger Randall Bozworth Tatum had managed to make me a part of the Great Lone Star State's glorious history. I didn't get long to contemplate my newly found revelation.

Lieutenant Beaumont's counterpart, a man only a few years older than me named Bedford Pickens, strolled up and said, "Captain Culpepper wants to talk with you boys right away. Think he might be about to send you out on your first real assignment, Dodge. If I know him, boys, this dance's gonna be a dandy."

5

"... HORSE AND COW STEALING, STREET SHOOTINGS AND SUCH."

I'VE NOTICED OVER the years, as how a man's mind has a tendency to erase good times and populate his waking thoughts with the horrors he often had to confront during life's long journey. Such was the case with the "dandy" of an assignment Captain Culpepper had in mind.

I champed at the bit to get back on the trail of Whitey and Raz again. But the events that awaited us, less than a hundred miles from Fort Worth, would pull me away from that mission and remain hidden from the general public for decades. Seventy years later, when most of what Boz and me accomplished together has been relegated to places so deep in my memory I have trouble bringing them to mind, the brutishness and blood of Sweetwater is as vivid as an open wound.

When we reported for our initial mission together, Beaumont sat on Culpepper's left, Pickens on his right. The trio looked about as serious as men who'd just been informed they suffered from gangrene and would each have to part with a leg, an arm, or something even more valuable. We had no way of knowing at the time, but the events of the few minutes spent with our superiors that morning were merely the beginnings of what would eventually become a long list of celebrated Boz Tatum and Lucius Dodge outings.

The captain cleared his throat and roared, "For some months now, I've been in receipt of one letter after another from a storekeeper over in Sweetwater. Gentleman name of Burton Hickerson feels the town has serious problems. Truth is, I'm about to get tired of having to read through a seemingly endless litany of whining complaints. His entreaties have become more strident with each missive. Latest communication, received yesterday, runs some eight pages, and is witnessed by almost fifty of the hamlet's three hundred permanent residents. Those folks claim to suffer at the mercy of an outlaw family headed by a gentleman named Titus Nightshade. Think you boys should take a ride out that way. See what you can discover."

"Whattaya think we're a-gonna find, Cap'n?" Boz asked.

Bedford Pickens leaned into the conversation. "Mr. Hickerson's catalog of individual grievances is a long one, boys. Charges of horse and cattle theft, terrorization of citizens in the night, and call-out street shootings seem commonplace events with this bunch. Not much of a way for us to tell exactly what you can reasonably expect to run up against. So, best be ready for almost any eventuality."

Boz cocked his head to one side. "Want us to look for something in particular, Cap'n?" He put a fair amount of stress on the word particular. "I mean anything other'n the horse and cow stealing, street shootings, and such."

Evidently Culpepper didn't want to discuss vague possibilities. Man stuck to the specifics. "You catch anybody stealing livestock, Boz, drag 'em back to Fort Worth soon as you're able. Otherwise, the God-fearing citizens of Sweetwater just might indulge in a little extra-legal cow-pasture justice of their own. I think everyone in Texas saw enough lynching before, during, and immediately after the war. Hell, I was a shirttailed kid back in '62, in Gainesville, when vigilantes hung nigh fifty folks in less than a week. You and Dodge gotta nip any such brutish behavior in the bud. I don't want the governor dragging me down to Austin to explain how such a thing happened on my watch. Can I make my feelings any plainer on this matter, boys?"

Boz shook his head, so I did the same. "Want us to read all them letters?" he asked.

Culpepper studied on Boz's query, for a second or so. "No, shouldn't be necessary. Probably better all round if you got the story firsthand."

Didn't waste much time messing around camp once we had our marching orders. Stopped by The Viper's Nest long enough to grab our war bags and saddle up. Boz broke open one of the chests sitting on his side of the tent and handed me a brace of Colt's Dragoon pistols in pommel holsters.

"They's loaded and primed, Lucius. Throw 'em on Grizz. Never know when you might need some more firepower."

Being as how I could barely walk with all the guns hanging on me already, I tried to give them back. "I've got my hip pistols, and the one at my back, along with the Henry. Carrying a bowie the size of a meat cleaver on my belt, and a six-inch toothpick in each boot. Got a steel-headed war ax tied to my saddle. Don't think I need any more weapons, Boz."

"But you just never know, do you, son? Always better to have one you don't need, than to need one you don't have. With five pistols you can rip off near thirty rounds and never stop to reload. Besides, tough to match these big ole Dragoons in a horseback gunfight. Your Henry's a fine weapon, but I ain't seen a man yet could fire one from a running horse worth a damn—lest he was part Comanche, or some other such land moccasin."

Never is easy to argue with sound reasoning. But his gift

presented me with a touchy problem. Game as Grizz was, the stringy mustang always got a bit testy when made to carry even a few ounces more than he liked. Between the added iron, extra food, cooking utensils, and camp gear Boz wanted to take along, I finally suggested we buy a mule. He liked the idea, and that's the way the thing shook out.

Boz said, "I know a dealer who likes to hang around Hugh Dugan's wagon yard on West Weatherford in Fort Worth. Bet he's got exactly what we need." So, we hoofed our way by the place, and arrived about the time this picture-taking feller name of Swartz got his box camera set up in the middle of the street.

He came running over soon as we stepped down, handed both of us a calling card, and said, "Gentlemen, I am a photographer, illustrator, and publisher of *Souvenir Views of Fort Worth*. Would you be willing to pose for me this morning?"

Boz grinned and winked. "Why not. My young friend and me could very well be the best-looking Rangers in all of Texas. Might as well let you preserve our native handsomosity for the sake of future generations. Hell, maybe a wealthy, semi-attractive widder woman who owns a saloon will see us. You have to promise to send 'em our way, if any come askin' 'bout us. Jest point 'em toward Company B's Ranger camp. We'll take care of things from there."

Swartz got a kick out of the joke. Said he'd write our names down, and make sure any interested females got informed of our whereabouts. Then he led us over to Dugan's office, where five other men, a woman, and little girl had already been posed.

He sat Boz on the corner of the plank boardwalk, and stood me right behind him. Kept mumbling about how he'd never seen that many guns on two men before in his whole life. Saw that picture in Swartz's Studio window several years later. Smaller and considerably less famous, our images rested behind a well-known rendering of Butch

Cassidy, the Sundance Kid, and their celebrated train robbing syn-di-cate. Them arrogant bastards got a case of the bigheaded stupidity by posing for that photo. Swartz put a copy on display and, before the Wild Bunch knew what hit, the Pinkertons swarmed all over them. Do believe their case of smiling bravado was the most dim-witted thing any gang of Texas outlaws ever did.

We purchased a fine piece of mule flesh named Butterbean from Boz's friend, Cretis Kincaid. Never did understand why Tatum liked the man so much. Near as I could tell, Kincaid had the personality of a teased tarantula and the social graces of a starved rat. But, have to give a man credit where credit's due. He took good care of his stock. Butterbean was a mite elderly, but sleek-coated and well-fed.

Soon as we got the extra weapons, ammunition, food, and possibles off our mounts and loaded onto the mule, Boz headed us north and west. He said, "Hell, it's only about fifty or sixty miles. We'll just mosey along and save the animals. Still won't take but a couple of days to make the ride. Nice little community, if memory serves. Mixed bunch of folks who migrated from Alabama, Mississippi, and Georgia back in '65. Think most of them came in with a group from Georgia that was simply trying to get away from the mess Sherman left on his march from Atlanta to the sea. They sure enough found the garden spot of north Texas. There's thirty artesian wells in and around the town, pumping water into some of the richest soil in this part of the state. Once heard a feller from up that way say he could stick a piece of stove wood in the ground and grow an oak tree."

'Bout the only way to stop Boz talking was to get his mind on something else. Course, then he'd rattle on for hours about whatever you'd set him out after. Not much of anything but rolling grassland west of Fort Worth. As a consequence, began to think ole Tatum would talk my ear completely off the side of my head by the time we got to Sweetwater.

We hit the two-rut Jacksboro Road and stuck to it for the most part. Gullies, riverbeds, and creeks tended to foster the only trees available to the eye. Infernal sun had cooked all the green out of the prairie. Anytime we took to the countryside, parched brittle grass crunched under our animals' feet, and straightaway turned into drifting waves of yellow dust. Soil of the roadbed and beneath the burnt-up vegetation looked like the bottom of an iron skillet seasoned over countless open campfires.

Late on the evening of our second day out, we came upon an area lush with trees and well-watered farmland. Grass turned green again, and seemed to grow on the tiniest piece of ground not touched by a plow, or where something else wasn't already planted.

Ambled into Sweetwater about an hour before sundown. Came up from the south and had to cross the covered bridge over Walnut Creek. I liked the rumbling sound our animals made as they clomped beneath its arched roof. Noticed how the clear, fast-running stream below virtually encircled the entire town like a horseshoe. Almost all the buildings stood along a main thoroughfare that ran straight as a chalk line from south to north.

On the right, almost as soon as you came off the bridge, was a good-sized church topped with an impressive steeple. Building looked newly whitewashed and sparkled in the dying sunlight. The pious and faithful who sat in pews along that side on Sundays had a great view of the creek.

As we got closer to the center of town, rode by a livery stable and blacksmith operation. Passed at least three saloons on either side of the street. Bashwell's and the Texas Star were on the east. The sign above a rough joint directly across from the Star proclaimed itself as Shorty Small's. Town had several stores, including Hickerson's Dry Goods Emporium, where the post office, the telegraph office, a barbershop, and the local lockup had spaces in parts of the same sizable building.

Opposite them, on the western edge of the square, was an outfit called Bruce Brother's. Not nearly as imposing as the Hickerson operation. A respectable presence nonetheless. Bit further up, and almost in the woods, sat a building that put me in mind of a one-room schoolhouse.

From all available appearances, town of Sweetwater looked like the kind of place anyone would want to live. Kids trotted along behind our horses, and giggled when Boz spit a stream of tobacco juice their direction. Dogs lazed on the boardwalks not bothering to rouse themselves to protest our invasion of their territory or the flies bedeviling their ears. Well-tended horses, singly and attached to buggies and spring wagons, stood at hitch rails all along the street. Others sought shelter from the sun beneath a patch of grand-looking oak trees, growing in the middle of a grass-covered central square, plopped down right in the heart of town. Cool, shady, and inviting-looking, the spot was decorated with a Civil War cannon and plaque dedicated to Southern men who'd died valiantly during the Unpleasantness.

Folks on the boardwalk saw us first. Word must have got around right away that strangers had arrived. Gawkers streamed out of every doorway, or hung from open windows, and watched as we passed.

Reined up in front of Hickerson's, Boz muttered, "That damned bridge sends out a warning sure as a cavalry bugle. Whole town must have heard us when we crossed it."

Prosperous-looking gentleman wearing a spotless apron and starched white shirt with fancy garters on his sleeves came out of the store and said, "You boys looking for anyone in particular?"

"Hickerson," Boz said. "Burton Hickerson."

Man in the garters wiped his hands on a piece of rag, and looked uncomfortable. "I'm Burton Hickerson. What can I do for you?"

"Name's Randall Bozworth Tatum. This handsome young feller here's my partner, Lucius Dodge. We're Texas

Rangers from Company B over in Fort Worth." He turned and pulled sealed papers from his saddlebag. "Letter of introduction from Captain Waggoner Culpepper," he said as he leaned forward and offered the note to the merchant. "We hear you folks been havin' some problems, and need help."

Believe the smile on Hickerson's face could have lit up that side of the town's square at midnight. "Step down, gentlemen. I can guarantee our entire community will be most pleased to hear of your arrival." Guess he thought better of such an all-encompassing statement. He scratched his chin and said, "Perhaps I should revise my welcome by saying those citizens of Sweetwater who matter will be pleased with your arrival. Do come inside."

We left a nice-sized crowd buzzing around in the street. Hickerson ushered us through his store. Past the flour, pickles, rakes, hoes, and a variety of saddles, boots, clothing, and all manner of canned and bottled goods. Stock was located behind two counters that ran the entire thirty feet of wall space on both sides of the building. Several large tables in the center bulged with a variety of sundries for those with loose spending money in their pockets.

Melon-headed boy in the aisle, whose eyes looked a bit too far apart, stepped aside and bobbed his head. He leaned on a well-used broom, doffed his raggedy cap, and as we passed, said, "Evenin', fine gennemums. Good evenin' to yez. Fine evenin', ain't it. Right fine evenin'."

Hickerson paused and placed a protective hand on the boy's shoulder. "This is Lenny Milsap. Lenny lives in the shed, out back of the store. Cleans up for us, and runs errands. Everyone in town knows Lenny. These are Texas Rangers, Lenny. They've come to help us."

Milsap held his cap over his heart, threw his head back, and weaved around like wheat blowing in the wind. Went to talking to himself again. "Rangers. They be Texas Rangers, Lenny. Done come to help Mr. Hickerson. Maybe save us from the dark people. Yes, save us from the dark ones."

Hickerson smiled and patted the unfortunate boy's shoulder. We followed the storekeeper through a door and into a comfortable-looking room that appeared to double as a parlor and kitchen. An attractive, well-dressed lady stood at the stove and stirred the contents of a large iron pot.

Boz sniffed the air like a Kentucky coon dog that had died and gone to heaven. "Whatever you're a-cooking there smells mighty good, missus."

Hickerson waved us toward the table. "Please sit. Marie, these men are Rangers Tatum and Dodge. Captain Culpepper has finally responded to our concerns."

The lady nodded. "You've arrived just in time for supper, gentlemen. We have vegetable-beef stew and jalapeno pepper cornbread. And for dessert, hot apple pie."

Boz pulled a chair, sat, and held his hat against his chest. I thought, for a second, he was praying. But then he grinned and said, "Well, missus, they's a feller what cooks for us, over in Fort Worth, name of Biggerstaff. Been eatin' from his bill of fare for nigh on six months. Don't remember anything he's cooked up so far smelled as good as your stew and cornbread. And my God, that apple pie already has my poor mouth a-waterin'. Hope you've done cooked up enough for eight or ten people. My young friend here has a right healthy appetite. As you can readily see, he's still a growing boy."

She laughed at my obvious embarrassment, and sassily snapped back, "Well, just have to see if we can fill him up, won't we. Long as he don't have a stomach the size of a rain barrel, I think there's plenty to go around."

Hickerson said grace over the groceries, then launched right in on the town's complaints before I could get the first spoonful to my mouth. "Little over three years ago, a busted-up piece of wagon, held together with rawhide straps, rumbled across Walnut Creek and stopped right in the middle of the town square. Scruffy Nightshade bunch set up camp under the biggest live oak. Man, woman, gang of kids, all kinds of animals. Bet they had twenty dogs. Kids went to work with hatchets and chopped limbs for firewood out of that precious hundred-year-old tree. Sheriff had to stop the beastly little savages, or they would surely have killed it. He made them corral all their animals too. His efforts at controlling the rowdy family worked for about a day. Typical of the Nightshades. Everything with them works for about a day. Sometimes two. Then they'll start something else that's usually twice as bad."

Boz slurped at his spoon a couple of times, before he responded. "Sounds like you felt these Nightshades were a problem from the git-go."

Mrs. Hickerson, who'd taken the seat opposite me, didn't have a plate or bowl, and sat with hands folded in her lap. I knew the lady would eat after we'd finished. She said, "No, they weren't considered a real problem at first. In fact, most expressed a degree of pleasure at the prospect of having another Southern-bred family in our community. Just about everyone in town tried, in one way or another, to make them feel welcome."

Not exactly sure how much Boz expected me to contribute, but he didn't look at all surprised when I chimed in with, "Why would you welcome a family whose very first act involved destruction of town property and disruptive behavior?"

Mrs. Hickerson smoothed the apron covering her lap. "Well, given that nearly every family in Sweetwater arrived from some part of the still-smoldering South in a similar state, we wanted to be neighborly. But every effort on our part met with the most foul and belligerent kind of response. Besides, we had no way of knowing the Nightshade clan was a bunch of yellow-dog traitors who sided with the North during the great War of Yankee Aggression."

"Can you give us an example of their quarrelsome behavior?" I asked. "Something you would consider, as Mr. Hickerson has said, typical."

She didn't have to think long. "Well, my friend Ellen Wilson tried to invite them to church for the Sunday service and fellowship." She hesitated. Her face and ears reddened. "The language those Nightshade girls used on Ellen would have made a Georgia moonshiner blush. Ladies standing nearby couldn't even bring themselves to repeat the outburst of filthiness they heard that morning. I finally dragged the encounter out of my friend Ageline Whitaker. Never would have believed girls that young knew such words."

Soon as she said girls, twice, my ears just naturally pricked up. "Mrs. Hickerson, are you saying the female members of the family cursed your friend?"

"Absolutely. Language so hot, Sweet Lord, it's a wonder that offensive rant didn't set their wagon ablaze and scorch the trees around it."

Hickerson listened and nodded his agreement like a deacon on the front row at a fire-breathing hard-shell Baptist tent revival. He held his hand up as if to stop his wife's testimony and said, "Fortunately, less than a week after they arrived, Titus, paterfamilias of the churlish tribe, purchased several plots of land about a mile off the Jacksboro Road south of town. We still haven't found out how he managed the transaction. No one in these parts will admit to the sale. Land certificates he showed came from a Fort Worth bank. I've heard a number of folks express an opinion questioning whether the documents might be counterfeit."

Boz picked at his teeth and muttered, "Has been known to happen. Exact thing that caused the Regulator-Moderator War over in Shelbyville, some years back."

Hickerson shook his head. "Guess it don't matter. You see, we celebrated when the whole rambunctious crew vanished from the square, one morning, and threw up a ramshackle log house beside Little Agnes Creek. Thought we'd pretty much got rid of them. Couldn't have been any further off the mark on that one." He stopped, and looked sneaky for a few seconds. "You boys rode right past their place on your way into town. I'd be willing to bet they're already aware of your arrival. And only God knows what they'll do."

Marie Hickerson leaned toward me and whispered, "Yes, and only God knows what goes on out there in that den of iniquity. The stories we've heard could turn a body's hair white."

"What kind of stories?" I asked.

Hickerson and his wife swapped furtive glances. He nodded as if to approve her yet-to-be-told tale. "Well," she said, "that oldest gal, Nance, appeared to be with child when they arrived. But no one here ever saw a baby, or heard for certain what might have happened to it. There have been rumors, though."

"What kind of rumors?" Boz sputtered though a mouth stuffed with a third slab of cornbread.

The lady got more conspiratorial, cupped her hand beside her mouth as though afraid some unseen person might hear. "Lady of my acquaintance tells as how she saw Nance stop in the woods, deliver the babe while holding the reins of her horse." She paused, clutched her throat, and said, "Then smashed the newborn's tiny skull with a rock."

Boz coughed and spit chunks of yellow meal and peppers into his hand. "Sweet Jesus, missus. That's murder if'n I ever heard of one. Saw a jail when we came into town. Did your resident lawman investigate the charge?"

Burton Hickerson pushed beef and vegetables around in a still-steaming bowl with his spoon. "'Bout three months after the Nightshades arrived in town, our sheriff, nice feller named Charlie Fain, up and disappeared. No one has seen hide or hair of the man since. Scared everyone so bad, the town council can't get any of the locals to accept the job. We've tried to hire a new man, but haven't had any luck. Talk was that anyone taking the job just might disappear too. People around here are scared to death. Nightshades come to town, and everyone runs for cover."

Marie Hickerson shook her finger in our faces. "And boys, what we've told you thus far is merely the first rattle out of the box. Good many people hereabouts believe those girls are all soiled doves, and that ole Titus is nothing more'n a whoremonger. Lots of strange faces on our streets since that family arrived. Hard-looking men. Rustlers, thieves, and probably worse. Burton and I could go through the entire story, but think it would be better for you to speak directly with those who've encountered the Nightshade bunch, and lived to regret it."

Boz leaned back in his chair, and stretched. "Given what we've seen so far, a body would never guess Sweetwater suffered under anything like the kind of antagonism you've described."

Hickerson stared into his bowl. When he looked up, ominous lines crackled around his eyes and mouth. "Well, Ranger Tatum, just you wait till the Nightshade gang comes to town. Amazing how swiftly the citizens of our beautiful piece of heaven can disappear from the streets, not to be seen again until Titus and his bunch of thugs head back to Little Agnes Creek."

Marie Hickerson's voice dropped like a bucket of ice on a frozen well rope. Sounded unearthly, prophetlike, when she said, "You seem like nice young men. Do be careful. The Devil is coming to Sweetwater and won't be satisfied until he's collected many an unsuspecting soul. You can take my word on this, there's a bloody time ahead. It's been creeping this way since the day that evil family, and their friends, arrived. Everyone in town has had his hackles up, and knows that all the rude behavior, beatings, gunplay, and livestock theft will eventually lead to Satan's bloody wrath. Sure as chickens can't lay square eggs, there's gonna be hell to pay."

6

"Seemed Like a Good Idea
at the Time."

AFTER MARIE HICKERSON'S rib-sticking dinner, Burton led us over, opened up, and helped Boz and me get settled into the abandoned sheriff's office. Just enough room for two cots, a well-used desk, a pair of run-down chairs, a potbellied stove, and an iron-bound cage. Four metal bunks, lined with straw, hung on chains from the cell's ten-by-twelve-foot basketlike walls.

Sweetwater's lockup looked brand-spanking-new to me. Hardly any noticeable corrosion, but covered with a fine layer of dust as though it'd never seen any use. The sad clapboard building appeared to have been constructed around the ominous-looking lockup.

Seldom-used hinges on the calaboose door squalled in protest when pulled open. "Sheriff Fain ever lock anyone up in your town's *juzgado* before he vanished, Mr. Hickerson?"

Our host threw me a satisfied smile. "Prior to the arrival of Titus Nightshade and his band of brigands, we never really had much use for a jail."

•

"That a fact," I said.

"Yep. Mainly kept up just for show. You know, the kind of thing you scare kids with. Once in a great while, one of our youngsters would get caught trying to look down a little girl's pantalets, or tipping an outhouse over, or pilfering hard candy out of my store. Ole Charlie would pinch their ears, and run them in here for a lecture on how he'd lock them up for life if they ever got caught doing anything else wrong. Tactic worked, mainly."

Boz slapped his leg with his hat. "By Godfrey, that's exactly the kind of life's lesson more of our young people need these days. Rambunctious little shits over in Fort Worth run the streets and alleys like wild animals. City marshal and county sheriff spend almost as much time trying to corral strong-willed, high-spirited kids these days as they do keeping south Texas brush-poppers in line who blow through on their way to the railheads in Kansas."

Pulled one of the chairs from the desk and sat myself down. The antiquated rump roost groaned and squeaked like a week-old shoat. "Well, Burton, you've got a pretty good idea how Boz feels about the matter. Personally, I wouldn't want to spend five minutes locked up in a booby hatch like this one. Bet if we pitched a couple of the Nightshade tribe in here for a spell, might take some of the starch out of the whole crowd."

Hickerson shook his head. "They're a pretty feisty bunch, Mr. Dodge. The women are as bad, or worse than the men. And, honest to God, I do believe Titus's wife, Dusky, is the worst of the lot. Woman can cut loose with some of the bluest language I've ever heard come out of any female's mouth. Even those girls roaming the streets of Hell's Half Acre, over in Forth Worth, can't hold a candle to her in the swearing department." He thought about what he'd said for a moment, amended his ruminations with: "Then again, oldest daughter Nance runs the old man a pretty close second. She's tougher than her brother Jack, and I've never seen him back away from anything. That boy looks like a coiled rattlesnake all the time. Angriest human being I've ever been around."

Guess Hickerson finally realized we'd just about run out our string for the day. He started for the door, but stopped just before pulling it shut behind him. "Don't mean to tell you fellers how to do your job, but if left to me, I'd start by talking to House Rickards—Sweetwater's blacksmith. He's the one who got the first taste of just what kind of trouble comes when you cross the Nightshades. Hope you Rangers sleep well because, once you start asking questions around here, your whole lives are gonna change. Be on your toes. Number of folks who got on the wrong side of the Nightshades ended up on the receiving end of a hellacious beating in the middle of the night. Take my advice and stay together, boys. You'll live considerable longer."

His kind wishes for our pleasant repose didn't pan out. Thundered like damnation, and lightning fell like pitchforks all night long. Never did rain, though. Next morning, after some fried bacon, a fairly decent cup of coffee Boz liked to call belly-wash, and half-a-dozen damned fine biscuits he cooked in a Dutch oven, we strolled down the main thoroughfare to Rickards's thriving blacksmith operation.

The street had begun to busy up by then. Women in gingham dresses and sunbonnets watched us pass, and whispered behind their hands. Kids carrying schoolbooks, with lunch bags thrown over their shoulders on leather straps, snatched furtive glances as they headed to the north end of town, and a day's measure of pure torture chained to a school bench. Saloons, stores, and other businesses had already opened. When we tipped our hats, most folks acted cautious, but friendly.

Smithy's shop reminded me of the barn behind my family's house in Lampasas. The long, rough-cut boards had weathered to a color resembling the soil where the building stood. At some point, the façade appeared to have once been painted red, but time and the extremes of weather had stripped most of the crimson cover away, and left the front wall looking like a large slab of crusted iron fronting the street.

The coarse outside walls were covered with an array of tin signs and metal parts taken from a variety of farm equipment and implements. Inside, pegs, nails, racks, and shelves held a clutter of harnesses, straps, buckles, yokes, bridles, and confused wads of other rigging. In many areas, the litter's depth made sections of the walls impossible to perceive. Much of the leather and metal had seen no use for so long a time, it had dried, cracked, and appeared beyond any hope of recovery.

Got to say, House Rickards looked less like the poet's image of a shoe bender than any man I've ever known to work at the profession. He was short, stringy-muscled, snowy-haired, and damn near sixty years old. If the man had worn a white shirt, string tie, and eyeshade, I would have gladly sworn he was a bookkeeper.

His heavy hammer rose, fell, and tapped out a metallic tune. Covered in sweat and ash, he moved though his work like a dancer. Smell from the smoky fire, heated metal, animals, and the company of other men worked like a magnet that pulled in an appreciative and ever-changing crowd. Without being told, I knew his audience came, and went, like the sparks that flew from the flaming shoes Rickards hammered into shapes that precisely fit each animal's foot. His whittle-and-spit congregation occupied an array of crates and boxes around the forge, and nodded their approval of his talent and skill. They stuffed their pipes, and contributed to the growing pile of splintered wood shavings at their feet.

Available places to take a seat led me to believe the group could have numbered as high as ten or eleven. I knew, having seen similar scenes all my life, men would sit, scrape slivered chunks off a pine picket, talk for a spell, then, like gypsy travelers, move to new and more interesting conversations—no matter where in town they might be located.

Few seconds before we walked up on them Boz whispered, "Pull your vest back so they can see your badge. Always be forthright with folks like these, Lucius. No need to antagonize them if we can keep from it, but let 'em know we're here, and expect 'em to cooperate with our efforts on their behalf." Then he grinned real big and said, "But whatever else you do, ole son, keep one hand on your pistol and make damn sure you watch my back."

Learned pretty promptly that morning, when official business reared its ugly head, Boz Tatum didn't mince words, or put up with much in the way of obfuscation from those he chose to interview. He walked straight up to House Rickards like he owned the shop and the smithy worked for him.

"Mr. Rickards, name's Bozworth Tatum. Young friend here's Lucius Dodge. We're Texas Rangers from Company B out of Fort Worth." Made something of a show when he pulled his vest away from one of Alfonso's heavy silver stars pinned to his chest. "If'n you can spare the time, we'd like to talk with you for a spell."

Chatter and laughter from the half-dozen whittlers dried up like rainwater during a west Texas drought. Got so quiet there, for a minute, I could hear glowing coals in the forge crackle and snap. Rickards propped a set of iron horseshoe tongs against his anvil, jerked a grimy rag from his waist, and wiped at the rivers of sweat streaming down his neck.

"What about?" For a man not much bigger than my younger brother, the elderly blacksmith had a voice that sounded like something coming from an angry panther.

"We understand you've had less than satisfactory dealings with a family name of Nightshade," Boz said.

One of the knife-and-pine picket bunch snorted, "Hell, boys, that describes damn near everybody in Sweetwater." He chuckled. His friends must have liked the joke. Twitters and snickers escaped some of them as well. "Ole House there just happens to be the first of a long list of folks around these parts who've had 'less than satisfactory dealings' with that bunch of ruffians. Yessir, be willing to bet near'bouts everyone here can relate a tale concerning them evil bastards and their witchy women. But such yarns mightn't be very smart health-wise, you know."

Rickards tossed his grubby rag onto the anvil beside the tongs. "I ain't afraid of that bunch, in spite of what they done to me. Ain't afraid of no man. Or woman. Including Nance Nightshade or that wolf-bitch she calls mother."

I decided to act something like a Ranger myself, and said, "What exactly did they do to you, sir?"

He eyed me with a bit more than run-of-the-mill suspicion and shoved gnarled hands behind the bib of his leather apron. "Feller name of Sparky Hazard lived out yonder on the Jacksboro Road not far from where Titus and his family live. Used to come by and sit with all my friends here. Guess them Nightshades had been out in the woods about three weeks, or a month, when Sparky stopped for a visit with us one day and said he was havin' trouble keeping firewood. Said he thought some Injuns might be skulking around in the woods near his house. Felt they was a-stealing from him. So, between the two of us, we figured out a way to put an end to it."

All six of Rickards's friends stifled giggles. Some laughed out loud. Graybeard sitting closest to me said, "Weren't nothing more'n a joke. Anyone else would've just let the thing go. But Titus, Jack, and Arch took the whole business as some kind of personal insult."

Dried-up geezer wearing a Boss of the Plains hat hacked more kindling onto the pile with a foot-long bowie, and said, "Just one of them fanciful thangs that seemed like a good idea at the time. We all got a kick out of it. The whole bunch of us laughed like folks from an insane asylum while we watched House do it."

Guess Boz finally tired of being left out of the joke, and

brought the discussion back to where he wanted when he said, "Mind lettin' me, and my partner, in on the trick? What'd you do?"

Rickards shook his head and toed the dirt. "Drilled out about a dozen sticks of stove wood and spiked them with gunpowder. Nothing more'n big ole firecrackers really. Sparky took 'em home. Stacked 'em under his shed on top of the regular stuff. That night, 'bout half of 'em disappeared. Early the next morning he heard an explosion over toward the Nightshade place. Some folks here in town claimed they heard the blast too. Can't testify to that part myself 'cause of all the hammerin' and other racket around here. Don't matter anyhow. Titus, Jack, Arch, and Nance stormed up to Sparky's house, dragged him out in the yard, and beat the hell out of him. Whipped up on him long enough that he told 'em I was the one what made them woody poppers. He disappeared a few days later. Ain't seen him since."

Boz looked like a man who couldn't believe what his mind had already worked out. "You gonna say they came after you?"

Rickards's head snapped up. Sounded like a man spoiling for another fight when he said, "When the Nightshades ride into town, they all like to hit the bridge across Walnut Creek at the same time. Makes a sound like rolling thunder. I heard 'em coming. Just didn't know what they had in mind. All four of 'em brought their horses to a jumping stop 'bout where you're standing, hopped off their animals, and kicked the hell out of me."

Got to admit it came as something of a surprise when his head dropped in embarrassment. Didn't expect such a reaction from anyone as feisty as he first seemed. He kinda mumbled, "They got me down on the ground and kicked me like a stray dog, Rangers. Worst came from that gal, Nance. She wears boots with hammered-silver tips on the toes and Mexican rowels the size of ten-dollar gold eagles. Them sons of bitches really hurt. Think she was the one what busted a couple of my ribs. By the time all four of them pissed-off thugs took a turn on me, I couldn't even get up."

Boz said, "Did they say anything to you at all?"

"Not till they'd finished. Titus stood over me and whacked a silver-headed riding crop against his palm. He hissed, 'My damned stove went through the roof and landed in the creek, you iron-pounding son of a bitch. You ever pull another stunt like this, and I'll let my boys, and girls, finish you off for good and all.' Then, they mounted up and left me laying here in the dirt. Went fogging over to Shorty Small's Saloon and spent the afternoon, and into the night, drinking. Hadn't been for some of my friends, I'd probably have laid out here in the cold and died. That was three year ago. Only good thing about my particular encounter with them hood-lums seems to be that once they've damned near stomped you to death, they tend to leave you alone, and go looking for their next victim."

Boz shook his head. Could tell he was getting angrier by the second when he said, "Typical goddamned bully be-havior. Sweet Weeping Jesus, I do hate a bully. Sheriff was still here at the time. Did he try to do anything about either of the beatings?"

Whittler, with one of those ancient five-pound Walker Colts sticking out of his belt, said, "I wuz in Shorty's that night. Had me a spot in the corner. Don't think anyone even noticed I was there. Hell, they was all excited and laughing 'bout how they'd just beat the bejabbers out'n Sparky and House. That gal, Nance, stood at the bar and drank straight whiskey with the men. I do believe she's the first woman I ever seen what goes around wearin' pants and straddlin' a horse. Good-looking gal, but damned unla-dylike behavior, if'n you ask me."

The side trips had begun to wear on Boz. "Get to the point, friend. Did the sheriff try to do anything?"

Feller carrying the Walker leaned over and spit before he answered. "Well, Titus and his clan had been at the bottle, pretty hot and heavy, for almost an hour 'fore anything happened. Sheriff Fain came in right after some fellers found House. Charlie barely got his head in the door when Jack Nightshade pulled his pistol and whacked the poor man across the mouth. He never knew what hit 'im. Knocked 'im colder'n a log-splitting wedge in January. Busted three of his teeth. Man never recovered. Disappeared 'bout a week later. Anyhow, the whole gang just kinda sashayed out, took their time saddlin' up, and proceeded to shoot hell out of the town in general. Been doin' the same kind of vicious shit ever since. Bastards seem to take particular pleasure from scarin' the hell outta women and kids."

Shriveled-up gent, who looked about a thousand years old, rolled a wad of cut-plug tobacco from one cheek to the other. His voice crackled and split like the dried pine at his feet. "Done got to the point where a body cain't even git out on the street some nights. Too damned dangerous. Them sons of bitches git good an' drunk, and git to shootin' at anything that's a-movin'. Put one through the brim of my hat one night when I wuz on my way home from prayer meetin'. Most folks round here is skeered to death of 'em. But as you can see, that don't include none of us. Like House said, once they've beat the snot out of a body, or if'n you're older'n the Red River, they tend to leave you alone. Guess they figure them such as us ain't much of a threat."

Rickards scratched at a crusted spot on the back of his hand. "You want a lesson in how to terrify a body, just stroll over to the Texas Star and talk to Cap'n Euless Whitecotton. He usually stakes out his spot by eight or nine in the morning. Be there all day. He's an easy man to find. Almost always sits in the corner opposite the pianner. Got his leg shot off in the Devil's Den at Gettysburg. Came to Sweetwater for some peace and quiet, but mostly to get away from men like Titus Nightshade. Didn't do him no good, though."

Boz allowed as how we'd taken enough of their valuable time, and thanked all those attending the devotional at

Rickards's shop that morning. As we headed for the Texas Star, he said, "Don't seem to have much trouble letting their feelings be known. I've seen situations like this where everyone in town was so terrified they wouldn't even talk to a Ranger. Doesn't appear to be a problem in these parts. Leastways, not yet."

I watched the street while he stood at the Texas Star's batwing doors and checked on everything inside. Sure as big yeller dogs live in Arkansas, a one-legged former trooper, in the remnants of a Confederate cavalry captain's uniform, nursed his drink at a corner table away from everyone else.

Tattered soldier spotted us soon as we ambled in. Looked mighty uncomfortable when confronted by two heavily armed men who strolled right up to his table. Boz tugged at the brim of his hat, introduced us all over again, and surprised me with the deference in his voice when he said, "Cap'n Whitecotton, we've come to try and help folks out with a problem we understand you've had some past experience with. Much appreciate the effort if you'd tell us anything you can about the Nightshade family."

The broken warrior fidgeted with his drink like he had trouble deciding whether he wanted to talk with us or not. Kept squirming around in his chair, but eventually motioned for us to take a seat. Could barely hear him when he said, "You boys don't have any idea what you're getting into here." His soft Southern accent, and an abundance of whiskey, rolled words around, smoothed the edges off them, and spread them inside my ears like butter on my mother's hot biscuits.

He kind of caught us by surprise for a second or so. I said, "We're trying to find out if there's any substance to complaints made by almost a hundred of the town's residents. House Rickards told us you'd had less than pleasant dealings with the Nightshade family."

Whitecotton's pale, lifeless eyes bored into mine. "Less

than pleasant dealings. That's an understatement if I ever heard one, young man. Let me ask you a question, son. Ever met someone who seemed to hate you from the first second they laid eyes on you?"

Boz rolled a smoke, and eyeballed me as I answered. "Yessir, think I have. My father and mother took me to Lampasas once a month when they went in for provisions. Second trip, I ran up against a bully named Pottsy Billingsly. Dragged me into an alley and beat hell out of me. Got to the point where he was waiting on the boardwalk in front of the general mercantile every time we went to town. Just couldn't seem to get enough of whipping my ass."

Captain Whitecotton leaned back in his chair, and grinned. "Yes. Well, same thing happened with Titus Nightshade and me. Man hated me from the instant we met. Takes uncommon pleasure at bullying me at any opportunity. I try to avoid him. Last time we accidentally ran into each other was a few weeks ago. I made the mistake of thinking I could go back into Shorty Small's saloon. Always liked Shorty's place because he don't have no piano. Less noise, you see. Didn't realize Titus was inside. He always lit in on me anytime he walked in the door. So, I ceased going over there."

He paused, scratched at the stubble on his chin, and sipped at his drink. "Made a simple mistake in judgment by going back. I knew better. Titus was hunkered over a spot at the bar. Didn't think he saw me. Tried to hobble around him. He kicked my crutch out from under me, and poured the contents of a spittoon over my hat. Screamed as how I was nothing but yellow Confederate scum. Said I should have died at Gettysburg. Told me, if I ever came back into Shorty's again, he'd shoot me like a cur dog."

Boz scraped a lucifer to life, fired his smoke, and said, "You believe him, Cap'n?"

"Oh, yes indeed, sir. Yes indeed. Have not one doubt in my mind the next time we meet someone will surely die.

You see, Ranger Tatum, Titus has made the mistaken assumption that I'm afraid of him. Afraid he'll do exactly as he threatened."

I couldn't let that one pass. Sounded right skeptical when I said, "You aren't afraid of him?"

"Oh, hell, no, young Ranger. I have no fear of death. Saw more dying during the war than most people will in a lifetime. Prayed for my own death thousands of times since. Titus didn't fight, you see. He ran. Been running since before '61. I've often thought perhaps that's why he hates me so much. I remind him of his cowardice. Hard thing to live with, cowardice."

He lifted his whiskey tumbler and gingerly threw down the rest of the scorching contents. Placed his glass on the table, refilled to the lip, and watched as the liquid began to dance and jiggle about. Sound of thunder rolled our direction, swept under the batwing doors, across the floor, and up the legs of our table like a visitor whose shadow brings fear and hatred as well.

Whitecotton's empty eyes darted over our shoulders in the direction of the doorway, then to the heavy glass window fronting the saloon. "You're in luck, gentlemen. The object of all your inquiries has arrived."

Boz and I turned. Four or five riders rumbled past the Texas Star. Made my skin crawl when the captain said, "God save the good people of Sweetwater. The Nightshades have come to town again. Let us pray for deliverance."

Chair legs squealed against the polished floor as Boz pushed away from Whitecotton's table. "About time we met these folks, Lucius."

My partner didn't say so, but beneath his seemingly calm exterior, I got the impression an explosion brewed. The kind of shattering flare-up that had a tendency to end in gunfire, death, and weeping women.

7

"He'll Kill Me Right Where I'm Standing."

WE STOOD ON the boardwalk in front of the Texas Star, and watched as five men dismounted and tied their animals to the hitch rails in front of Shorty Small's. The formerly teeming street had emptied of any other foot traffic. Women, kids, even the dogs had simply vanished like mist under a warming sun.

An uncommon quiet descended, and the morning's light breeze slipped into the woods and hid. Watched as window shades in some of the shops and stores were lowered. Only person in evidence, other than us, was Lenny Milsap. Clouds of dust swirled around his constantly moving broom as he worked near Hickerson's front entrance. He turned, spotted us, removed his raggedy cap, and waved.

Boz pulled each of his weapons and checked the loads. "Might want to give all yours a look too, Lucius. Better safe than sorry, I always say. Never know what might develop into a fight. Wouldn't want to drop the hammer on an empty chamber at an unfortunate moment."

A runty bulldog of a man I took to be Titus Nightshade led the group inside. A black felt hat hung down his back on a leather thong. His block-shaped head squatted on thick shoulders. Stringy gray hair hung down past the collar of a white shirt that had gone to a well-used pale yellow. He topped a rough-stitched leather vest off with a faded red bandanna the size of a pillowcase. Wore stovepipe chaps and sported work boots decorated with silver spurs. A brace of pistols finished out a costume his followers had tried to copy with varying degrees of success. Everyone in the group bristled with an array of weapons. One lanky drink of water wearing a palm-leaf sombrero sported fancy, bone-handled Colts.

Soon as they disappeared behind Shorty Small's door, Boz stepped into the street. He silently pointed to the spot where he wanted me. I followed a few steps behind and to his left. Don't know why, but that dusty, cow-country boulevard seemed a mile wide.

Our brief trek turned into one of the longest walks of my entire life. Hell, when you don't know what to expect, time has the uncanny ability to turn into maple syrup in February, or double greased lightning. Just have to take it as it comes. But that morning, my education in such matters had barely begun. By the time we slid into the roughest-looking liquor-selling establishment in town, my whole body hummed like a picked banjo string.

All the riders had bellied up to the bar. Soon as Boz pushed the cantina door open, everyone inside stopped in mid-drink, and turned our direction. Boz whispered, "Just follow my lead, son. Gonna feel these boys out a little. See what's what. Might get rough." He stopped, and I almost bumped into him. Barely heard him whisper, "Actually, I'm pretty damned certain things are gonna get messy before we leave today. Be alert."

I glanced from face to face and, for the first time, realized the fella wearing the palm-leaf sombrero was a girl.

Shook me right down to the soles of my boots. Slim-hipped, dressed like a man, heavily armed, and a damned good-looking woman. She leaned against the bar, and held an empty shot glass in her free hand.

Young man about my age that could have passed as the pistol-toting good looker's older twin said, "Well, well, well. Just what in the blue-eyed hell have we got here?"

The bulldog I figured for Titus Nightshade huffed, "Must be them Texas Rangers we done heard 'bout. You boys Rangers?"

Boz strode right up in the blockheaded feller's face. Got so close, I thought for a second he was gonna kiss Night-shade right on the lips. Kept my place, hands on my Colt's butts, and tried to look vicious.

"Name's Randall Bozworth Tatum. And you are correct sir. We're with Company B out of Fort Worth."

Rough-looking jackass, who had no family resemblance to anyone else at the bar, stood beside the elder Nightshade. He hooked his thumbs in his pistol belt, puffed out his chest, and snorted, "We don't be needing no goddamned Rangers round here. Why don't you take your ugly asses on back to Fort Worth, 'fore I have to kick the shit out of both of you."

The smart mouth's audience started to laugh. Boz slapped that poor yammering fool so hard he would have only seen stars for the next week, if he had just let it alone. But as the flaming handprint started to rise on his cheeks, I guess something in the bullyboy's brain snapped like a dried cottonwood limb. He made a half-assed reach for the gun in his belt. Boz pulled one of his, whacked the poor son of a bitch on the nog-gin, and reholstered so fast I wasn't sure I'd actually seen what I saw. Pistol-whipped goober dropped like a felled tree, ricocheted off the foot rail, and slumped against the bar.

Titus Nightshade waved off the others in his party. He stared down at my partner's left hand. Muzzle of Boz's belly gun was pressed against Nightshade's pecan-sized heart. Snatched both my weapons out, and covered everyone else soon as I realized what he'd done. Decided right then and there, my friend's skill with firearms surpassed anything I'd ever witnessed, or imagined. Not only that, but he hardened my continually growing belief that Randall Bozworth Tatum knew absolutely no fear.

If looks could have killed, the fair-haired girl in the sombrero would've turned both of us to blackened smoldering cinders. She leveled Boz with a hate-filled glare. Her face turned the color of rising blood. Slender hands anxiously hovered over the bone-handled guns on her hips. Finely etched, pouting lips quivered. The pupils, in eyes so brown they appeared black, narrowed down on me like birdshot.

She yelled, "Goddammit, Pa, do something, or I will." Sounded tough enough. But something around her eyes betrayed a softness she put out considerable effort to hide.

The old man didn't even blink, and barely breathed. "You and Jack stay still, Nance. This here Ranger feller ain't no Sweetwater storekeeper, blacksmith, or farmer. He'll kill me right where I'm a-standing. Settle down, or you'll be buryin' me tomorrow. Let it go."

For about a second, thought I just might have to shoot Nance Nightshade. The realization startled me. Shooting a man was one thing, a woman something else altogether. Since stunningly good-looking blond women tended to be few and far between at the time, the thought of having to kill one confused the hell out of me. I tried not to let my perplexity show. Not sure how good a job I did.

Then, in a voice as calm as water in a rain barrel, I heard Boz say, "He's right, missy. Give me the slightest reason and I'll plug your ole man so fast, he'll be bakin' in Satan's favorite oven before you can blink twice." Then his lips curled back over his teeth like a hungry wolf's and he snarled, "Guess you're not quite as stupid as you look, Nightshade."

Insulted, the old man gritted his teeth so hard it sounded

like cracking walnuts. He raised up on his toes. Boz pushed him back down with the muzzle of his pistol. "Lots of rumors 'bout you and yours, sir." *Sir* came out like an insult. "Hear tell you like to run roughshod over the fine God-fearin' folks around these parts. Complaints filed with Captain Culpepper in Fort Worth tell a story of continual brutality, lawlessness, call-out gunfights, even horse and cattle theft. Been several robberies of Baynes Stage Line in these parts. Number of people here'bouts feel you might have knowledge concerning those thefts."

Gray-haired brigand shook all over. You'd of thought he had a killing case of malaria. "You suppose I give a good goddamn what these sheep think? If so, you're stupider than you look, you badge-totin' bastard. Besides, nobody can prove any of what you just said. Ain't no witnesses ever gonna come forward and testify agin me, or mine."

Boz grinned, and took two steps backward. "That might well be true. But my young associate and I are here to make inquiries about you, your family, and friends. Probably be strolling by your place on Little Agnes Creek for a visit in the near future. Better hope we can't find out anything we can prove. Make one misstep, and I'll haul you back to Fort Worth and jail, or hang you faster'n minnows can swim a water dipper."

Boz motioned for me to move out behind him. "Come on, Lucius. Our business with these gentlemen, and the lady, is finished. Today." He tugged at the brim of his hat and said, "Miss, good day to you. Mr. Nightshade, I'm sure we'll talk again in the near future."

Soon as we got outside, he hustled us back across the street to the Texas Star. Pulled at my sleeve and led me to an empty hitch rail. We leaned against it and he said, "Let's roll a smoke, and see what happens when they come out."

Minute or so crawled by before the smart-mouthed goober Boz had cracked on the head stumbled through the batwing doors with a friend under each arm to hold him up. The girl followed, carrying her wounded compadre's hat. Nightshade came out last, and did the evil-eye routine on us. Took them about a minute to load up their wounded running buddy and get mounted.

The still-fuming girl peeled away from the rest of the group and came tearing over at us. Her father tried to stop her, but didn't do any good at it. She reined up so sharp, dust and clods landed all over our feet. Still madder'n hell when she shouted, "You ain't seen the end of this dance. Not by a damned site. Ain't no one gonna get away with putting knots on the head of a Nightshade rider. I'm gonna personally see you bastards pay heavy for this."

She glared at me for the longest. Like I was the one who'd buffaloed her friend. I grinned, and shrugged. That really ripped the lid off. Shook all over when she yelled, "Damn you, you self-righteous son of a bitch."

Heard her father call out, "Come on, Nance. Let the matter go. We'll have our turn. Sooner or later, everything that goes around comes back."

Then, as God is my witness, angry gal tried to spit on us. Couldn't get up enough moisture, I guess. Fact that she made the attempt was more shocking to me than anything else that happened that day. Boz chuckled as she kicked away, and caught up with her father and friends. He said, "Fiery woman. Fiesty as a bag of wildcats. Good-looking too. You might want to get to know her better, Mr. Dodge."

I could not fathom such a suggestion. "Sweet Weeping Jesus, Boz. Nance Nightshade probably hates you, and me, more than any two people in Texas right this minute. Be willing to cover all bets she'd cut my heart out with a soup ladle, if she had half a chance."

He laughed, and slapped me on the back. "Seen many a lifelong relationship start with more venom. Hell, boy, I could tell right off, Nance Nighshade thinks you're downright irresistible."

Got me to thinking he might be right. For all her piss and vinegar, that hard-to-detect softness around the lovely Miss Nightshade's eyes stayed with me long after I'd pushed her blistering speechifying to distant corners of my memory.

8

"Ezra, Git Yore Gun. . . ."

FOR THE NEXT two or three days not much happened. Lulled me into the mistaken belief that maybe Boz had thrown something of a real scare into ole Titus and his bunch—all of them except the old man's wild-eyed gal, Nance, of course. By then, I had come to the conclusion Nightshade's oldest daughter wasn't afraid of much of anything in this world, and perhaps held little in the way of fear for most of the demons that surely inhabited Perdition. Then I thought, hell, Lucius, you're spending way too much time chasing that girl around in your dreams and fantasies.

The days came, and the days went. Scorching heat let up a bit, and the weather got right pleasant for an hour or so every morning. Boz and me strolled around town like natives, and made an attempt at acting like actual lawmen. We visited nearly every business owner. Talked extensively with each of them about the problem those willing to express an opinion referred to as "the damned ruthless Nightshade bunch."

Storekeeper Burton Hickerson had been bull's-eye accurate in his assessment of the renegade family's impact on his neighbors. Town folk despised the belligerent outlaw clan, and their ever-changing pack of worthless friends and cohorts. We tried, but didn't find a single citizen who had even one good, or uplifting, thing to say about any of them—men or women.

I suppose a lady name of Shadle summed the town's feelings up best when she shook her fan open, hid behind the lace trim, and in a voice burdened with cornpone and wisteria, whispered, "Trash. Worst kind of trash I've ever encountered in my entire life. Whole bunch ain't nothing but an ugly blot on the South and Southern ways. I've not witnessed one act of kindness, or indication of any breeding, since the day they wobbled into town in their greasy, broken-down wagon. 'Fore God, they're the least chivalrous assortment of men in my memory. And, Good Lord Almighty, the behavior of Dusky and those girls is nothing short of scandalous. Drinking in saloons. Wearing pants. Straddling horses like men. My, oh, my."

She leaned closer and, in a hiss I could barely hear, said, "I've heard tell their shack over on Little Agnes Creek is nothing more than a house of ill fame. Dancing and carousing goes on all night long, sometimes. Fiddle-playing, whooping, and hollering you can hear all over Parker County. Lord help us if that benighted clan is the best Alabama has to offer. God save that poor, defeated state and all her pitiful inhabitants." While fourteen years had passed since the end of what my mother always referred to as the Unpleasantness, feelings like those of Mrs. Shadle still ran strong and deep.

Boz said about the only thing we could do was listen to each individual's complaints and nod like we understood their concerns. "We'll just keep digging around. And hope we eventually find something serious enough to hang on some of the Nightshade gang. One of 'em will trip up, sooner or later."

In our spare time, we became something akin to celebrities in the minds of Sweetwater's army of youngsters. Boz loved to draw a crowd by handing out hard candy. Man exhibited all the attributes of a ten-year-old anytime sugar was involved. He formed a particular attachment for Lenny Milsap, and the smile of a blue-eyed, sandy-haired waif named Eliza had the power to soften his leathery heart and light him up like kids' sparklers on Independence Day.

After bacon, eggs, and coffee, on the third or fourth day, we dragged chairs to the boardwalk, in front of the sheriff's office, and rolled ourselves a smoke. Morning had come up a bit cooler than usual. Boz allowed as how a stretch in the shade would be mighty fine. We could take in some fresh air before the whole town got up, started moving around and stirring up the dust.

Propped our feet on the hitch rail and pushed back for the utmost in comfort. Pulled our hats down over our eyes, and started out to snooze the morning away. Guess we'd only been there taking our leisure for a peaceful few minutes when a farmer, whose homespun pants came almost to his knees, rode into town and reined up right in front of us. A double-barreled 10-gauge shotgun rested across his animal's withers.

Bobbed his head in a bashful greeting, removed a battered hat, and ran the sleeve of a grimy shirt across his face. Sounded almost apologetic when he said, "You fellers them Rangers folks been tellin' 'bout?"

I glanced at Boz, and waited for him to take the lead. He squinted, thumped ashes from his smoke, and picked a piece of errant tobacco off his lip. Winked at me and said, "You are correct, sir. How can my young *assistant* and me be of help?" Winked with the other eye when he said *assistant*.

Plow chaser slid off his animal, and stood with the hat in one hand, the shotgun in the other. He resembled an Arkansas cotton farmer broken by fate, who'd come to visit greedy bankers and beg for a loan of money. Toes of his feet kept scrunching up like he was trying to grab hold of the ground. Remember wondering if he thought he might fall off Texas and fly over to the Nations, or something.

Sounded about as serious as cholera when he finally said, "Name's McKee. Have a spread seven or eight mile out the Jacksboro Road. Yestiddy mornin', wife says as how she hears squealing from the pigpen. She says, 'Ezra, git yore gun and git down there—right now. Coyotes must be at the sow and all her shoats. We lose them pigs, could turn into a mighty lean winter.' So, I grab up my double-barreled blaster, and do my best imitation of the Comanche tiptoe past the barn and out towards the sty. Built 'at 'ere haven fer hogs far 'nough from the house so's the smell and flies ain't so much of a problem, you see."

Boz looked like a man who wanted to pull all the hair out of his own nose rather than listen to such nonsense. Ezra McKee never missed a beat. Kept talking like his tale of pigs, sties, smells, and flies was more important than anything else happening in the entire state of Texas that morning.

"Kinda sidled up to a tree behind the barn and noticed near'bouts six or seven horses bunched around my pig-pen. Gang of fellers sat on the top rail of the fence, and was a-hollering to beat the band. You'd a-thought they was a celebratorious sack race going on, Indian leg 'ras-selin' contest, or somethin'. Finally, seen this gal, least-ways looked like a gal, down in the slops with my sow Maggie. She chased that hog round and round. Screamed and cussed a blue streak the whole time. 'Bout the third or fourth trip, she whipped out a pistol and begun shoot-ing. Emptied that'n and pulled another'n. Musta capped off eight or ten rounds altogether."

Boz nodded and sagely pulled at his chin. Sounded almost sympathetic when he said, "Killed poor ole Maggie, huh?"

McKee shook his head. "No, sir. Not right off anyways. Guess all the mud, and such, musta messed with that there gal's aim or sumpthin'. Pig wouldn't go down. Gal holstered them pistols and jumped on Maggie's back. Whipped out a big ole knife and went to stabbin' like somethin' insane. Took her nigh on ten minutes, but she finally kilt ole Maggie. All them fellers, sittin' along my fence, cheered like a horse they bet on done went and won a race. Took 'em a spell, but the thievin' bastards loaded Maggie onto a pole drag and hightailed it."

He ran completely out of steam with the murdered porker's untimely departure from the glories of porcine life. Couldn't even speak for almost a minute. Then, in a husky, sad voice, he said, "Don't know what my kids are gonna eat this winter. Damned hard to live on squirrels and hickory nuts round here. Cain't eat the shoats. All ten of them ain't as big as one of Maggie's hocks. Kill any of my cows and we won't have nothin' to sell next spring." He shook his head back and forth like a tired dog and, almost to himself, added, "Ain't never ate no horse. Never been that desperate. Yet."

Boz shot me a bemused glance and said, "You know, Ezra, I think my young friend here should ride out to your place, and take a look around. Maybe he can get your hog back. You got any idea who done went and murdered poor defenseless Maggie?"

"Looked like that Nightshade gal, Nance, to me. Course I watched from a ways off, and have to admit my long sight ain't nearly as good as years past. Besides, didn't stay, around much after the slaughter."

"Why not?" I asked.

McKee's back stiffened, and some fire flickered behind his dead brown eyes. "Left right after they started tryin' to load Maggie up, 'cause I've had my share of dealin's with them Nightshades, and their company of friends, afore. Feared if'n I stayed around, they'd spot me sooner or later. Same bunch cotched me out on Caney Creek two year ago. For absolutely no reason a-tall, they roped me round'bouts my neck, and drug me all over hell and half of Parker County. Sons of bitches laughed the whole time. They thought I wuz deader'n Stonewall Jackson whens they finally cut me loose. Bobbed around in the water like a turtle with a cracked shell for sometime 'fore I gained strength enough to pull my poor busted-up self onto the bank. Took me near three months to completely recover from that 'un. Done tried being real careful round them folks ever since. But killin' Maggie went beyond the pale. I've got young'uns to feed, and ain't had no paper money in my pocket for a whole year. That hog might'a meant the difference between my kids eatin' and starvin' this winter. Cain't have that, by God. Them bastards can beat me and drag me around in muddy water, but they cain't go messin' with the lives of my children."

I felt right sorry for the man. Said, "We'll see what we can do about this, Mr. McKee."

Surprised both of us when he shoved his tattered hat back on his head and snapped, "I'd surely appreciate your kind assistance, Rangers. You see, next time any of the Nightshade bunch tries to buffalo me, or comes on my property, I can guarantee you boys they's gonna be a killin'. Maybe more'n one. Ain't about to spend a lot of time waitin' for upcoming outrages. Next dance I'll shoot to kill first, and pay the devil his due afterwards." Then he climbed back on his bony mule and waited.

Boz walked me down to Rickards'. We'd stabled our animals with him. House took better care of Grizz than any man I've met since. Blacksmith developed a particular affection for Butterbean. Turned out kind of a mutual thing. Think the mule loved the old man as well.

My partner slapped me on the leg after I got mounted

and said, "Don't take any unnecessary chances, Lucius. Try to stay away from the Nightshades, if you can. Ride on over to this pitiful soul's place. Poke around a little. Try to act like you know what you're about. Anything you do should make him happy. Maybe even put off the killing he mentioned. Best if one of us stays in town just in case something pops up here. If you're not back by tomorrow afternoon, I'll come looking for you."

The jaunt to Ezra McKee's ranch took us south on the Jacksboro Road for six or eight miles. Turned west on a barely visible cattle trail for another mile or two. As we rode along, my guide revealed in conversation that he worked body and soul raising a herd of horses and cows on his small ranch. And he complained that the size of his family had resulted in more farming than he really cared for. But, as he noted, with more than a little regret, a man does what he must when the future of his children rests in the balance.

Found the main house for his spread nestled against a free-flowing creek lined with a stand of fifty-foot cotton-woods. Imprint of a strong-willed woman was obvious on the entire visible operation. Given his scruffy appearance, I could never have imagined Ezra McKee's home would be so neat, and well kept.

As if by magic, children appeared from behind virtually every rock, tree, and stump. Pair, who looked like twins, stumbled from the barn carrying a bucket of milk. Counted seven by the time I stopped. Eldest girl sported a seasoned Yellow Boy rifle across her arm and, in my less-than-learned estimation, must have been at least fifteen or sixteen years old. Remaining flock of McKee's offspring descended in age from her.

Mrs. McKee, holding a baby on her hip and a Walker Colt in her free hand, stood in the doorway of the house. Tired and worn ragged by life, the woman still had a dignified look about her that evidenced itself in the obvious pride she took in her home and children. She was tall, dark-eyed, and willowy of figure, and a sunburned weariness had draped itself over the once-beautiful woman's chiseled face.

McKee's excited brood yammered so much, and so fast, I couldn't understand much of anything said. Family fogged around their father as he slid off the mule. Could tell by the way he caressed the backs of their heads, ole Ezra had meant every word when he said messing with his kids would most certainly end in a killing.

Soon as he got the excited bunch quieted down a bit, the oldest girl said, "They come back, Papa. You couldn'a been gone more'n an hour or so. May have took some of the horses. Two or three, I think. Cain't be sure. Scared Mama and the little ones so bad, I've been keepin' 'em close to the house. Nightshade flunky called Underhill rode up here in the yard and yelled out how the next time they visit, he might have to kill some kids just for the hell of it. Said he figured he'd be doing the county a favor by ridding this area of baby vermin. Big-mouthed bastard didn't stay around long after I sent a pair of blue whistlers past his ears."

Look on McKee's hollow dejected countenance could have jerked tears from a glass eye. Man trembled and shook as he stumbled for his wife and baby. The couple clung to each other like drowning lovers. Kids latched onto their parents' legs. Some of the youngsters giggled, others cried.

Proud rancher motioned me toward the churning mass of humanity, and tried to introduce all of them. Presented his wife to me as Irene. Today I couldn't tell you all the kid's names on a bet. Never forget the oldest girl, though. Auburn-haired, green-eyed, and deceptively tough, she was obviously her father's favorite.

"Martha Francis, this here's Mr. Dodge. He's a Texas Ranger. Come out to help. That bunch from over at Night-shade's won't be bothering the McKee family no more."

Offered my hand and said, "Pleased to meet you, Martha Francis."

Not a glimmer of timidity in the girl's conduct. She grabbed my ungloved paw, threw me a glance of green-eyed fury, and said, "Don't call me Francis. Only person who calls me Francis is Ma when she's angry about something I either did, or didn't do proper. Don't know why Pa always introduces me that way. Everyone calls me Martye, Ranger Dodge."

She kind of caught me off guard. Given the beaten behavior exhibited by Ezra, her fiery lip came as something of a surprise. Tried to smooth the way a bit. Affable as possible, I said, "Sounds good to me, Martye."

She wasn't in a friendly mood. "Hope you don't turn out to be the same kind of coward as Sheriff Fain. That tubby gob of chicken shit rode out here twice before, when Pa complained about the Nightshades. Beer-bellied coward never did a thing to help us out—first cousin to Moses Rose as far as I'm concerned. Then he ran like a scared rabbit, right after one of Nightshades' henchmen pistol-whipped him in that rat's nest saloon of Shorty Small's. Ever since then, the whole town's been scared to death of them sons of bitches."

Mrs. McKee tried to step in and calm her spirited daughter when she said, "Now, Martye. There's no need for profanity. Mr. Dodge doesn't know you that well yet. Please excuse her, sir. My daughter's conduct is the result of an unrefined backwater upbringing."

The feisty little gal had her stinger out, and was spoiling for the opportunity to put bumps on somebody's head. She snapped, "I don't care what this man thinks of me, Ma. We've had to put up with that clan of egg-sucking prairie snakes for three years. 'Bout time someone with the right level of authority, and grit, took notice."

Thought I'd get away from her when Ezra led me out to his pigpen. Regrettably, my luck didn't hold. She followed, and ragged on me the whole time.

I'd just scouted around some and found sign leading to

the north when she snapped, "You done wasted thirty minutes, Ranger Dodge. I coulda told you which way they went. If this trail don't lead right to the Nightshades' front porch, I'll eat one of them Mexican barn hornets raw. No salt. Straight up. You gonna go after 'em, or stand here with your face hanging out, and gandering at the tracks?"

Couldn't help but smile, which didn't do anything but make her even madder. I said, "Don't you ever calm down, darlin'?"

Her lips peeled back and she snarled, "You don't know me well enough yet to call me darlin'. Besides, if you don't put some hurry-up into this, they'll have Maggie butchered and et 'fore night falls. Pile of pork that big ain't gonna keep. Thievin' sons of bitches could be cookin' her right now."

No profit to be had arguing with the girl. Besides, I never much liked being abused by good-looking females. Mounted up and started following the track. No difficulty there. Pole drag left deep cuts on the baked soil, and considerable blood sign along the way as well.

Not sure what I expected, but the Nightshade ranch couldn't have been more'n three or four miles from McKee's place. Surprised me when I came upon their house. Poor Ezra's unfortunate closeness virtually assured the kind of harassment bullies, and thugs, never seem to get their fill of. Reined up in a stand of trees on the south side of Little Agnes Creek, and pulled my long glass.

Appeared as though the entire band had gathered behind the house around a spit turned by a constantly changing parade of children. The carcass of a recently slaughtered hog cooked in its own juices over a smoky, slow-burning fire. I counted eleven people in the yard. Figured that covered Nightshade, at least seven kids, and a couple of extras. Spotted Nance helping her father baste the pig from a bucket of some kind of sauce.

Swept the glass over the crowd, one last time, and kinda

mumbled to myself, "One of you boys must be Underhill. And I'd bet the other'n is probably the one Boz whacked on the noggin."

Damn near scared me speechless when this voice out of nowhere whispered, "Well, you gonna do something, Ranger Dodge, or just sit here with your face hanging out?" Last time I got myself armed that fast involved a running gun battle with Comanches out on the Llano Estacado.

9

"Are All You Rangers This Badly Informed . . . ?"

MARTYE MCKEE SAT bareback on a pinto pony and stared into the open muzzle of my pistol. If she had moved about an inch closer, the tip of her nose could've fit inside.

I eased the hammer down, holstered the gun, and hissed, "Goddammit, girl, how in the blue-eyed hell did you get this close without me knowing? Sweet Weeping Jesus, I damn near blew your head off."

She smiled, and in a voice dripping with sarcasm said, "Slipping up on the likes of you ain't that hard." She patted the pony's neck. "Sneaky, here, has the lightest feet in Parker County. I can ride her right up to the Nightshades' back porch, in broad daylight, and they won't hear me."

Soon as I stopped shaking, tried to get her to go home. Girl wouldn't give an inch. Snapped at me like she wanted to bite my ears off. "I ain't gonna. You can forget it. Besides, you can't get our hog back alone, and I've got a plan."

"Well, that's just by God peachy. Not sure I really

expected to 'get your hog back.' Randall Bozworth Tatum, my senior in this matter, warned me to be careful around this bunch of hard cases. But you've got a plan. Does this *plan* of yours involve getting me killed anytime today?"

"Maybe, but I don't think so."

"You don't think so?"

"No. If you do what I've got in mind, we can get Maggie and be back on the ranch so fast they'll still be standing around arguing with each other about what happened to 'em this time tomorrow."

Well, she actually did have a fairly good idea about how to handle the situation. Dangerous, but a pretty impressive scheme for an Indian-wild, pony-riding, barefoot country girl. All came down to the notion that she expected me to ride up to the Nightshade house and reclaim her family's slaughtered porker, while she and her Yellow Boy covered me from the safety of the willow-covered creek bank. And although Boz's warning, not to confront Titus and his band of thugs, rang in my ears like cathedral bells, Martye McKee's "I by God dare you, Lucius Dodge" attitude got the better of me.

Before I waded Grizz across the creek, pointed and said, "You see the bucket sitting on top of the spit?" She nodded. "Can you hit something that small from here?"

She looked at me like I'd sprouted a third head. Groaned and said, "I could put lead in a target that size from twice this distance, shooting over my shoulder with a two-hundred-year-old cracked mirror."

Had to smile, but used the back of my hand to conceal my mouth. "As best you can, get out of sight, Martye. When you see me point at the bucket, I expect splintered wood in the air, immediately, if not a damned sight sooner. No room for carelessness here. You understand?"

"My Glorious God. Are all you Rangers this badly informed about the mental powers of the womenfolk of Parker County? This whole dance was my idea to start with." She pushed herself up on the pony's back, leaned toward me, and rattled off one word at a time. "I think my pea-sized brain comprehends what you want me to do, Mr. Dodge." Then she grinned and winked. God, but women could be a mystery for a young man blessed with limited familiarity in the study of those creatures.

Pulled up on the far side of the shallow creek, kept mumbling to myself like an aged grandpa with hardening of the arteries. Couldn't believe the emerald-eyed little devil could set me talking to myself like she did. Course my experience with women, and girls at the time, could charitably be described as elementary at best. Only female-type person of my *close* acquaintance, at that point in my life, was my mother. Trust me when I tell you, Matilda Dodge exhibited none of the attributes of Fort Worth's soiled doves, Nance Nightshade, or the spunky Miss Martye McKee.

The brazen clan of hog thieves must have been watering at the mouth so much they didn't bother to notice my arrival. I damn near rode right up in the middle of them. Guess the prospect of a free meal let their bellies get the better of their questionable judgment. Only good thing about the whole situation was when I noticed they'd leaned their rifles against the fence, and the top rail was gaily decorated with a number of unreachable pistol belts.

Two rough tables, dressed out with wooden bowls and pewter utensils, had been jammed against each other to form a single ten-foot-long eating surface. Piles of corn, taters, hoecakes, and beans waited while the cook basted the stolen hog with a rag wrapped around a long pole.

"Smells mighty good," I said. Whole bunch jumped around at the same time like I'd fired a cannon. "Bet Ezra McKee's gonna be glad to get her back."

Titus held the meat-basting stick like a magic wand. Kids of every imaginable age gathered around their father and threw daggered looks my direction. He dropped the rag-and-pole contraption into a bucket on the ground and said, "You got a lot of nerve coming out here alone, Ranger Dodge. Must be feeling mighty wolfish."

Leaned on the pommel of my saddle and tapped a finger against one of Boz Tatum's Colt's Dragoons. "Rumors from most of the folks in Sweetwater would lead me to believe this is a right dangerous area, Mr. Nightshade. As a direct consequence, I've decided never to travel in these parts alone."

"That a fact?"

"Yes, sir. That's a fact."

"Well, then, where's the rest of your help?"

"All around you."

A knowing smile flitted across his thin, cracked lips. "What if I don't believe you, Ranger Dodge?"

"Well, why don't you go ahead and do something stupid, Mr. Nightshade. But be advised. Quarrelsome action of any kind might cost you your life, perhaps the lives of some of these others as well. Besides, don't need but one Texas Ranger for a pissant-sized outfit like this one anyway."

There's an amazing thing about bullshit. Once a body starts slinging outright lies around, nervy mendacity begins to take on a life of its own. Sounds almost like the truth. More convincingly you slather on a tall tale, the more prone the gullible and softheaded are to believe you.

Nance boldly pushed through the pack of younger siblings to a spot near her father and said, "This is Nightshade land. No one comes in here and threatens us."

Tipped my hat her direction. "No threat, Miss Nance. Plain facts are, you folks stole Maggie there from your neighbors, dragged the hog over here, and, from all appearances, almost have her cooked and ready to eat."

Nightshade's oldest daughter shook her finger at me. "You cain't prove a word of that scurrilous lie. My brothers raised this hog from a shoat. Took 'em four years to get her up to slaughterin' size." That old saw, about females getting better-looking when they're angry, turned into living proof right in front of me that morning. Flames in Nance

Nightshade's eyes flicked my direction. I could feel the heat and smell the smoke.

'Bout then, a wild-faced woman with yellowed teeth came busting out of the house carrying a pot of boiling water. Dusky Nightshade had the kind of look on her you only see in real bad dreams.

She hustled across the porch, and stopped on the bottom step. Still a good thirty feet away from me when she squealed, "Let me scald him, Pa. Let me scald the badge-totin' son of a bitch. Cain't let the likes of him come in here and threaten my family."

Titus held up a reassuring hand and said, "Calm down, Dusky. I'll take care of this."

Crazed woman's gaze raced all over me like a swarm of red ants. She fidgeted with the simmering pot for several more seconds, then scurried back inside behind a cloud of steam.

Answer seemed more'n obvious when things settled down again and I asked my next question. "Why didn't you wait till the first frost? I know you folks ain't from Texas, but I've never heard of anyone from Alabama slaughtering hogs in this kind of heat. Ain't necessarily safe. Never has been."

Man I'd taken to be Nance's older brother Jack, during our brief meeting in Sweetwater, slithered up to his father's side. "We ain't trying to preserve any of this pig. Just gonna eat the meaty beast. Now, why don't you take your worthless self on outta here, 'fore I have your sorry carcass loaded on our spit behind the sow."

Well, that piece of smart-mouthed bullyboy behavior ripped the rag off the bush. Tapped Grizz with my spurs, and pushed the kids out of my way. Step or two more and the big rumped animal would have ended up standing on top of Titus Nightshade's feet.

Turned the horse slightly sideways, leaned over so I didn't have to shout, and said, "I'm tired of our time-wasting discussion. Just came from the spot where your family killed

McKee's animal. Tracked you and yours right to where I see her being cooked. You've got exactly one minute to start getting Maggie on the back of that spring wagon I spotted over by the barn. If that don't happen, something like this will."

Pointed at the bucket sitting on top of Titus's spit. Iron-bound wooden shell splintered into a shower of broken shards. Youngest kids ran screaming for the house. In the confusion, I pulled both pommel guns. Covered Titus, Nance, and Jack.

The old man vibrated with indignation. "You ain't got no right to treat us like this. By God, we're just as entitled to lead our lives the way we want as any of the other sons of bitches here'bouts. We got rights too, you bastard."

Used a pistol barrel to push my vest back and reveal Alfonso Esparza's handmade star. "This, and the state of Texas, gives me the right. Now load 'er up."

Not much arguing after that. Whole clan worked like field hands as they hefted the pig, spit and all, into the wagon. Nance, over the objections of her father and brother, decided she'd drive it back to Ezra McKee's place and return with their six-foot piece of cookin' iron.

We'd managed to get about a mile away from the house when Martye thundered up. Flashed me an ear-to-ear grin. "See, I told you my plan would work."

Nance Nightshade's face went scarlet. "This was your company of Rangers in the trees?"

Smiled when I said, "Never mentioned a company of Rangers, Miss Nance. Simply alluded to the fact that I don't travel alone in these parts."

"Well, if I'd known this little bitch had anything to do with—"

She never got a chance to finish. Martye stood on her pony's back like a circus rider, and jumped right into the middle of Nance Nightshade's lap. Knocked the hot-mouthed gal sideways, and out of the wagon seat. They landed in a pile, right at Grizz's feet, and went to scratching and screaming like a pair of branded bobcats. Slapping and hair-pulling lasted so long, I finally had to step down and break them apart. Didn't help the cussing much, though. They kept that up all the way back to McKee's ranch. Nance gave McKee's whole clan a hell of a tongue-lashing, while Ezra and his brood unloaded their pig. Then she whipped her team away like bat-winged demons chased them.

Naturally, McKee was glad to get his poor murdered sow back. His wife set to doing everything she could think of to preserve some of it. I figured they would have to eat most of the meat. He forced a roast on me when I saddled up for my ride back to town.

Martye followed me all the way to the Jacksboro Road. Pulled up right after I turned north. "You've got to go back home, Martye." She looked like I'd hurt her feelings or something. But maybe the split lip and black eye simply fooled me.

"You comin' back anytime soon?" she asked.

"Don't know. Maybe so. Maybe not."

"You gotta come back."

"Is that a fact? Why do I gotta come back."

She leaned over, grabbed me around the neck quicker'n she'd jumped on Nance Nightshade, and kissed me like to-morrow would never show a bright sunny face. Broke the kiss and said, "That's why, Ranger Dodge. Figure we know each other well enough now. Seein' as how you got Maggie back, and all."

Whipped her pony away, and left me sitting in the middle of the road wrapped in a cloud of dust with her breath still in my mouth. Looking back, I think Martye's impetuous behavior surprised her as much as it did me. Being as how women posed an unsolvable mystery at the time, I couldn't do nothing but shake my head like a dog with ear mites all the way back to Sweetwater. Notice I said "at the time." But, honestly, friends, even after all these years, I'm not sure I can actually say my knowledge on the subject has improved much a-tall.

10

"Did I Kill the Back-Shooting Son of a Bitch?"

I MADE TOWN just in time to keep Boz from coming out looking for me. He got all bug-eyed and fuzzy-necked when I told him about my heroic rescue of Maggie, the murdered hog, and the mischievous assistance of Martye McKee.

"Damn, Lucius, you rode right up to their house and took the swine back?"

"That is exactly what I did, Boz."

"Well, ole son, you've got more hard bark covering your ass than I thought. Don't know if I would have had nerve enough to confront the tiger, in his own den, this early in the game. On top of that, I've never had much personal inclination to die over the disposition of a future meal. But what's done's done."

He thought the whole incident over for a minute or two, grew an impish grin as he rolled himself a smoke, and said, "You do realize, of course, this sorry tale will get spread around, and probably follow you to the grave. I can hear the leaky-mouthed blather now. Every time you walk into a well-known watering hole, anywhere in the state, people will whisper behind your back. They'll say, 'That's him. Lucius Dodge, famed savior of slaughtered sows.'"

Have to admit, he'd hit on an aspect of the Maggie skirmish I'd never so much as given a thought. And while he waxed eloquent with a smile on his lips, I still didn't like the sound of my prospects for the future. In an effort to jokingly steer him away from my porky misadventures, I said, "Have any problems while I was out in the big, dark and lonely, establishing a hard-earned reputation as Texas's foremost pig retriever?"

He chuckled, snatched his hat off, ran fingers through thinning hair, and shook his head. With the hand-rolled dangling from his lips, he said, "Well, I kept my rambling talks going with folks here in town. Honest to God, Lucius, I can't remember a time when I've heard such venomous hatred come from people. Truth is, given what they're saying, don't think we've seen anything close to the real, true, and genuine Nightshades in action yet."

No doubt in my mind what he meant, and the following day we got a fair idea of how things that have been building for months, or years, can turn bad in a heartbeat. All started about the time we'd almost finished cooking coffee and frying bacon. Slightly cooler weather still held, and we looked forward to another lazy morning, outside in our chairs, waving at the locals as they passed. Couldn't have been more than a minute or two from having our breakfast ready, when gunfire caused Boz to lose his grip on a skillet of hot grease. Honest to God, the pistol shots sounded like the fight was in the room with us.

Boz cussed a blue streak, and hit the jailhouse door with his crossover gun out and ready. I followed. First thing we saw was two men rolling around in the street a few steps away from the Texas Star's doorway. Before we could reach them, they both sat up and fired at almost the same instant.

Shooter closest to us flopped back like he'd been hit with a coal shovel.

Took about another second for me to realize the feller, still able to prop himself up on one elbow, was Captain Euless Whitecotton. The former Confederate cavalry officer had dropped his pistol, and groped at a wound in his left side just above the belt.

"Did I kill the back-shooting son of a bitch?" Whitecotton gasped as I bent over him.

"Not sure, Cap'n. Boz is checkin' now."

Whitecotton's wife ran up and squealed like someone had plugged her too. Fell on her wounded husband's chest, and wept like a baby as a crowd bunched up around them. I turned, and noticed none of those gathered around us seemed very interested in the plight of the other shooter.

Boz stood, as I walked over to check on Whitecotton's apparently dead attacker. My friend stepped aside, and revealed the well-ventilated corpse of Titus Nightshade. Stunned don't even come close to my reaction.

Boz grinned and said, "Something of a shocker, ain't she? Appears our friend Cap'n Whitecotton's one hell of a shot. Poor wretch of a cripple put two, maybe three, in Nightshade's heart that you could cover with a ten-dollar gold piece."

For a minute, or so, I couldn't get my chaotic brain to make my mouth work right. Don't know exactly what I anticipated, but the oozing corpse of Titus Nightshade wasn't part of any of my expectations. Boz shook his head, stepped up on the boardwalk in front of the Texas Star, and took the dram shop's owner, Nathan Macray, by the elbow and walked him back inside.

I followed and heard Boz say, "Did you see what happened here, Nate?"

Booze-slinger shook his head, a time or two, and tried to weasel out on the thing. "I don't want to get involved in this killing, Ranger. Think the best practice, all the way round, is to leave it be."

Tatum watched as Macray fumbled around to his regular spot behind the polished mahogany bar. "Ain't gonna work, Nate. Everyone in Sweetwater knew Cap'n Whitecotton hit your door soon's you opened up every morning. Hell, I've sometimes noticed him sitting out front waiting before first light. He ain't missed a day's drinking since Lucius and me got to town. Now, I want to know what happened, and you're gonna tell me. You get my drift here, ole son?"

Macray hefted his liquor-expanded gut onto a stool, and leaned on the bar like a man who'd recently run a footrace. He slid shaking hands over his sweaty pate, wiped them on a filthy apron, and let out a ragged breath. Poured a double shot of snakebite medicine and threw the whole dose all down in one gulp. Held his head in both hands and talked to the empty glass.

"Whitecotton come in just like he always does every livin' day. Little earlier than usual, but that ain't nothing out of the ordinary. 'Stead of taking his regular seat in the corner, though, he sidled up here to the bar. Stood in the spot closest to the door. Guess he hadn't been here more'n ten, fifteen minutes, when Titus blew in. Kinda unusual for him to come alone, but he's done as much before. Think he'd already been at the bottle. A half-blind Sunday school teacher coulda seen he was red-faced drunk, madder'n hell, and spoiling for a fight."

Boz said, "How do you know he was looking for a fight?"

Macray glanced up like a man irritated, all to hell and gone, over such a stupid question. "Every time Titus Nightshade came through my door, he was looking for a fight. And if he saw Whitecotton, you could bet money there'd be words 'tween the two of them. Mostly from Nightshade, but, ever once in a great while, the cap'n made his feelings real plain as how he wasn't to be trifled with. Suppose ole

Titus was probably the only person in these parts bold enough, or stupid enough, not to recognize how dangerous a man he'd picked to provoke."

"They have words this morning, Nate?" I asked.

His gaze swung my direction for about a second, then dipped back into the bottom of his glass. "Yeah. They had words. Door'd barely hit Titus in the ass when he yelled, 'You yellow-bellied Confederate dog. I cain't believe you still have nerve enough to show your sorry ridge-running ass in my town.' Then, he stumbled over to Whitecotton and kicked the poor one-legged bastard's crutch out from under him. Damned thing went flying across the floor and bounced off my pie-anner. He'd done as much at least once before."

Boz said, "That it? That what caused the shooting?"

Nervous bartender poured another fortifier, and sucked the fiery liquid down in a single breath. "Hell, no, that ain't all by a long shot. Whitecotton hopped over to the crutch, leaned on a chair, and gathered his third leg up again. Titus was a-cussin' him the whole time. The cap'n finally got started for the door. Titus cussed him some more. Said filthy-mouthed things what could get any man shot dead. Then the crazy son of a bitch pulled his gun on Whitecotton and said, 'Think it's time to kill you. Worthless, crippled trash like you shoulda died in the war years ago. Think I'll finish what God started.' The cap'n turned, and tried to talk his way out of the thing again. Titus wasn't hearin' anything Whitecotton had to offer. Cap'n said, 'I don't want to fight with you, Nightshade. Might as well put your gun away.' Didn't help his case any, though. Personally, think ole Titus had himself all primed for a killing, and wasn't about to be denied."

I said, "That when the shootin' started?"

"Well, kinda. The cap'n went and headed for the door again. He'd almost made his way outside, when Night-shade shot the man. Looked like the bullet went in his left side, kinda low on the back. Came out his front, and hit my door. Sorry trick. Ole Titus paid for his treachery, though. Cap'n came up with his pistol, and fired under the arm holding his crutch. Hit Titus in the chest. Knocked him back a good two steps. But he grabbed at the spurting hole, recovered, and stumbled outside after Euless. Cap'n had lost his footing, tripped over his crutch, or somethin', and tumbled down the steps."

"Don't suppose you waited behind the bar for the two of them to finish up killing each other?" I said.

"Hell, no. Ran to my window and watched Titus rip off another'n. He missed that time. Cap'n rolled over and plugged ole Titus again. That's when he fell off the porch, and they ended up almost toe-to-toe in the street. 'Bout then, I spotted you boys coming out of the sheriff's office. Think y'all can testify to anything you seen after that."

Boz pulled his hat off and slapped it against his leg. "Anyone else see what happened, before the whole she-bang ended up on the street?"

Voice from the table beside the piano said, "I seen the whole dance. Start to finish."

Thought we'd pretty much met everyone in town. But I didn't recognize the gent hiding in the corner. Boz strolled over to the table, and pulled me along with him. We could still hear a subdued buzz from the street, but, inside the saloon, our spurs sounded like jingling thunder as we moved his direction.

"Watch the door," Boz whispered over his shoulder. He pulled a chair away from the table, put his foot in the seat, leaned on his knee, and said, "Who are you, sir?"

Early morning tippler poured a drink from the bottle on his table. With a trembling hand, he brought the glass to his lips. Sucked about half of the liquid down, then gently lowered the tumbler back to a wet spot in front near his free hand. So low I almost didn't hear him, he said, "Name's Bob Horton."

"Disagreement went about the way Nate described?" Boz asked.

Horton pushed his hat back, and leaned out of the shadowy corner. "Happened exactly the way Mr. Macray said. He ain't tryin' to pull any wool over your eyes, Ranger. Like most folks here'bouts, Nate knows what this means. Jack, Nance, and their friends will doubtless blame the whole thing on him. Very likely, they'll burn the Star to the ground. Maybe the whole damned town. Wouldn't surprise me in the least."

Boz snapped, "Well, we're getting ahead of ourselves a bit, Bob. Still haven't heard who *you* think started the shooting. So far, all we've got is the second, or third, chapter of an ongoing argument between two men who hated each other."

Horton pulled tobacco from a vest pocket. Took his sweet time rolling a cigarette. Fired up, inhaled the first lungful, and as he blew smoke our direction said, "Euless Whitecotton hasn't had energy enough to hate anyone since the war. Only person here, this morning, that hated folks was Titus Nightshade. Sorry, friendless son of a bitch has yet to meet anyone he didn't hate. I personally hope he's roasting on Satan's favorite spit in hell."

Boz got impatient. "You gonna tell me the rest of it in your own words, Bob, or did you pop off at the mouth because you wanted some attention?"

"Swear before Jesus, there ain't nothing else to tell, Ranger. Nate hit the nail right on the head. I seen it exactly the way he said. Euless Whitecotton is totally blameless in this one. Course, that ain't gonna mean much when Nance and Jack find out Titus done went and bought it. Gonna be hell to pay over this killin'. Gonna be hell to pay." His voice trailed off like a man lost in the frightful realization that awful events awaited him around unseen corners in his life.

We headed for the door, but stopped when Horton said, "Heard one thing Nate didn't mention. Leastways, I think

I heard it. Nightshade kept mumbling something under his breath about pigs. Lost pigs. Stolen pigs. Something like that. Didn't make any sense. Still don't. But I've heard him ramble like that before when he'd been drinking and wanted to pick a fight. Like he had a cocklebur stuck in his craw, couldn't spit it out, and wasn't happy till he'd made someone else's life miserable. Pigs. Incredible."

Boz shot me a worried glance, shook his head, and whispered, "Well, I guess some of us know what was botherin' him, don't we?"

By the time we made our way back to the street, someone had shown a bit of consideration and covered Nightshade's body with a ratty piece of canvas. Large pool of blood had already soaked through. A solemn cluster of adults, and half a dozen kids, stood nearby, whispered, and pointed at the corpse.

We followed a small knot of the overly concerned to a house near the school at the north end of town. Friends carried Whitecotton home, and sent for the only local resident with something like real medical experience. F. Scott Bryles, called "Doc" by most, practiced a combination of folk remedies, veterinary hocus-pocus, and actual medicine. Heard he'd studied somewhere back East, and served as a Confederate field medic during the war. Enough for me that Burton Hickerson trusted the man.

Stuck around for a spell, and determined the cap'n had indeed been shot in the back. He stayed conscious long enough to confirm the whole story, almost word for word, the way Nate Macray and Bob Horton had described.

Poor back-shot bastard passed out when Doc Bryles pushed his way through the crowd and upended a bottle of whiskey into the swollen, open wound. Agonized yelling, gasping, and bleeding sent most folks outside for fresh air. Seemed like a fine time for us to make our exit as well.

Boz decided we'd best get ole Titus out of the street. He said, "Wouldn't want to let the family find him still stretched out in the mud, blood, and horse manure. Probably serve to make 'em that much madder. Besides, dogs be goin' at the carcass soon, if'n we don't get him up."

We rolled Nightshade's body in the tarp and carried him to the sheriff's office. Laid the corpse out on the boardwalk, till we borrowed a pair of sawhorses from Burton Hickerson. Took the door off the outhouse behind the office to make a temporary funeral platform. Then we dragged our chairs outside the way we usually did, but set up a few steps away from the body. Boz brought his short-barreled shotgun with him. Leaned the big popper against the wall behind us.

We enjoyed the quiet, for a few minutes, before I said, "You reckon we should ride out to Little Agnes Creek and tell his family what happened?"

My partner shook his head. "No need. Bet they're on the way to town right now. Probably knew what transpired within minutes of the shooting. Likely had tale-carryin' friends on their doorstep while smoke from Whitecotton's last shot still hovered over the bodies. Don't want to alarm you, Lucius, but you'd best get ready for a tense confrontation when they arrive. Tell you what we'll do. Soon's we hear them hit the bridge, you take my shotgun, and get back into the office. You can cover me from the window."

"Damned if I will. Gonna stay out here. We'll face whatever comes together."

"No, son. I ain't tryin' to be noble, or nothin'. It's just that this here sit-chi-ation will work out better if they don't know you're around, till I want them to. You can do a lot more good coverin' me with the shotgun from inside, than out here. That way, you can have 'em under the gun soon's they ride up. She's primed with buckshot. At this distance, you can make quite a mess, if they start anything. Besides, if one of 'em manages to shoot me, I want you to kill as many of 'em as you can. *Comprende, amigo?*"

Told him I understood, but the plan still didn't sit well

with me. Figured my place was out on the street by his side, no matter what the odds might be. But when the thunder from the creek rolled over us like a cannon barrage, he slapped me on the leg, handed me the shotgun, and motioned me inside.

Called over his shoulder, "First one makes a move for his pistol, don't be bashful, open up with both barrels. Kill as many as you can."

11

"Woman Has Witchy Powers."

"SOON AS YOU close the door, Lucius, cock that scattergun and stand in the window so they can see you when I point 'em your direction. I'll take care of the rest."

I'd barely had time to turn around good when they came storming up. Three oldest Nightshades, Jack, Nance, and Arch, led a party of at least seven others. Some of them obviously weren't family, but everyone in the gang was packing iron and itching for a fight.

When the dust settled, and things quieted down some, Jack said, "You got our father under that there nasty piece of rag?"

Boz didn't get out of his chair. He sat with one hand on the butt of his belly gun, the other on his hip pistol. "Yes, it is. Unfortunate for you, and him, I'm sorry to say. But, yes, it is."

Nance pointed at Boz with a braided leather riding quirt. "We want the man who murdered Pa, and we want him right by God now. Gonna string his sorry carcass up to the tree, over yonder in the square, after we fill him full of holes. If he's inside, bring him out." Damned good thing she couldn't have spit ten-penny nails, or her blistering tongue would have pinned Boz to the boardwalk like a sinner on a cross.

Calm as a horse trough in a drought, Boz stood and pushed the chair back with his foot. "Not today, you ain't. Near as I've been able to determine, Titus picked this fight, fired the first shot, and paid a heavy price for a clear-cut case of deliberate back-shootin' belligerence."

Stringy-haired kid, I took to be Arch Nightshade, stood in his stirrups. "Who told them black-damnable lies? You turn 'em over to us, and they'll change their Rebel tune—and right sudden. Git finished carvin' on one of 'em with my bowie, and won't be no one else spreadin' such bald-faced fiction. Won't take me more'n a minute to put such sorry lies to rest."

Boz didn't miss a beat. "No fiction to this one, son. Your pa picked a fight with a better shot. Witnesses saw Titus come into town drunk and lookin' for trouble. He found exactly that. Now he's dead, and that's the end of the story."

Jack Nightshade's flushed face gave him the appearance of a man whose head was about to explode. "Just be damned if that's the end. This bunch of stinkweed-growin' plow pushers have had a festerin' hatred for us since the day we got to town. Been laying out waitin' for a chance to kill one of us. We'll have payment, in blood, for my father's murder. No one's gonna kill a Nightshade and expect to go through this life unpunished."

Jack's right hand hovered over the pistol on his hip like he couldn't wait for the blasting to start. In spite of Boz's instructions, seemed like a good time for me to get a little closer to the action. Pushed the jailhouse door open with the shotgun's barrel, and took one step onto the boardwalk.

Brought that big double-barreled man-killer to my shoulder, aimed for the three Nightshades on the front row, and said, "Time for you to calm down, Jack. You folks have got too many fingers wandering toward weapons for my taste. First one of you touches a pistol, I aim to cut the three of you out front in half."

Let my less than delicate threat sit on them a few seconds, then went on with, "I can't truly believe your grief has made you stupid, on top of all your other less than admirable traits. Think all of you should take a gander at the open muzzle of this 10-gauge, and let the darkness you see at the back bring some enlightening reason into your life."

For about five seconds, the whole scene got so quiet thought I could hear the cogs turning in all their questionable thinker mechanisms. Half a minute later, a whipped, defeated look gradually settled on the faces of those in the leading rank.

Nance touched her brother's arm with the quirt and said, "Careful, brother. These men *will* kill us." She turned to me and snapped, "Jack is something of a hothead at times, Ranger Dodge. We'll just take Titus's body, and be on our way."

She twisted around in her saddle, and said something I didn't rightly hear. Several of the other riders stepped down, moved forward, and retrieved her father's body from our makeshift resting place. They managed to bend ole Titus in the middle enough to get him draped over an extra horse. Then remounted, turned, and headed out of town a lot slower, and with considerable less thunder and lightning, than when they rode in.

Feel fairly certain she didn't mean for Boz or me to hear, but amidst the noise and movement, Nightshade's hot-blooded daughter leaned toward her brother and said, "Don't worry, Jack. We'll get 'em. I swear 'fore Jesus, we'll get 'em back."

Sidled up next to Boz. He squinted at me from the corner of his eye. "Didn't stay inside like I told you."

"I know. Got concerned for your safety."

He chuckled. "Well, not altogether sure I told you right.

Got their undivided attention when you stepped up close with that butt-ugly scattergun. Don't know if you noticed or not, but think I saw real fear in young Jack's eyes for the first time since we got here."

"You sure 'bout that?"

He scratched his chin. "Could have been little more than a combination of anger and disbelief over his father's unexpected departure, or maybe indigestion from this morning's *huevos rancheros.* But looked like fear to me. Course none of my amateur face-reading means much in the long run. We'll just have to wait and see how the whole doo-dah shakes out. To be on the safe side, though, let's follow these angry dogs, Lucius. Gotta make sure they don't bite anyone on the way home."

His suggestion surprised me some. But, once we got to a spot where we could survey the enraged clan through our long glasses and not be seen, I realized he'd made the right decision. Watched as Titus's agitated family carried the old man's body into the house. Couldn't see exactly what happened after that, but tradition called for the women to wash and redress him for burial. Probably laid him out in the front room, or wherever a reasonably cool spot could be found. I know for certain sure, they had to work fast. Ain't nothing worse than a festerin' carcass lying around the house for two or three days. Gets to smelling a shade ripe in just a matter of hours.

Just a few minutes before sundown, Nightshade's oldest boys, and several men I didn't recognize, carried the corpse, wrapped in a multicolored patchwork quilt, to a spot on the creek about a hundred yards from the house. Half a dozen of them, with shovels and picks, made right short work of a deep hole under the shade of a live oak, and lowered the body, with the aid of what looked like a set of lines from wagon harness. Piled rocks inside the hole, then shoveled all the turned earth on top.

Mourners didn't spend much time over the grave, once

they got him in the ground, though. Mighty little praying got done at that burial. Whole family hustled back to the house, and set to celebrating. Fiddle music, dancing, whooping, hollering, and drinking went on loud, long, and well into the night. Sometime around ten or eleven, when the wake was in full swing, we headed back to town.

Boz cast a parting glance over his shoulder. "Maybe they learned something from this experience."

"You really believe that?"

He snickered. "No, Lucius. I don't. The way I've got this situation figured, Euless Whitecotton's desperate defense of his own life has probably lit a fire under the Nightshades that'll end up scorching everyone in Sweetwater. Like ole Bob Horton said, 'There's gonna be hell to pay.' Might be later than sooner but, trust me, it'll happen. These kinds of disagreements get goin' good, and the blood flows like water. We just might be in for a flood."

Two weeks passed, and nothing out of the ordinary occurred. The town pushed the murderous events of that day aside, and got all worked up over the coming wedding of a double set of twins from two well-known, and much-liked, local families.

The identical Boucher brothers, Tom and Ed, had proposed to, and been accepted by, the McKinney sisters, Barbara and Susan. Nuptials, planned for months prior to the Whitecotton-Nightshade dustup, had some members of both families suggesting a postponement of the event. Naturally, the overheated and anxious young lovers wouldn't consent to any such delay.

Concerned heads of each family stopped by the office, brought food offerings, and invited us to attend. Unable to resist the opportunity to grace any drinking and eating shindig with his boisterous presence, Boz readily accepted on our behalf. After due consideration of the opportunities to meet young ladies, dance, and have a fine meal to boot,

I gamely agreed with his decision. Like the rest of Sweet-water, we soon looked forward to the event with consider-able anticipation.

As Boz so aptly put it on at least a dozen occasions, "Lots of free bonded-in-the-barn tarantula juice at these countrified swarees, Lucius. Combine that with fresh-faced farm girls and all the jiggin' you can do—Merciful Father, she'll be a night to remember, my friend." He'd slap his belly, make sounds like a rutting hog, and let out a robust hoot. Deep down the man was something less than the absolute personification of polite behavior. Set me to wondering if I might be forced to shoot him in the foot, be-fore the celebrating finally drew to an end.

Seemed as though the town's entire population turned out for days before the big knot-tying, and each man, woman, and child took a personal run at helping the con-cerned families decorate the church house. Every so often, we'd stroll by, look over their progress, and offer sugges-tions. To this day, I don't believe I've ever witnessed a more heartfelt expression of a community's joy over such an occasion. Difficult to estimate how many hours of labor got expended on the bridal arch placed over a soon-to-be-flower-covered altar.

Country folk, from as far as ten miles away, rode in for an opportunity to lend a hand. Accidentally bumped into Martye McKee on the church steps, late one afternoon. Leastways, I thought it was an accident. She stood bare-footed, one plank below me, batted ebony eyelashes, did a little I'm-just-so-embarrassed-I-can't-hardly-stand-it act, and said, "Been here all afternoon, Ranger Dodge. Had hoped you might stop by. Thought we could do some more sparkin' out behind the church house. There's a nice lovers' spot I know of."

Held my hat in my hand and kicked at the porch with the toe of my boot. Couldn't believe the girl managed to discomfort me the way she did. "Now, Martye. That kiss we exchanged, a few days ago, was completely your affair. Can't say as I had much in the way of anything to do with that hastified romantic interlude."

"Oh, is that so, Mr. Dodge?"

"Yes. That is absolutely so."

She picked at a button on the front of my vest and ran a glistening tongue around cherry lips. "Am I to assume you didn't care for my kisses, Mr. Dodge? Not sweet enough for your sophisticated Fort Worth tastes?"

Have to admit her coquettish act was most likely having the exact effect she wanted, because things started to get right warm just below my belt buckle. But my pony-riding, semi-Comanche, white gal still managed to catch me by surprise again. Got me to squirming around under an inquisitive finger she used to dig inside my shirt.

Pretty sure the green-eyed beauty knew exactly what she was about. Devilish gal winked and said, "Well, you done waited too late today anyhow. My ma and me have to get back to the ranch 'fore nightfall. But I'll be back for the weddin'. Meet me at the lightnin'-split oak, out back of the church, after the big doings."

"Not sure that'd be a good idea, Miss McKee."

She flipped up my string tie, stuck her finger in my mouth, and wetly breathed into my ear, "I'll show you somthin' you ain't never seen before, cowboy." Then, she grabbed me by the ears, locked her lips to mine, and damn near sucked the spurs right off my boots. Held me for what seemed like an eternity. Broke the slobbery kiss with a resounding smack, giggled, darted across the brittle grass, and jumped onto her pinto's naked back like a painted savage. Left me standing in a cloud of red-hot Texas dust, shaking like a windswept leaf, with the smell of her breath clinging to my upper lip.

When the day of the big event finally arrived, the chapel bulged with people. Behind the crowded building, tables laden with enough victuals to feed Fort Worth adorned an area designated for the joyous reception scheduled to follow. A sizable area of grass had been scraped away and lightly watered, for the evening's dancing and foot-stomping. Some of the menfolk had collected pots, cans, and other noisemaking devices for a shivaree after the eating and celebrating.

Boz and I rated a seat at the festivities just behind those of the brides' and grooms' families. As a consequence, we had to spend time the afternoon before at Hickerson's picking out fresh outfits. Bought me a gray bib-front shirt, wine-colored bandanna, and bleached palm-leaf sombrero. Boz went for a fine-looking ready-made shirt, string tie, and leather-seated riding pants. His old canvas trousers had seen better days, long before we met. When Mrs. Hickerson finished decking us out with our spanking-fresh duds, we looked first-rate—if I do say so myself.

Even went so far as to spring for a serious scrubbing and shave at Delmar Clyde's Barber Shoppe, Tonsorial Parlor, and Bath House. Turned out that, under a thick layer of Texas topsoil you could have plowed and used to grow a fine crop of cotton, my newly acquired trail running amigo was a right distinguished-looking gentleman. When scoured, barbered, trimmed of nose hair, slathered in tonic, and decked out in his freshly purchased trappings, Boz Tatum could have passed for a governor, a Texas state senator, or at least a gambler, or bawdy house owner. Swear to Jesus.

Handsome lady, named Mrs. Leota Louks, flooded the church with the wedding march from an imposing, hand-carved German pump organ. The grooms awaited their brides under the town's remarkable arch. Ear-to-ear smiles decorated those young gentlemen's freshly scrubbed faces.

The striking brides made a splendid double entrance, amidst ecstatic twittering from all the ladies in attendance. Numerous whispered comments reveled in the stylishness of high-collared dove-gray dresses, imported from New

York City especially for the blissful occasion. I sat on the end of the pew next to the aisle, and when those girls swept past me, subdued moans of envy escaped some of the unattached men, and boys, nearby. Across the walkway, a ruby-lipped Martye McKee twirled her hair on a nervous finger, and made puckery-mouthed kissing signals at me. I tried to ignore her, but Lord God, she'd become a force in my life to be reckoned with.

Preacher Elton Jones had barely managed to get his final pronouncement of the bindings out, when the shooting started. Windows broke all around us. Men, women, and children dropped to the floor accompanied by splintered glass and screams of disbelief. The gunfire tended to be of a general nature, and seemed to come from all sides of the building at the same time. Glittery fragments flew in every direction like ice falling from a home's eaves when the thaw finally comes after a brutal storm.

Course, I went to reaching and grabbing, only to realize my weapons hung from a peg in a small room just inside the church house door, where the bell ringer did his weekly duties. Couldn't believe I'd allowed Boz to persuade me such silliness was a good idea, but the Reverend Jones had insisted no one be allowed in his house of worship with a pistol strapped around his waist.

Boz'd threatened to wear a shoulder rig he favored. But his raggedy coat looked out of place over his new outfit, so he discarded the idea. My partner pressed himself as flat to the floor as a ribbon snake and, under his breath, cursed like a drunken sailor about having been so stupid as to not keep at least one pistol hidden on his person. Don't think he ever made such a mistake again.

In less than a minute, the town's carefully crafted wedding celebration was reduced to splinters. Bullet-peppered doors dropped from their blasted hinges, and the walls took on the appearance of a foreign cheese that sports all them mouseyfied holes. Martye crawled to my side, placed her head in the crook of my arm, stared into my eyes, and made not a single sound. Her unruffled demeanor was impressive, to say the least.

Blasting and screaming died down after two or three minutes. The shooters finally retreated across Walnut Creek. Angry townsmen crowded into the church's bell room for their checked weapons, then raced outside to nothing more than a lingering cloud of grayish-black dust and the sound of retreating hoofbeats.

Mr. Hickerson, and other members of the congregation and business community, stood unbelieving, and stared at their much-abused church like men stunned by a bad dream come true. The frenzied architects of the destruction had also stolen abundant amounts of the wedding party's foodstuffs from the tables outside, then upset the painstakingly decorated counters, and trampled over them with their horses.

Hickerson shook his head. "How'd they manage to get so close, and no one saw or even heard them? Just can't imagine."

Leighton Bruce, owner of the only other real mercantile store in town, said, "Appears to have been carefully planned. Looks almost like a cavalry action. Stole their way up to the meetinghouse, pilfered all the food they wanted, then started shooting. Parishioners were so busy and excited about the wedding, no one noticed."

Right soon, the cry went up from one of the other attendees, "It was that damnable Nightshade bunch. Sure as hell's hot. They've been a-waitin' for the chance to mete out a nasty dose of bloody revenge for Titus getting plugged."

Stocky feller who wore a suit and vest he'd outgrown by more'n a few years said, "Time we cleaned out that nest of skunks. Whole family is like a bad tooth. You have to rip the sucker out by the roots, suffer for a bit, and then you can git on with the rest of your life. Snuff Jack Nightshade and, I'll guar-awn-damn-tee, things'll get considerable peaceful round these here parts."

Rapidly growing crowd mumbled and nodded its collective agreement. Boz tried to calm 'em down. "You boys need to take a breath. 'Fore you know it, someone's gonna say somethin' he'll end up regrettin'."

Tall, thin, ropy-necked horse wrangler who worked for House Rickards yelped, "Well, by God, if'n ain't no one else's gonna say it, I will. Let's braid us up 'bout three or six good pieces of oiled Kentucky hemp, and pay them evil sons of bitches a hot visit. If'n we let'em get away with shootin' up our church, what's next? Cain't have such foolish behavior, by God."

Boz grabbed me by the arm, and we pushed our way into the middle of the angry crowd. He had to yell, that time. A fractious buzz hovered over the irate assemblage like a hive of rudely disturbed bees. "That's just what I meant. Want you boys to count to ten, breath deep, and start thinking straight again. Looks as though we can say, for certain, no one got hit during the shouting, shooting, and general mayhem. No missing animals have been reported to me. And, most important of all, your women and kids are all safe and sound. Right now, what we seem to have is little more than an unnerving prank, pulled off by a band of unknowns that have yet to be positively identified."

The horse wrangler had felt the power derived from mouthing off in public and liked his newly found importance. "That ain't gonna do, Ranger. Ain't no man living can rub a feller's rhubarb like this and be allowed to git away with such lawless disrespect."

I held my hands up, and tried my own shot at putting a coat of oil in the water. "We haven't said anything about letting whoever is responsible get away with this. Give me and Ranger Tatum a chance, and I can assure you those responsible will be brought to book."

The stout chap in the tight suit felt left out of the action, and yelled loud enough for everyone within the range of a cavalry bugle to hear. "This bunch has been a-spoiling for an ass-kicking for sometime now. You Rangers have only been in town a few weeks. Look what has happened since you arrived and can personally bear witness to. We've had to deal with such shenanigans for years. Far as I'm concerned, it's way past time for some harsh retribution for their rude behavior."

Not sure where the voice of reason originated, but someone shouted, "Let the Rangers handle this. Leastways if they git killed, won't matter much." Didn't care for the shouter's final assessment of my importance in Sweetwater's tiny world, but his short, sweet speech had the desired effect. Men began to nod and mumble and drift apart— good signs from any potential mob.

Hickerson brought the whole dance to an end when he stepped up between Boz'n me, and put his arms around our shoulders. "Friends, these are capable men sent by Captain Horatio Waggoner Culpepper in Fort Worth to handle this state of affairs. I say we stand aside and allow them to do their job."

A grizzled old-timer slipped through the crowd, and stopped in front of Boz. "Young fellers, this here sit-chiation ain't gonna get better anytime soon. Might as well be aware as how most folks round here kinda like the suggestion about lettin' Judge Lynch dole out a dose of oak-tree justice. Best take some sincerely offered advice and git this cleared up, soon as possible. If not, we'll take care of it ourselves. Been a spell since I done any night ridin', but behavior like what we've seen today can bring past deeds out of hidin', right damned speedylike. Git my drift?" That time we nodded.

The still grumbling mob began to break apart, and soon most folks had headed for home. Martye caught me by the elbow, pulled me behind a live oak near a spot where the tables had been sitting, and just about kissed the tar outta me. Thought my lips would stick to her face when she finally broke loose.

She said, "You go out to the Nightshade place again, Lucius Dodge, be careful. I might not be around to keep you out of harm's way, this time. Make no mistake about it, they're a dangerous bunch and, given the opportunity, will kill you in a heartbeat. Don't ever trust Nance. Turn your back on that woman, and you'll likely end up deader'n Davy Crockett."

"You needn't worry 'bout me, little girl. Pretty sure I can take care of myself—no matter what comes my way."

"Yeah, well, you keep right on thinkin', and watch out for Nance Nightshade." She pulled me closer and whispered, "The woman has witchy powers. Kind men can't resist. Be aware. Keep you wits about, Lucius. If you don't, she'll kill you. Then, as God is my witness, I'll have to kill her."

12

"... I'LL KICK YOUR ASS. TILL YOUR NOSE BLEEDS."

TOWN GOT CONSIDERABLE subdued after all the shooting and hell-raising. Small clusters of folks huddled in doorways, or under awnings, and muttered amongst themselves as Boz and me passed. Some pointed and offered hushed remarks to their neighbors behind trembling hands. Got me to thinking on how their actions had the power to give a man some right uneasy feelings, if he wanted to think on them long enough. Didn't care to waste any real effort on it myself. Had to get ready for our ride out to Titus's ranch. Not sure why, but a cold, lifeless image of Nance Nightshade kept weaseling its way into my brain. Disturbing thought, so I did my best to push the dreadful apparition aside.

Walk from the church really didn't amount to much by way of distance, but seemed to take forever. Nothing like the inquisitive eyes of angry, agitated people convinced you ain't gonna live much longer to slow time to something like molasses in a Vermont winter.

Once we made our way to the relative tranquility of the

office, Boz and me spent close to an hour getting loaded and primed for what awaited us on Little Agnes Creek. First time I'd noticed a right grim aspect to my partner's personality. His normal joshing around, and funning, disappeared. Found his gloomy attitude a shade on the worrisome side, but figured he'd perk up as soon as we confronted the Nightshades about their most recent slap in Sweetwater's collective face. Just knew any kind of action would sharpen his wits and perk him up.

We'd stepped back outside and were about to get mounted when, to my absolute awestruck wonderment, the grizzled, ghostlike vision of Crow Foot Stickles ambled down the street. I would have recognized his ramrod outline from half a mile away in a blowing sandstorm. Man gave off all the confident grit of a desert in August, and glowered at the world from a bored countenance that resembled a thousand-year-old Arizona cactus. His platter-sized sombrero, crimped in a fashionable, but self-made, rustic style, along with the scarlet sash and heavy silver spurs, were set off by a studded gun belt and ivory-handled Richard's conversion pistol in a belly-high cross-draw rig.

Crow Foot was something of an old-fashioned dandy, when you got right down to it, even if he heatedly refused to own up to a personal weakness for the kind of stylish splendor used to cover a body well past its prime. Kept his hair, chin whiskers, and mustaches free of vermin and well trimmed. Claimed the *ladies* liked them that way. Have to admit that while his arrival surprised the absolute hell out of me, I secretly rejoiced at the prospect of news from family and home he surly carried with him.

Drew his mule, Mildred, to a halt at the hitch rack, crossed a leg over his saddle horn, and went to cutting on a plug of his preferred chaw. He favored a local Lampasas brand called Uncle Jake's Tejas Twist. And, while he rarely chewed in the presence of women, he was seldom without the stuff when in the company of men.

Crowfoot had no use for horses. More than once I heard him opine on the equine animal's inherent skittishness, belligerence, thickheadedness, and underestimated ability to kill its poor stupid riders. "Give me a mule any day of the week," he'd grumpily lecture. "Far better companions and a damned site more dependable. Ain't never broke none of my bones a-fallin' off'n a mule. But, by God, I've been bucked off, stomped on, run into fences, dragged, pitched into trees and barbed wire, and generally abused by damned near every hammerhead I ever threw a leg over."

Have to say his confident, relaxed appearance stunned me to the point where all I managed to get out of my rubbery mouth was, "What in the hell are you doing here, you rapscallious old bandit?"

He smiled, pushed the tobacco into his mouth, and chomped around a bit till the wad found a favorite spot. "Yore mama done sent me to make sure her oldest remaining son ain't gone and got hisself kilt, or somethin'. You isn't daid or anything, is you, Lucius? 'Cause I'd be mighty sorry to have to go back to the Colinas and tell that sad, wonderful woman as how her wandering child done went and got his head shot full of holes, or worse."

I hopped off the boardwalk and whacked him on the leg with my hat. "Hell, no, I ain't deceased yet, you old horse thief. Step down, shake, and say howdy to my Ranger partner, Boz Tatum."

Two best friends I could claim in the world at that moment circled each other like a couple of suspicious scorpions. Dance went on for about ten seconds before they finally decided a handshake wouldn't cost either of them much of anything.

Boz said, "Didn't catch your name, sir." Kept his tone neutral. I listened for the slightest affront, but could detect nothing by way of a challenge. Good thing. Would have hated to see them go to spitting and gouging at each other.

But such events did occasionally occur when men who were strangers met for the first time.

"Crow Foot Stickles is the name. Chicken wranglin's my game. Leastways, seems as such since this here pullet flew the coop after his pappy went and got hisself shot deader'n Mad Sam Walker. Be a pleasure to report back to his mama that he's still with us, and appears to be a-prosperin' under the benevolent guidance of one of Tejas' finest. Sure Miz Mattie'll be pleased to discover he appears to be ridin' on a gravy train with biscuit wheels." Damned fine to hear him make light of his mission, and bring some cheer back to our circumstances.

Boz turned to me and, with a shade of testiness in his voice, snapped, "Didn't you send the dispatch I had you write explaining where you were, and what had taken place in Fort Worth? Told you how important it was for your family. Thought I done a right fair job of stressing the significance of that particular note."

"Honest to God, Boz, I posted the letter right before we left town for Sweetwater. It must have got delayed or something. Hell, Crow Foot probably hit the trail from Las Tres Colinas 'bout the time I dropped it in the mailbag on the Waco stage."

"Ain't seen, nor heard of, any letter. Leastways, yore mama didn't mention one. Just said, 'Crow Foot, find my boy and make sure he's not been harmed. If'n he's still living, make sure he stays that way.' Brother Burl advised as how things are goin' just 'bout as peachy as can be expected on the ranch. Tole me to say you shouldn't worry if'n I was to locate you."

"How did you manage to find me? Explained everything in my note, but never expected Ma would send you to look."

"Figured One-Eyed Whitey and Raz would head for Fort Worth. Only place worth stoppin' 'tween Lampasas and the safety of the Nations. Soon's word got around 'bout Bone and his two henchmen, knew you'd be right behind 'em.

Good thing I happened to stop in and visit with some friends out at the Ranger camp. They tole me all 'bout yore hastified enlistment. But, hell, got me to thinkin', and I reasoned as how you musta figured it'd be easier to kill Whitey and Raz if'n you had some law hangin' off 'n yore chest." Boz and me both smiled at his unlettered ability to ferret out the real reason for my association with Company B.

"Don't suppose you wasted so much as a minute's worth of your time in Hell's Half Acre, did you, old man?" Winked when I asked the question, because I already knew the answer.

"Well, now, Lucius, I mighta spent somethin' of a thrillin' interlude visitin' with my good friend Gold Tooth Alice Crowder. She's a fine woman what got forced into the life of the crimson Cyprian. An unfortunate circumstance I would gladly rectify were it not for the fact that it has befallen me to live the life of an ancient, rootless, broken-down rover and cowboy. Besides, the woman gives the best bath this side of St. Louis. And, by the time I made it to Fort Worth from the Colinas, I'd begun to feel a mite crusty. Ain't nothin' worse'n feelin' crusty. In my more than humble opinion, that is."

"Well, Crusty, you made Sweetwater just in time to help us out with a festerin' problem," I said. "We're confronted with a family of miscreants named Nightshade that live a short piece outside town. Little more'n a few hours ago, they disturbed the town's peace by bustin' up a much-anticipated wedding. Shot so many holes in the church house, Boz claims the congregation might have to start using the building for a flour sifter. We're fixin' to take a ride out to Little Agnes Creek. Wanna string along?"

Crowfoot grinned, pulled his pistol, and started checking the loads. "Only thing I like more'n a hot woman on cool sheets is stompin' the hell out of evil bastards what deserve it. Takes some pretty sorry sorts to break up a sacred event as hallowed as a wedding. Besides, I've been hearing 'bout this Nightshade bunch for two, or three, years now. Have friends who live a bit west of here over in Poolville. They've been grumblin' 'bout cattle borrowin' ever since ole Titus and his tribe arrived in these parts. Bet you they ain't nothin' like a few bullet holes to set them straight."

Mention of ole man Nightshade brought an awkward silence. Hush lasted so long, Crow Foot finally snorted, "Well, hell, boys, did I snap a suspender, is my barn door open, or what?"

"Titus got shot graveyard dead a couple of weeks ago. Pulled down on the wrong man," said Boz. "Remaining family's been fairly quiet, up till today. Have to figure the gunplay at the church was little more than their version of vengeance." Boz thought a bit before he continued. "But blood will have blood. They ain't finished by a damned sight, boys. Be willing to bet they've got something gory in mind, and given what we already know of their past history, the hooraw this morning amounted to nothing more'n a warning of things to come."

I assumed we'd said about all that was needed and started for Grizz. But Boz came up with an absolutely stellar idea that would never have entered my pea-sized brain. "Tell me somethin', Crow Foot, how'd you like to be sheriff of Sweetwater, Texas?"

Ole Stickles looked like a man who'd just been hit in the face with a wet saloon mop. "The hell, you say. Never been nothin' like a peace officer afore. Did my share of Rangerin' back when the Comanche was still runnin' wild, but ain't sure I've ever had any desire to carry a badge."

Boz slapped my old friend on the back, then squeezed his shoulder. "Most folks 'round here feel the Nightshades were responsible for their last lawman's disappearance. Pretty sure I can get you hired for as long as we're in town. Be mighty helpful and, what's more, it won't be anything permanent." He grinned. "Whattaya say, old-timer?"

"Oh, I guess that'll be all right. Besides, probably

impress them Nightshades if'n we all show up sporting a badge of some sort. Been my experience they ain't nothing like the long, officious arm of the real law to get the undivided attention of bad folks. 'Sides, I know this bunch for thieves. They ain't made no reputation as gunmen or killers as yet, has they?"

"Not yet," Boz said. "But after this morning's dustup, won't surprise me much when it happens. I had hoped Titus's unforeseen departure from this life would make them give a bit more in the way of careful thought to their actions. Guess I was wrong."

We hashed the situation around for a few more minutes, then strolled over to Hickerson's. Bore witness while Burton, as representative of the town council, swore Crow Foot in as Sweetwater's newest high sheriff. Things were going along pretty good till our storekeeping friend said, "What's your given name, Mr. Stickles?"

A degree of hot surprise crept into Crow Foot's voice. "Why?"

Burton's sheepish, nervous look darted to each of us in turn. "Can't swear you in using a nickname, or nom de plume, as it were."

Crow Foot's confusion went all the way to his boot heels. "Nom de ploo-me. What the hell's that? Been accused of a lot in my life, but never of bein' a nom de ploo-me."

"Just a French word for false name," Hickerson said. "Gonna need your real, actual, and full name for town records and such. You understand, don't you?"

Crow Foot scratched most of his entire head. Started with the beard, went to his side-whiskers, mustache, then to the thick mat under his sombrero. He even dug around in his ears, for a bit, before letting the thing go. "Leander Gladstone Sanborn Stickles, by God. And, I swear 'fore Jesus, if one of you boys lets this particular cat out of the bag, I'll kick your ass till your nose bleeds."

Came as such a shock to me, my comment kind of

darted out of my mouth before I could stop it. "Damn, Crow Foot, if I had a ten-dollar name like Leander Gladstone Sanborn Stickles, think my chest might swell up so big I wouldn't be able to walk down the street 'thout knocking folks off the boardwalk."

"That's just exactly what I mean, goddammit. Never fails. Soon's some smart-alec like you hears my real, actual, honest-to-God name, I usually end up in a fistfight. Spent the first twelve, or so, years of my life rolling around in my own blood over my mother's favorite label. I got hung with a string of old family monikers and the discards of long-dead uncles. Hell, boys, the woman named my brother Aaron Jacob Stickles. Nice name. Jack never had a single giggling reference to the handle she threw his direction."

I could tell Boz suffered from a prodigious effort to keep from falling down laughing. He nervously suppressed the snigger, to a point, but couldn't resist asking, "Where'd Crow Foot come from?"

"My grandpap. He thought my gait funny. Said when I wuz a kid tryin' to learn how to dance, I looked like a drunk crow. I liked the name he gave me a bunch better'n bein' called Lee-ander or Gladdy-stone. And boys, if'n you want to git my dander up, all you gotta do is even think 'bout callin' me Sandy. That particular handle is just so sissified, she has the power to make the hair stand up on my back. Call me that'un, and yore for damned sure in for an ass-kickin'."

Hickerson tried to hide stifled amusement, and his wife had her face buried in an apron. He coughed and pinned a six-pointed star to Crow Foot's chest and said, "Well, Sheriff Stickles, I can assure you the secret is safe with my wife and me." My old friend's red-faced nod put the discussion to bed. We headed for our horses and the uncertainty of what waited out on Little Agnes Creek.

13

"WHAT THE HELL YOU
LAWDOGS WANT THIS TIME?"

THE RIDE OUT to what the citizens of Sweet-water believed was the Nightshade clan's combination ranch house, hideout, dance hall, and gossip-reputed whorehouse ended up being noticeably less tense than I expected before Crow Foot's appearance on the scene. Having another badge and gun on the raid elevated our expectations of success. My old friend's presence helped greatly with my personal feelings of well-being. Could tell by his manner that Boz's banjo string had also loosened up a turn or two.

A rod or so off the Jacksboro Road, we stepped down while I drew a map in the dirt of the area around ole Titus's rude dwelling. Boz said, "Since you've made one trip out this way already, you can lead us in. Crow Foot and me will hang back till we get to the creek. Then, I'll take over from there. You remember anyplace along the way that could be used for an ambush, Lucius?"

"Not much to hide behind till we get to the Little Agnes. Creek bank is pretty thick with blackjack oak, willow, and cottonwood. Have to come at the house from the south. Lazy stream is pretty shallow right now. Barely made Grizz's knees at its deepest. Could go downstream, and sneak over there. Do a long circle, and come at 'em from the north. It'd take us at last an extra hour or so, but you might want to think on it."

Boz discarded that idea out of hand. "No need. They'll probably be expecting us to do that exact thing, being as how it's the opposite of your first visit. We'll go at 'em from the creek, the way you did, Lucius." Then he locked us in a steely gaze. "You boys keep sharp. Faced off with this type more times than I care to count. What we want out of this, more'n anything else, is to make it back to Sweetwater tonight where we can have a nice piece of beefsteak and a beer at the Texas Star. Once we confront 'em, put your hands on your pistols, get ready for a fight, and let me do the talkin'. Understand?" We nodded our agreement, and saddled up again.

Don't suppose it would have mattered how we approached the Nightshade den. Turned out exactly the way Boz expected. Whole clan was ready for us, and came pouring out of the house soon as we got on their side of the watery barrier. Place looked like an anthill some mean-assed kid had just stomped on. Did a casual count, and came up with fourteen of them. Jack and Nance headed up a bunch of folks that included at least five faces I'd not seen on my initial foray, or during their trip into town to retrieve ole Titus.

All five of the new ones had the look of men that buckshot would roll right off their bare chests like water off a baby duck's back. My heart went to beating pretty fast when I realized just how deep the hole we'd jumped into really was. I've lived a long time since that afternoon, but I've never seen that many children, under the age of twelve, so heavily armed. The red-faced, snot-nosed little shits carried pistols, rifles, and knives of damned near every sort I'd ever seen. And the worst thing was, those kids appeared anxious for the shooting to start so they could kill all of us.

Lot of noise at first, but Jack and Nance finally shushed them down. Nance hooked her thumbs into her pistol belt and said, "What the hell you lawdogs want this time? Ole Man McKee and his bitch daughter lose some chickens?" Nervous snickers danced our way from the pack of kids. "That smart-mouthed little Martye been a-telling lies on us Nightshades again? Or did you fellers ride out just to socialize? Might as well know, we ain't got no tea and cookies for the likes of you." She locked me in a wicked gaze. "Or maybe you came miles out of the way to help us cook another pig."

Boz had stopped a few steps closer to the house than Crow Foot and me. He stretched forward in his stirrups and, when he spoke, I could barely hear him. No doubt about it, the man was as serious as cholera and real unhappy about being confronted by that many hostile guns in the hands of children.

"You folks caused quite a stir in Sweetwater this morning. Scared the hell out of damn near everyone in town. Did a journeyman's job of bringing a fine wedding ceremony, and reception, to a screeching halt. Damaged considerable property, and made off with most of the food."

Jack Nightshade yelped, "What in the blue-eyed hell are you mumbling about? We ain't been off'n our property in damned near a week."

Little brother Arch bounced up to the front of the Nightshade litter, and stopped beside his older sibling. Nervy boy held a Winchester next to his leg. "Yeah. We been right here. Don't know what you're going on about. Ain't seen nothing. Ain't done nothing. Ain't been nowhere. Why don't you sons of bitches get the hell off our property, and leave us alone?"

Nance must have noticed Crow Foot's badge. She lifted a defiant chin in his direction. "Who the hell's this newest law-bringin' bastard. That looks like Charlie Fain's badge you're wearin' there, old man. Where'd you get it?"

She'd mouthed off and said the exact wrong thing to a testy old coot like Crow Foot. Boz might have warned him to keep quiet. Didn't matter. Sounded like a grizzly from the back of a three-cub den when he growled, "You watch your quarrelsome mouth, girl. Don't let all these wrinkles and scars fool you. One of you heathens starts anything today, and I'll kill at least five of you before you can spit."

Boz turned in the saddle, and tried to glare him into silence. Didn't make one whit's worth of difference. Crow Foot had launched into a rant, and them Nightshade kids were about to learn one of life's more important lessons: Never brace a man you don't know.

Old warhorse snapped, "Let me tell you somethin', girl. You think paradin' all these kids out here's gonna cause me to hesitate if'n you start pitchin' lead my way, you got another think comin'. I don't care if half of you is still suckin' at the teat. Bring a loaded gun up my direction, and I'll send any, or all, of you to Jesus so fast your diapers will catch fire like a fresh-lit pine knot."

Jack's face went scarlet and, for a spell, he looked like a man in the midst of a stroke. I thought his head might explode. "Damn you. This is the second time one of you lawmen has come on our property and threatened us. Ain't nobody else around these parts had the nerve to show such brass."

Boz made a subdued effort to calm the situation. Cool as the bottom of a post hole, he said, "Well, son, you Nightshades have had your way here'bouts for some years now. Might as well get used to the fact that those days is over. The Texas Rangers have arrived. They's even a new sheriff in town. Best get used to the fact that anytime something amiss takes place within a hundred miles of Sweetwater, we're gonna be out here asking questions."

Crow Foot just couldn't keep his mouth shut. "Yeah, and kickin' your whole family's collective ass, if'n we have to."

Jack quivered like a coon dog trying to pass a six-pound cannon ball. He turned to a bearded, lanky feller leaning against the door frame. Dressed in a coat and black felt hat, the stranger tore himself away from his resting place and pushed some of the kids aside. Entire clan immediately made a path, as the newest brigand in the mix moved to the front of the crowd. Heavy silver spurs chinked and jingled. He stopped between Nance and her brother. Pulled his inky frock aside to reveal a pair of handsome Smith & Wesson pistols.

Nance and Arch grinned, as Jack got all Shakespeare dramatic and said, "Like you lawdogs to meet a good friend of our'n. This here's Snake River Tom Runyon." He turned and made a sweeping motion with his arm like a full-blown Eastern stage actor. "These here other boys are Tom's traveling companions. All of 'em be associates of our recently assassinated father what got sent to heaven by that murderer from Sweetwater. Just stopped by to say howdy, and visit. Think maybe Tom and his friends might even be persuaded to stay over for a spell."

Pretty sure I'd never heard of Snake River Tom Runyon, at the time. Don't believe Crow Foot had either. Leastways, he didn't act like the introduction affected him one way or the other. Only sign Boz registered amounted to a slight stiffening of the shoulders, along with an ever-so-delicate move in the direction of his belly gun.

Runyon grudgingly tipped his hat like a man who wanted to send us all to hell on an outhouse door. "Afternoon, Rangers, Sheriff. Mighty fine of you *gentlemen* to stop by and warn my good friends about the kind of worthless trash who'd shoot into a church house full of people." He removed his hat and held it over his heart. "My dearly departed ole pappy preached the gospel. Just can't abide anyone who'd do such a despicable thing. Unsettling, downright unsettling, if you ask me. Desperadoes, such as those, should be punished to the full extent of the law's ability to do so." Man had a voice that sounded like it came from just outside the gates to Satan's playground. "Think you'll have to look elsewhere fer them bad men, 'cause we've been right here all day readin' the Bible, prayin', and praisin' God. I swear to Jesus."

Boz squinted hard. "Been a long time, ain't it, Tom? Seems like only yesterday I put a bullet in your less than sorry hide over in San Angelo. Last time we ran you out of Texas, I heard you settled for the green hills and prairies of Montana and Wyoming. Done ventured out of your regular stomping grounds, ain't you?"

Runyon's face went scarlet as he stuffed his hat back on his head. "Ain't no reason to get temperamental, Boz. Me and the boys is just as innocent as newborn babes."

Tatum came damned near to laughing out loud, but he covered it up by coughing into his hand. "Hear tell, some folks up around Billings might want to talk with you about trains, stolen gold, and such. Even heard a scurrilous rumor that the city fathers of Casper, Wyoming, think you murdered several individuals who might not have been able to get themselves armed, or turn around in time to keep from getting shot in the back. Bloody events happened a number of years ago, but I'd be willing to bet the marshal up there would still love to have a sit-down with you."

The black-draped gunman threw Boz a contemptuous smile. "Just a pack of sorry damnable lies, far as I'm concerned. You know how it is, Boz. People make mistakes. Some see things that never happened. Knew a feller up in Cut Bank who swore he seen cigar-shaped things with blinking lights flyin' 'round in the sky at night. Other folks think too much. Seems like everywhere I go them thinkin' bastards are the ones what cause me the most problems. But none of that matters a damn, one way or 'tother, because there ain't no paper out on me, or my boys, up in Montana, or here in Texas. We can go, and do, as we please. Right now, it's our pleasure to visit with grieving friends—the

Nightshades. Help them mourn the passing of a sainted father, gentleman, and good neighbor."

Boz snapped a glance my direction, and another over at Crow Foot. Creaking leather sounded like battlefield gunfire as he leisurely shifted in his saddle, and brought a hand around to the cantle and nearer his belly gun. Then, he turned a challenging frown on one of the strangers, mixed in with the clutch of Nightshade children milling around on the porch. "That you a-hidin' up there amongst the kids, Latigo?"

Skinny wretch with a long scar on his scabrous face yelped, "Maybe. Maybe not. Ain't got no reason to insult me like that, Boz. I ain't done nothin' to you. Lately."

"Lucius, Crow Foot. Meet Latigo Cooley. His real name's Ernest Poorman. Ole Ernest never could accept what God made him, so he changed his name and set out on a life of evil doings. Two other deacons in attendance today include Jesse Dodd over on the left, and Leo Kershaw on the right. Neither one of 'em worth the gunpowder it'd take to fill a nit's ass."

With that audacious insult, Jack's smile vanished like spit on a blacksmith's glowing forge. "Look here now, Tatum, I don't care if you are a Ranger. You ain't got no right to ride in here and insult my family's friends."

Crow Foot laughed out loud. "If'n this is the best you can do for friends, son, you might want to invest some more time lookin'. You can outshine this bunch with a single visit to the docks of Houston. They's an abundance of whores and killers down there who'd gladly call you friend, if the price proved agreeable."

By then, I'd reached the point where the rapidly growing tension had me wound up tighter than a knotted rope. Whole fragile jawbone session kind of popped like a soap bubble when the cantankerous clan's loony matriarch stormed to the front steps and cut loose with a string of curses that would've made my mother cover her ears in shame.

Dusky Nightshade shook her corncob pipe at us. Looked like a witch using the leg bone of a black cat, in some sort of hellish ceremony only performed at midnight when the heavens were laced with lightning. "Goddamn you lawmen," she screeched, "and all them other sons of bitches like ye."

For the first time since we'd met, Boz looked absolutely thunderstruck. Got to give him credit, though. He recovered mighty fast. "Calm down, Mrs. Nightshade."

"You can go straight to hell, Ranger. Don't be a-tellin' me to calm down." She waved the pipe dismissively as if to rid herself of things she didn't want to see. "Yore kind has been a tribulation on my family for longer'n I can tell. Persecuted us fer untold years back in 'Bama. Got to the pint where we couldn't even cook up a batch of home brew, once in a while. Alabama dirt farmers even complained 'bout our fiddlin' and dancin'. Sweet Jesus, life ain't worth livin' if'n you cain't fiddle ner dance. Came to Texas to git away from yore type of jackass. But did we? Hell, no. Now, you've stood by and 'llowed one o' them snake-fornicatin' bastards from Sweetwater to kill my Titus."

Crazy woman's hair-covered upper lip quivered. She got all misty-eyed for a few seconds. Wiped away a tear and snapped back to life. "Come out here accusin' my sons, daughters, and their friends of crimes 'gin that same bunch of shit-eatin' dogs. I want all of yen's off'n my property, and be damned lively about it. Don't come back till ye can prove such broke-brained charges."

Got to hand it to Boz. He didn't flinch. Let everything quiet down again. Then, real low and real slow, he said, "We'll leave when our business here is finished, missus, and not a second sooner. So far, we've not had anyone come forward to say for certain they saw you Nightshades hoo-raw the wedding. But, believe me, if and when we do, we'll be back. In the meanwhile, should I so much as hear of someone stealing fleas off any of your neighbor's dogs, you can count on seein' me so fast it'll make your head spin." He started to turn away, but stopped and added, "Next time I have to come out here, you'd best be prepared to give up someone for the jailhouse. 'Cause I'll be taking one, or more, of you back with me. Anyone not understand what I just said? Any of you who didn't hear me?" Whole bunch milled around, picked at their clothes, and toed the porch planks like a gang of embarrassed kids who'd been caught behind the barn looking in one another's britches.

Boz eased his horse back two steps and said, "Let's get on back to town, boys. Ain't nothing else for us here. You go first, Lucius. Crow Foot will follow, and I'll come over last. Soon's you get on the other side, son, pull your rifle. They'll be less inclined to act if they're already under the gun."

So, that's how the mouthy confrontation finally shook out. We took our time crossing Little Agnes Creek, but whipped 'em good once we'd achieved some degree of safety. Slowed down as soon as the Jacksboro Road came back into sight.

Crow Foot got to cackling like a crazy man, and soon we'd all took a turn hooting and slapping our legs. He snorted, "Damn, boys. That's about as intense as I've seen in a spell. Them's some right testy folks. But, you know, I never felt like they really intended on doin' anything other'n run off at the mouth."

"Is that a natural fact?" I snapped. "Scruffy, tree-dwelling jugheads scared the bejabbers out of me, Crow Foot. Thought for sure they might go to pitching lead just any second. Especially after ole Mama Nightshade went nuttier than a box of soft-shell pecans before our very eyes. God Almighty, don't take but about a minute's worth of her to help you understand why the rest of them are buggier'n a blanket full of dog ticks."

Boz got his wish. He sprung for steaks, and all the trimmings, at the Texas Star late that afternoon. We'd each just managed to slice into individual slabs of beef the size of a wagon wheel when a delegation of nigh on twenty of

Sweetwater's leading citizens showed up, and noisily gathered around our table.

Burton Hickerson led a solid-looking group that included the owners of Bashwell's and Bruce Brother's. I didn't recognize everyone in the assemblage, but if anybody who could claim to be somebody in Sweetwater didn't attend the meeting, I couldn't have told you who that might have been.

Most surprising member of the hastily convened congregation, though, was Shorty Small. For some reason, it never occurred to me that the owner of the Nightshade gang's favorite hangout might have more than a bit of incentive to want them out of his hair.

Burton stepped forward with his hat in his hand and spoke directly to Boz. "My friends, neighbors, and business associates were wondering why you didn't arrest anyone during your trip out to Little Agnes Creek, Ranger."

Boz ran a finger around in his mouth, and took a swallow of his beer. "Well, Burton, being as how no one could positively identify those who fired into the church, and being as how the Nightshades denied it, and being as how they have friends out there who support their story, wasn't much we could do other'n what we did. Warned 'em we'd be watching their every move, and made certain they knew dire consequences would follow if any more violent behavior befell citizens hereabouts. Think our words of warning got their attention. Can't imagine you folks will have to sit up nights worrying about much of a response from them, for a spell."

Josiah Bruce pushed his way to Burton's side. "You boys haven't been around these parts long enough to make such an assessment. We have. Seen it all before. The Nightshades will pull a trick like shooting holes in the church house, run to the safety of their stronghold, deny they had a hand in the lawlessness, and wait. Usually only takes a few days before they show up in town again, looking to punish us for daring to raise objections to their behavior."

Shorty Small chimed in like a man pained by the fact that

he even had to speak. "Josiah is right as rain on this one, boys. Inside a week, them evil sons of bitches, and their angry women, will show up in my place for a daylong session of drinkin', cussin', hell-raisin', and general belligerence. No doubt I'll make plenty of money, 'cause they always pay in gold coin for their pleasures. But I'm not sure the abuse is worth it. Ain't been a time yet they didn't threaten to kill me, at some point during one of their visits. They revel in their outlaw behavior, and don't have one whit of conscience talkin' 'bout it when the only person listening would be easy to find and rub out."

Boz must have decided he wouldn't get to finish his meal for a spell. He tossed his napkin onto the table, twisted around in his chair, and locked eyes with the whole bunch of them. "Look, fellers, whatever might have occurred with Jack, Nance, and the rest of 'em don't mean anymore'n a paper bag full of east Texas goat shit as far as I'm concerned. They've been warned by Randall Bozworth Tatum, and the great state of Texas, to be on their best behavior. Trust me when I tell you if a single event occurs in Parker County that can attach itself to the Nightshade family, we'll be on them like ugly on an armadillo."

I barely heard him speak, but Hornus Bashwell sure got my attention when he said, "You might well have put the fear of God in them, Ranger. But then again, you could just be fooling yourself. We know those people. And if you think they're done with us for not inviting them to the wedding, reception, and dancin' afterward, you've got another think a-coming. They'll definitely be paying the town a call soon, and if what you've said about your discussion with that bunch of renegades is accurate, you can bet the ranch they'll be madder'n a gunnysack of teased rattlesnakes. Personally, I don't want to be around for that next visit. It's gonna be hell on wheels, boys."

14

"THESE MEN HAVE BLOOD IN THEIR EYES."

HORNUS BASHWELL'S VISIONARY procla-mation came true exactly six days after we laid it on the line for the Nightshade clan. Unfortunately, Boz, Crow Foot, and me weren't in town when it all came down like thunderation on those poor folks.

Early that morning a feller named Webster Wilhoit, from the tiny community of Jeeter, out on Denton Creek about ten miles north of Sweetwater, led us on a wild-goose chase for a band of outlaws he claimed had stolen some of his horses. Turned out, all we had was his word on the matter and no evidence he ever owned any horses.

Crow Foot saw through the ruse within an hour of our arrival at the lying slug's watch-pocket-sized ranch. Wilhoit's claims of theft had their basis in a personal dispute that'd been bubbling around for some years. Not all that much different from what we were confronted with in Sweetwater. Most obvious dissimilarity I could note, after we'd done all the investigating we needed to do, was that the folks in

Jeeter might not have liked each other much, but they hadn't descended to Sweetwater's level of murder and mayhem—yet. We figured such behavior couldn't be far behind, because Jeeter had even less in the way of law enforcement available than Sweetwater, before our arrival on the scene.

Being sidetracked like that made Boz madder'n a two-tailed scorpion. He griped all the way back to the office. "Damned amazing how these grudge-carrying snakes come out from under every rock within miles when they hear there's a Ranger somewhere nearby. Hell, I should have known better soon as Wilhoit rode up. Every stump-jumping yokel with a gripe against one of his neighbors can't stand it unless he can spend time bending some agreeable lawman's ear with a load of personal bitterness and irate bullshit."

We'd been out fumbling around in the briars and brambles on our snipe hunt a good part of the morning when we finally owned up to the error of our ways, and headed back to Sweetwater. Could hear the uproar before we got to Walnut Creek. When we popped out on the other side of the covered bridge, the ruckus sounded like all the ranch-raised folk in Parker County had trekked in from the countryside, and were madder than hell on a pitchfork. Passing stranger might have thought a town full of drunken preachers had found red-horned Satan camped out in their backyards.

Made our way up Main Street and passed several groups of heavily armed men. Every saloon had its own gathering of the obviously agitated, belligerent, and soon-to-be-sloppy knee-walking drunk. Members of each crowd turned and eyeballed us as if our small posse intruded on a private get-together. Shouting from so many people, and general noise contributed by their various animals, made it difficult to determine what all the activity was about. Good deal of the riffraff's open anger seemed pointed our direction, which only confused us further.

Crow Foot turned to me and hollered, "What in the hell

do you reckon happened, Lucius? Ain't seen this many people in town since I got here."

Could tell Boz didn't care much for what he saw either. "This ain't good, boys. These men have blood in their eyes. Can't imagine what's got 'em this riled up."

Someone in the swarm of citizens camped out front of the Texas Star yelled, "'Bout, by God, time you lawmen came back. Where the hell you been? Whole town coulda done got murdered in their beds by now."

Sizable gathering took up most of the street in front of Hickerson's Store. Burton stood on the boardwalk and tried to quiet a seething pack of about twenty-five or thirty angry men who waved their guns and seemed intent on shouting him down.

Every time Hickerson moved more than a few steps, his slow-witted helper, Lenny Milsap, swept the vacant spot left behind. Boy looked happier than a two-tailed puppy in a box full of brothers and sisters. Ain't nothing like a bit of responsibility to make a man feel wanted.

Boz rode through the middle of the mob, and dismounted at the hitch rail. He grabbed the frantic storekeeper by the arm and hustled him inside. Crow Foot and me hotfooted it behind them as fast as we could leg it. Boz didn't stop pushing Burton until they'd arrived in the private room at the back of the busy mercantile.

You could hear the concern in his voice when Boz said, "What the hell's going on here, Burton? Looks like every cow-chasin' horse wrangler in the county's done gone and got hisself pissed off, drunk, and armed up for a fight."

The flustered merchant looked like a man in the midst of a deep personal crisis. A series of raw emotions danced across his face. He flopped into a chair behind his dinner table, and held his head in shaking hands for damned near a minute before he finally looked up again. "It's bad, Ranger. Real bad. The town's leading citizens have lobbied Cyrus Baynes for almost two years to get added on as a regular daily stop for his stage line between Fort Worth and Jacksboro. As you well know, they only visit town once every other week now. The contract would amount to a financial boon for the town by way of perhaps twenty men employed at a Baynes layover, the sale of horses and feed, food and lodging for travelers, and maybe even a new hotel or bank. Hell, the economic benefits for our area are virtually limitless, and that doesn't even bring a sorely needed connection to the outside world into consideration."

Boz got impatient. "You can give the 'ain't Sweetwater a great place to open a business' speech a rest, Burton. Get to the point. My hair's turnin' gray."

Hickerson slapped the tabletop. Got all red in the face. "Well, dammit, Ranger Tatum, the point is, someone stopped Baynes's noon stage on its way to Jacksboro, and killed the driver and express agent. All happened about a mile north of town. Moses Hand found those poor boys shot to Jesus. Killers made 'em kneel down next to the front wheel on the driver's side of the coach. Moses said it appeared they'd been executed. After a personal examination of the bloody scene, I tend to agree with him. Those men didn't have no more chance than butterflies in a cyclone. Shot like dogs. Some folks, here in town, claim they heard the gunfire. Can't testify to that myself, but those assertions came from reliable people. 'Bout two hours ago, me and a posse of Sweetwater's founders located the empty strongbox on the side of the road less than a hundred yards from the scene of the murders."

I said, "He's right, Boz. Sounds about as bad as it gets to me."

Hickerson kept going like he didn't even hear me. "Jesus, boys, we've had three killings in a matter of weeks. That's more dead people in a shorter span of time than any other instance I can remember since 1852 when me, Bashwell, and the Bruce brothers established the town."

Crow Foot asked the most obvious question. "You folks got any idea who did it?"

Hickerson shot him a mocking look, and contemptuously snorted. "Hell, yes. We have more than a good idea. Who do you think did it, Sheriff Stickles? Want to place any bets? You think maybe Euless Whitecotton got out of his sickbed and did it? Get you damned good odds on anyone other than that bunch out on Little Agnes Creek."

"You sound pretty well persuaded the Nightshades did these killings?" Boz sounded tired.

Grabbed my Ranger friend by the sleeve and pulled him over to a corner. Crow Foot followed. "We need to find Moses Hand, Boz. Whoever that might be. Got to hear this tale directly from him. Looks to me like the spark has already been set to Sweetwater's fuse, and there's gonna be a lynching, unless we do something damned decisive to stop it."

Crow Foot nodded, but surprised me when he said, "Why would we want to stop it? Let 'em hang the bastards—Nightshades or not. Save us the trouble of lockin' 'em up, then dragging the whole crew all the way over to the county seat for a trial. Mad as these people is, they just might turn on us, if'n we don't handle the situation, and pretty speedy."

Not sure he meant to, but my old friend managed to light a fire under me as well. "Damn, Crow Foot, I can't believe you'd even entertain such an idea."

Boz snapped a glance back at Mr. Hickerson. "Where's Moses Hand? We need to talk with him."

"Well, Mose likes his privacy, Ranger Tatum. Lives about three miles north of town on Denton Creek. That's why he was the one who came upon the killings like he did. He was on his way to town at the time. Comes in once a week and stocks up on necessities here in my store. Been ranching out that way since before Sweetwater came into existence."

Burton was a likable enough sort. He just couldn't get to

the point without making a speech. That time I interrupted him. "We've got to talk with Hand sometime today, Burton. Don't require a personal history right now."

A brief look of disappointment, at not being able to finish his lecture, flickered in the man's eyes. "Well, as luck would have it, think he's in the Taxas Star. Unless he's decided to have nothing more to do with what's going on in the street, and headed for the ranch. Not much chance he'll take part in any of the rash behavior you see building outside." He stopped for a second, then got downright serious. "But if I were you boys, I'd be careful how I approached the man."

Struck me as an odd thing to say. "What does that mean?" I asked.

"Mose is the kind who doesn't like to be crept up on, surprised, or brought to anger. Best tread softly, gentlemen. Been a number of cattle thieves around these parts who found out it didn't pay to *borrow* cows from Moses Hand. He's a dead shot with a Winchester or Colt, and dangerous even when unarmed."

Thought came to me that we had a more immediate problem than some powwow with a rancher named for one of the King James Bible's major characters. "Look, boys, we've got a street full of folks outside who'll shortly have enough whiskey-powered steam built up to do something reckless of the oak-tree justice variety. Think we'd best nip this whole situation in the bud right now, and talk with Moses Hand later."

Everyone nodded his agreement. Boz scratched his chin. "Gonna have to take action right quicklike. Might have to use some force. Fact is, I think we should probably grab up the most vocal rabble-rousers we can find, throw them in the calaboose, and sort the whole mess out tomorrow."

Burton Hickerson made a motion at Boz like a kid in school trying to get the teacher's attention. He'd obviously had second thoughts about something. "Talk to Mose first, Ranger Tatum. Get him to help. Everyone in these parts knows the man. Most are afraid of him. If he steps in, folks with as little as a shot glass of sober brain cells will cut and run."

Sounded like more than a good idea. So we left Hickerson with his thoughts, and hit the street again. Milling crowd had stirred up a curtain of gritty dust laced with the odors of sweat, cheap whiskey, and even cheaper audacity. Men darted between the gathered groups in an effort to miss as little of the inflammatory speechifying as possible. One or two fellers led most of the rabble-rousing, and seemed well on the way to getting the crowd more excited by the minute.

We headed for the Texas Star as people all around us hooted and jeered. I heard comments like, "Where you yeller bellies a-goin'?" and "'Bout time some of you badge-wearin' bastards showed up. We're gonna need somethin' like law around when we catch up with them Nightshades."

Waltzed into Nate Macray's one-man liquor-pouring operation only to find things had busied up to the point where he'd been forced to press two new bartenders into service. Boz almost disappeared in a thick swirl of tobacco smoke as he forced his way through the crowd, leaned over, and asked where we could locate Hand.

Macray pointed to Euless Whitecotton's regular spot in the corner. Remember thinking later all we'd of had to do was give the place an eyeballing from the door, and we'd have easily spotted him. Hell, he was the only black man in the place. Maybe the whole town. Maybe the whole county. Leastways, I'd not seen any others till then.

As we strolled toward the table, I spotted a darting glance from his direction, and a hand that moved to the grip of his pistol. Under his breath Boz said, "Remember, boys, show your badges, act like you know what you're doin', and be careful. Don't want any problems with this cowboy."

Easy for me to understand Moses Hand's discomfort at having three unknown men surround him, while he tried to indulge in a nice, quiet drink. But if we bothered him much, the case-hardened rancher didn't show it as he twirled a full dipper of whiskey with his free hand and silently measured each of us for a coffin.

Boz made an effort to put the man at his ease. "Afternoon. I'm Ranger Boz Tatum. Young feller on my right is Ranger Lucius Dodge. Old fart on my left, wearing the sheriff's badge, goes by the name of Crow Foot Stickles. Burton Hickerson advises that you might be willing to help us out with a small problem."

Hand offered up a crooked smile. "And what problem might dat be, Mr. Tatum." For a man not much bigger than a wrung-out dishrag, his voice was deep and dripped of the Old South—possibly the backwoods of Alabama, the delta country of Mississippi, or piney woods of Georgia.

"You can see what's happening from you chair. If we don't put a damper to what's going on here, like as not someone will certainly get strung up 'fore the sun comes out tomorrow. Ain't that much of a ride out to Little Agnes Creek. Drunk as these men are, Jack Nightshade and his family won't have any trouble making sure half of 'em end up as dead as those Baynes stage line boys." No panic in Boz's voice, but you could detect a degree of urgency.

Moses Hand appeared nothing like his evocative name. Man was short, skinny as a bed slat, sickly-looking, and the color of a chewed razor strop. He stared at the three of us from behind black eyes laced with a series of yellowish-green cobwebs painted over the whites that encircled them. More than anything else, the man looked bone-tired. Gave me the impression he suffered from a nagging case of jaundice.

His drooping eyelids slowly slid up and down as he sipped from the glass in his hand, then carefully lowered it to the tabletop. "Cain't say as how it'd matter much to me one way or 'tother if'n some of these crackers hung a few of them Nightshades, and managed to get themselves killed in the effort. That misbegotten family of thieves had only been in these parts a short time when my cows started disappearin'."

"You sure the Nightshades did the borrowing?" I asked.

He glanced at me, then went for another sip of his drink. Carefully lowered the glass to the same spot on the table. "Caught dat 'un named Arch takin' some of 'em. Boy couldn't have been more'n twelve or thirteen year old at the time. Switched his ass with a green cottonwood limb. Dragged him back home by the scruff of the neck. They wuz all livin' in a broke-down wagon, at the time. Dat old man they called Titus messed around and went to callin' me names. Made out like he might pull a pistol. Put the fear of God in him right on the spot. Tole him if'n any more of my cows disappeared, or if'n I caught his kids tryin' to take anymore of 'em, wouldn't be no talkin' 'bout the problem. I'd come back and kill him before he could blow out a coal-oil lamp."

Crow Foot grinned and said, "Lose any more cows?"

"No, sir. Not one. Ain't had no trouble out'n dat bunch since. But I do believe they might be behind the killin' of them stagecoach fellers. And if'n they ain't behind it, they know who done it. Course, I suppose dat don't give this bunch of drunks the right to lynch any of 'em. Have real personal feelin's 'bout lynchin'. If'n I doan never see another'n, it'll be way too soon."

Then, out of the clear blue, Crow Foot had an absolute stunning flash of brilliance. "How 'bout I make you my deputy. Don't have to be permanent, less'n you want. You know, maybe you can work with me for a week, or so, while you think it over. Mr. Hickerson said if'n I found anyone able, as the town's unofficial mayor, he'd have no objection to me hirin' another man. Been needin' one for a spell now."

Hand's jaundice-rimmed eyes lit up like Fourth of July sparklers. "You'd do dat? You'd take on a black feller as deputy sheriff?"

Crow Foot threw his head back and laughed. Then said,

"Hell, yes. Ain't got no personal prejudices along them lines. Long as you can use that pistol you've been fingerin' ever since we ambled over. Wouldn't make any difference to me if'n you had two heads. You cover my back, when the time comes. That's all that matters, 'cause I'll damn sure do the same for you."

Moses thought the offer over for about a minute. Rolled a smoke. As he fired up he said, "Does I gets a badge?" He grinned and shook his flaming match till the burned tip smoked.

Crow Foot fished around in one of his vest pockets and came up with a six-pointed star, almost exactly like the one Burton Hickerson had pinned on my old friend. He leaned over, attached the shiny symbol of authority to Hand's shirt, and said, "How's that strike you, amigo?"

Moses Hand stood, turned, and glanced at his reflection in a heavy mirror hanging on the wall. He smiled and showed a sterling set of pearly teeth. "Looks mighty fine, Sheriff. Mighty fine. I thinks we's gonna do right well together. And bein' as how I's a deputy now, you can call me Mose—if'n you'd like."

Boz, who looked somewhat surprised by the turn of events, took a deep breath. "Well, now that we've settled on a new deputy, let's us lawmen meander outside and see what's what. Maybe get a handle on the hoi polloi 'fore anything awful manages to percolate up and bust wide open."

The four of us marched onto the boardwalk just in time to watch the various groups of noisy, future vigilantes form into a single angry mass that moved to the front of Hickerson's store. Burton had their attention, and tried to talk reason. One man in the crowd seemed far and away the most vocal, and appeared on the verge of inflaming his neighbors to acts of violent retribution.

I pulled at Hand's sleeve. "Do you know the idiot out front arguing with Mr. Hickerson, Mose?"

"That two-legged jackass be Judas Tierney. Man's got a

lip like a Gatlin' gun. Owns a peckerwood-sized horse operation not far from the Nightshade place. He done went and lost several animals to 'em, over the past year or so. Leastways, dat's the story he'll tell you if you hold still long enough. But he ain't got nerve enough to do anything 'bout the situation by hisself. Bet my last dollar, he'd love to stir everyone up enough to go chargin' out to Little Agnes Creek and hang every damned one of them Nightshades, including the kids. Tell you somethin', Mr. Dodge, you shut him up and this whole drunken shebang will fall apart like a paper hat in a rainstorm."

We eased around the noisy mob. Tried not to get them any more upset than they already were until we could snake our way to the front and challenge the whole bunch at the same time. Boz and I came at them from one side of Hickerson's porch. Crow Foot and Mose slipped in from the other. Surprised the drunken herd when all four of us took positions behind Burton. Got real quite for a few seconds. Then Judas Tierney went right back to shooting off his whiskey-soaked mouth.

He assumed the mantle of a kind of crowd leader and cut loose like a man dead certain he had the support of his audience. "Well, looka here. The goddamned law finally showed its sorry face. We thought maybe you boys had done gone and skipped town. Typical behavior for your sort. Kinda thing we've come to expect from anyone 'round here wearin' a tin star. Figured you Rangers was already back in Fort Worth by now, or camped out somewhere in the big cold and lonely with Charlie Fain."

Boz moved down the steps to a spot about six feet from our insolent antagonist. Cooler than iced water he said, "You boys need to calm down some. Maybe sober up. Put your weapons away and let us handle the problem. No need for this kind of reaction yet. Just drag yourselves on back home, take a nap, sleep off some of the tarantula juice you've had today."

Tierney sneered. Upended the bottle in his hand and took a deep drag. Glanced over his shoulder at the crowd for encouragement and yelped, "Damned if we will. We come here for justice. That clan of thieves, and their filthy-mouthed, mattress-backed women, are long overdue for a serious comeuppance." Then he turned directly to the mob and shouted, "And, by God, we're just the ones who can give 'em what fer. Ain't we boys?"

The raucous pack of drunks roared intoxicated approval, but fell silent and sucked back like waves on a stormy beach when Deputy Sheriff Moses Hand darted past Boz, and whacked Judas Tierney on the noggin with the barrel of his pistol. Ole Judas dropped like a condemned man falling through the trap on a well-greased gallows. Didn't even twitch. Eyes rolled up in the back of his head like he was dead. Looked right surprised. Truth is, I thought maybe Hand might've cracked Tierney's brainpan or something.

Thank God it didn't take long for the rest of us official lawman types to react to our new deputy's impetuous act. Before the crowd could draw a second flabbergasted breath, they were staring into the open muzzles of eight cocked pistols.

Mose stood over Tierney's limp body, both weapons at the ready. "You boys go on home now. Party's over. Ain't gonna be no twisted-rope justice in Sweetwater today. Do like Ranger Tatum said. Hoof your way to the house, and sleep off this day's tubful of firewater."

Don't think the rowdy swarm would have got any quieter if death himself had walked right up in the middle of that pack of angry, confused dogs. One chucklebrain, whose head was evidently considerable bigger than his hat, must not have known Moses Hand as well as everyone else attending the spur-of-the-moment prayer meeting. He jumped right up in our runty black deputy's face, and said the exact wrong thing for the situation at hand.

"Yew gotta lotta got-damned nerve stickin' out on you

there, nigger. We 'ens jest might hafta string you up first, afore we go after them got-damned Nightshades. Fact is, if'n yew lawdogs doan put them pistols away, this jest might be yore last time to see the light of the Lord."

Audacious son of a bitch grinned in Hand's face—kind of grin that left no doubt how he felt about our new friend. Then, the gutsy jerk went and spit on the black feller's boots. Glanced back over his shoulder for the crowd's approval, the same way Judas Tierney had. Not much doubt he expected the rest of the mob to follow his lead, and do as they pleased.

Imagine the smart-mouthed yob's surprise when ole Mose whacked him too. Laid the barrel of his pistol right between the big dumb bastard's eyes. Dropped him like a hammered steer in a Chicago slaughterhouse. Boz followed suit with a rapid firing of four shots into the air over the mob's heads.

My God, but I wish you could have seen them scatter. Looked like red ants pouring out of a burning log. Bet it didn't take twenty seconds for that street to clear, but we stuck around for a spell longer with our guns drawn anyhow. Just to make sure they didn't come back, you know.

We'd been primed for a return match, for two or three minutes, when Mose holstered his pistols. "They ain't comin' back. Them ole boys has done went and had enough excitement for one day. Be talkin' 'bout this day's happenings for years to come. Tell they granchilrin 'bout the time they fought the big gunfight in Sweetwater, and what heroes they wuz. How they buffaloed the lawmens and lynched that black bastard." He flashed me a toothy smile, grabbed Judas Tierney by the collar, and said, "Think maybe you needs to sleep your'n off in one of Sheriff Crow Foot's cells. Maybe learn you a lesson."

Flicked my pistol barrel toward the man I didn't recognize. "What about this other one, Boz? Want to take him in for a spell in the cooler too?"

Tatum finally put his guns away. He was the last one of us to uncoil. Glanced at the bloody-faced wretch and couldn't help grinning. "Hell, yes. Lock both these morons up. Tomorrow we'll fine 'em fifty dollars apiece for inciting to riot, and turn 'em loose."

Crow Foot jerked the stranger up by the nap of his neck, snatched the pistol out of his belt, and said, "March your sorry, smart-mouthed ass over to the jail, yay-hoo. Gonna git to spend the night mouthin' off at cave crickets and cockroaches."

Most folks recognize their arrival at that point when it's best to keep your opinions to yourself. Then again, there are always some who just can't keep their mouths shut no matter what, and Hand's pistol-whipped adversary was one of them. He held a blood-soaked bandanna over the gash between his eyes and yelped, "Damned if'n ya'll gonna lock Frank Miller up in some two-bit, jerkwater Texas jail."

Crow Foot looked surprised, shocked, disbelieving. "My Sweet, Glorious God. Are you Frank Miller?"

The bloody-faced feller brightened up. "That's right. You heard of me?"

Crow Foot grinned. "Hell, no, I ain't never heard of Frank Miller, you dumb son of a bitch. Far as I'm concerned you're nothing more'n a future occupant of a cell in my jail. But I'm right pleased to know your name, Frank."

We hustled those boys over to the sheriff's office and threw them in the box. Slammed the barred door so hard everyone in town must have heard the metallic clang. Both of them whined and bellyached for hours. I thought the whole dance was over. But as events usually worked out during my first several years as a Ranger, I was mistaken.

We'd just found ourselves a place to sit, and take a breather, when Boz said, "Damned dangerous trick you pulled out there, Mose. Scared about ten years worth of hell out of me when you bounced you pistol off ole Judas's head. But when you walloped Miller too, I thought for damned sure we were all deader'n Santa Anna. Jesus H. Christ, next time you decide to pull a trick like that, let someone know what you're about."

Mose yanked at his tobacco pouch and shook out an already rolled handmade cigarette. Took his time searching every pocket for a match and trying to light up. Around the coffin nail dangling from his lips he said, "No need to worry, Ranger Tatum. All dem boys needed was a dose of sure-handed guidance. Seen their type many a time afore. Just regular folks. Most of 'em are farmers, ranchers, storekeepers, and such. Their kind don't really want no trouble."

I scratched a match to life, leaned down, and helped him get his tobacco lit. "They looked right serious to me, Mose. Don't know as how I'd want such a crew out for a piece of my hide."

Hand pushed his hat to the back of his head. Sucked down a lung of silky blue smoke and blew a stream toward the ceiling. Then he said something that has stayed with me through all the years that have passed since. "You know, Mr. Dodge, as you go along in this life you gonna find dat they's night riders, and then they's mobs. Them night-ridin' bastards is dangerous. Most times they cover their faces and do they evil from behind the safety of a mask. Secrecy makes them right audacious, sometimes. But a mob has a face. Usually forms up behind one or two men in the broad daylight. Do they business where everyone involved knows everyone else. Damned near impossible to stop masked night riders. But a mob is like a poisonous snake. Chop off the fanged head"—he waved dismissively toward our prisoners—"and what's left cain't do nothin', but wiggle and squirm till death comes."

We sat, puffed, and mulled that one over for a spell. I'd barely got relaxed when the jail's back entry popped open. Nance Nightshade stood in the open doorway, fist on one hip, and motioned at me. "Could I speak with you a moment,

Ranger Dodge?" She slapped a quirt against her leg and nervously shifted from foot to foot.

Looked to Boz for guidance. He nodded. Said, "See what you can find out, Lucius. Could be we can put a cap on this whole situation right here, before anyone else has to die."

I hopped up, stepped outside, and pulled the door closed. Said, "What can I can I do for you, Miss Nightshade?"

The jumpy girl grabbed the quirt at each end, and almost bent the thing double. "Took my life in my own hands by coming into town today. Given what I saw sneaking in, have to believe my unease isn't misplaced. But I had to make sure you badge-toters understood that the Nightshade family didn't have anything to do with murdering the Baynes Company's stage driver, or his shotgun guard."

"Well, Miss Nightshade, your story might be difficult to sell in Sweetwater right now. Less than an hour ago, my *badge-totin'* amigos and me broke up a mob that had blood in one eye and your family's stretched necks in the other."

She stopped twisting the quirt, and placed a quaking hand on my arm. "That's why I'm here. I'll admit to a deep-seated dislike for you law-pushing types. My family's brief meetings with you, and your friends, recently should be absolute proof of that fact. But I'm very concerned by what's going on today. Jack, Arch, and my mother have armed the kids, boarded up the house, and they're all primed for a fight I'm convinced isn't necessary. Any red-eyed rope-swinging mob showing up on Little Agnes Creek's gonna be damned sorry, but they just might kill some of the little ones when the shooting starts." Don't know why her obvious concern surprised me, but it did. I could see the turmoil in bloodshot eyes. They swam in liquid pools that were about to slosh over onto her cheeks.

"You're probably right about all that. But you needn't stay up nights in a state of sleepless worry. Boz and I won't let the town ignore the law. Won't be any lynch mobs around these parts, long as we have anything to say about it, Miss Nightshade."

She pushed sweaty hair from her eyes. Then said, "Can we make a deal? I'll call you Lucius, and you can call me Nance. Reckon that'd work?"

"Fine by me."

"Good. Glad that's settled." Her head dropped and, for several seconds, she thought about what she said next. "Tom Runyon and his bunch killed those men, Lucius. And the treacherous scum left the responsibility for the crime right on our front doorstep."

Then the look she threw me hardened. She put her hands on her hips, stepped to within a foot of my face, and said, "Sometimes you can't control people if they get crazy enough. I've seen as much before. It's the exact reason why we came to Texas in the first place. Us Nightshades had to leave our home in Alabama after my oldest brother, Ethan, got strung up for a crime he didn't commit. Nothing more than a sad story about a bunch of screaming drunks out for blood. And the opportunity to punish a family of blue-bellied Northern sympathizers they all wanted dead anyway."

Tried to be reassuring. Don't think I succeeded. "Believe me on this one. No need to trouble yourself any further, Nance. You can hang up the fiddle, 'cause we've jailed the two most vocal troublemakers, and the rest of 'em called it a day and went home. But that don't mean you shouldn't expect a visit from Boz and me. Go back to the ranch and get your family prepared. Tell them to stay away from town for a spell—leastways till we can go over the scene of the killings and maybe straighten this mess out. Good chance we can avoid additional trouble, if you'll do that."

She nailed me to the ground in a steely-eyed gaze punctuated by a single tear that dropped from the corner of her eye. "Hope you're right, Lucius. Anyone bring this fight out to my brother, and I can guarantee there'll be killings for damned sure. Don't know what kind of luck I'll have keeping Jack at home. As you well know, he tends to do as he pleases. But I'll try."

She didn't wait for me to respond that time. Simply turned, jumped onto a wiry mustang's naked back, and edged her way along the building to the street. She stopped at the alley's entrance, checked for movement in both directions, and silently slipped into the evening's rapidly dimming light.

I followed and watched as she eased down the street to Walnut Creek like a ghost. Lost sight of her when she disappeared into the open maw of the covered bridge. Didn't hear a sound after the darkened, cavelike entrance enveloped her.

Thought, at the time, my companions and I'd done a damned fine job. But as Crow Foot always liked to say, "A man should never count his chickens until after Sunday dinner. And if that ain't a fact, may a wild steer hook my gizzard." Or maybe he said something equally as convoluted and I just can't recall the exact wording.

Anyhow, little more than a week later, I would look back on my astonishing level of inexperience and optimism about such matters, and swear I would never let myself be fooled in such a manner again, even if I lived to be a thousand years old.

Crow Foot was right in his rustic assessment of the situation. But what he should have said was, "When it rains, you'll get wet if you stand out in the middle of the road." Or maybe something equally as tortuous for me to figure out. All I know, for certain, is no matter how bad you think things are going, any given situation can get a hell of a lot worse so fast, it'll make your eyeballs spin in their sockets like pinwheel fireworks on a holiday.

15

" . . . HE'S AN UGLY SON OF A BITCH, AND COMIN' FAST."

NEWLY APPOINTED HIGH Sheriff Crow Foot Stickles got downright officious about Judas Tierney and Frank Miller. Insisted those bellyaching boys stay in his jail overnight. Finally agreed to turn them loose after he and Boz talked their lawless behavior over. But if Boz thought he'd had the final word on the matter, he couldn't have been any further off the mark. Crow Foot let the rabble-rousers out of their cell, and then held what he called an "oh-fishal" hearing right there in the office.

He slapped each man with a ten-dollar fine for disorderly conduct. My God, you can't imagine the whining and moaning. Course neither one of them had any money—leastways that's what they claimed. Boz told them they could pay the penalty out at a dollar a week. Said they should thank whatever god they prayed to that Crow Foot hadn't charged them with inciting to riot. That one would've cost them fifty apiece and as much as a year behind bars down in the state penitentiary at Huntsville.

Crow Foot put them back on the street with one final piece of advice. "Don't let me catch you sons of bitches a-causin' trouble in *my* town again."

God Almighty, you would of thought the town's newest citizen had helped establish Sweetwater—a founding father or something, no less. Didn't matter, though. No one in, or around, town ever saw either man after Crow Foot turned them loose. Leastways us badge-toting boys didn't.

Morning after we confronted the mob, Boz started our investigation of the murders. Moses Hand turned into an invaluable plus for our side. Man knew Parker County, and the surrounding area, like the lines in the palms of his hands, and he surprised everyone by being an uncommonly good tracker.

We all made the trip out to the spot where the killings took place. Moses immediately found blood sign leading away from the scene. He said, "Be a-looking like maybe them stagecoach fellers musta put a blue whistler in one of the thieves. Could explain why the driver and guard went and got shot up like they did."

After we'd been on the trail for near half a day, Boz got on a thinking rip and decided he didn't want to leave the town completely unprotected. He sent Crow Foot back to Sweetwater. My ancient compadre didn't like the idea of not being in on any foreseeable action. Man loved the smell of spent black powder and the prospect of a good fight, but understood the necessity of having someone around to act as defender of the town.

Turned out Nance Nightshade told me the honest-to-God truth. Followed the four killers away from the murder scene. They headed north for the Red River, and tried to use Denton Creek to cover their escape. Moses was too smart for them, by a damned sight. I do believe the man could have tracked a granddaddy longlegs over a bed of river rocks. We ran hard for two days. Crossed the Red a bit east of Wichita Falls.

About noon on the second day past the Red, we reined up on the banks of a creek that emptied into the Cache River. Watered the horses, drank what we needed, and filled our canteens. Boz and Mose talked the situation over and agreed our prey was headed for the Wildhorse country.

Moses said, "These boys done be a-thinkin' that if'n they can make the Wildhorse River, won't nobody be takin' time enough to follow. Rough country for sure. Be hard to find 'em once they hide 'mongst all them timbered-up cuts and hidden breaks."

Boz scratched a grizzled chin. "Hard, you say? Reckon you can keep up with 'em? Stay on their tails in all this stuff?"

Our ebony-colored friend grinned and wiped his mouth on the sleeve of a tattered shirt. "Don't you be a-worrin' any, Ranger Tatum. Long as they keep the one a-leakin' his life all over the place with 'em, followin' this bunch'll be easy. But I don't think he's gonna last much longer. We be findin' them, whatever they does. And from the look of things, I'd say sometime tomorrow afternoon. Seems as like they's mighty proud of theyselves. Be a-thinkin' they done got away with murder and robbery. 'Pears to me, these bad boys done slowed their pace considerable. We should be about to surprise them faster'n you can beat a bull to a hole in the fence."

He took out ahead of Boz and me a piece, and I guess it couldn't have been more than an hour later when we ran across the barely living person of Jesse Dodd. Poor son of a bitch looked a whole bunch different from the day I'd first seen him at the Nightshade ranch. He was slumped against the trunk of a blackjack oak. A crusted stain started on the left side of his shirt, just above his pants, and cascaded down into a dripping boot. Someone had tied his animal's reins to a bush nearby—a cocked pistol lay beside him. Don't think he could have lifted the weapon and fired at anyone even if he'd wanted.

When Boz and me arrived on the scene, Mose had

kneeled beside the wounded bandit, and held a canteen to the dying brigand's cracked lips. Water trickled down ashen cheeks streaked with dirt, sweat, and blood. The wounded man moaned, and his eyes opened about the time we bent over him to see what, if anything, could be done.

Took near everything ole Jesse had left when he said, "Damnation, but I sure as hell hate to die in the company of a bunch of egg-sucking lawdogs."

His eyes closed, and he made that gurgling, chest-rumbling kind of sound that doesn't leave much doubt a man's time on this earth is almost over. He weakly covered the hole in his side with a blood-caked hand. His eyes popped open again, and wandered from one face to an other like he'd just woke up in a brand-new world. Out of nowhere he seemed to regain substantial strength. Made a move as if he might try to stand, but didn't. Fumbled around for his pistol. Mose pushed the weapon away with the toe of his boot. Only thing I've ever seen that can sustain a man in such a manner is hatred deep enough to keep him going—even when he's already in Hell, and just don't know he's dead.

"Can you tell us what happened when you boys robbed Mr. Baynes' stage, Jesse?" Boz squatted, and took a small pad of paper along with a stubby pencil from his pocket.

The ready-for-the-grave outlaw's gaze rubbered around for several seconds, and finally landed on the toes of his own boots. Must have steadied him up a bit—same as any common drunk who concentrates on a single spot to keep him upright. "We stopped that there Jacksboro coach. Looked to me like the robbin' was a-goin' right well, at first. Got them boys down. Thought we had 'em disarmed. Shotgun feller come up with an old Colt pocket pistol from somewheres."

His eyes snapped shut like God had slammed a door to the real world, and he drifted off into death's approaching haze. We all figured he might not come back that time. But he did, and went at the tale again. You'd of thought he never stopped. "Couldn't have been more'n three feet from the man when he shot me—twice. Latigo slapped the gun out'n the bold bastard's hand and whacked him on the head with a rifle barrel. Snake River Tom went crazy. Made both of them Baynes fellers kneel down in the ditch beside the front wheel of the coach. Shot 'em deader'n hell. All for nothin'. Express box was emptier'n a gourd. What a waste. Never meant for no one to get kilt. 'Specially me."

Moment or two of silence passed. Jesse's half-opened eyes glazed over. Tears ran down both cheeks. He started breathing hard. Got a beached-fish look and sound about him. Man couldn't have been more than twenty years old, and then, for just a second or so, he looked like a scared child. He turned to Moses Hand. Reached out and grabbed our surprised friend by the arm.

Between gasps for breath the fading bandit said, "Kentucky's . . . mighty cold . . . in the winter, Mother. Think maybe . . . I'll go to Texas . . . someday. Hear tell . . . sun shines . . . more there." He shuddered and gasped, "Cain't . . . get warm. Cold done gone . . . all the way through my bones."

He drifted off again, but came back for one final run at the world. "Tell Papa . . . mare's ready. Foal cain't wait. . . . It's a-comin' . . . right damned now." Thought his time was finally over, but then he sat bolt upright and grabbed Mose by the arm again. "Sorry . . . Mother. Tell Mary Margaret . . . I'm sorry." Then he stared at something over my shoulder and clear as a bell said, "My God, but he is an ugly son of a bitch and coming fast." Then all the air went out of him. Poor bastard flopped back against the tree slack-jawed, eyes wide open.

Boz slapped a quirt against his leg. "Damn, boys. 'Bout to think the poor son of bitch might've made some kind of bargain with the devil, and wasn't never gonna die." He snatched the dead robber's gun off the ground, untied the abandoned horse, and climbed aboard his own. "Let's get the hell out of here."

Being the least experienced member of the group, I asked what I thought was a pertinent question. "Ain't we gonna bury him?"

Mose stepped into a stirrup and settled into his saddle. "You want him buried, Lucius, then go ahead. Bury him. Far as I'm concerned, God will take care of what's left here today."

Boz turned and called over his shoulder as he moved on up the trail, "We'll pile some rocks on him when we come back this way—if there's anything left. Right now, we've got more important irons in the fire. They's still three of them killers ahead, and I want 'em dead, or captured, 'fore nightfall."

Managed to catch up with that particular band of sorry outlaws exactly the way Moses Hand said we would. Got to them before they made the tree line at the foothills of the Arbuckle Mountains. But I have to admit they didn't respond the way we'd have liked.

Being old hands at horseback gunfights with the Comanche, Boz and me hoped they'd turn, charge us, and make it easier to take some of them down. Instead, soon as the one riding drag spotted our posse, the whole bunch ran to beat hell for a stack of rocks some of the Nation's locals called Pinnacle Mountain.

We had a spot, just west of Lampasas, everyone in my part of the country knew as the Haystack. The two of them looked amazingly similar, if you ask me. Neither amounted to much in the way of a mountain, compared to those out West. But, if you closed one eye, and squinted real hard with the other, I suppose you might induce yourself to believe the Pinnacle's rudely heaped pile of granite amounted to something like the rocky crags of Montana, Wyoming, or Colorado.

I could tell those boys had been chased and forced to fight before. All three could pitch storms of lead over their shoulders, on a horse stretched out to its absolute limit. We followed them over rolling grasslands for several miles. Dust and black powder smoke made seeing them mighty difficult the closer we got. More than once, I thought my shots seemed to have found a home, but the blasting didn't slow the objects of our chase down any.

'Bout forty or fifty yards from solid cover they jumped off their horses. Tom Runyon and Latigo Cooley handed their reins off to Leo Kershaw. Then they kneeled and laid down a fiery wall of lead, while their compadre pulled the animals toward a cut in the base of the hill.

To this very moment, I feel pretty sure if Leo had managed to make the rocks, we would have had a hell of a time rooting them out. But, thank God, he didn't. Two brigands offering him cover jumped up and started hoofing it behind Kershaw, just as Moses Hand pulled off a minor wonder of a rifle shot. That rainbow miracle upended the fleeing Leo like a biscuit tin used for target practice. Big chunk of whistling lead hit him in the head and sent him rolling like a Chinese tumbler in a traveling circus.

When his skull exploded, and he went to flying ass over teakettle, them other two got a dose of newfound religion. With bullets peppering everything in their immediate vicinity, Runyon and Cooley stopped and looked right thoughtful. Didn't take more than a second, or so, for them to come to the only decision available. They threw down their weapons, and commenced to hollering about how they'd done gone and give up. Totally unexpected occurrence. I felt certain them boys would fight to the finish. Go down bloody. Punched full of holes. But I suppose seeing a friend's brains get splattered all over heaven and earth can bring about a serious change of heart, no matter the circumstance.

Said more than a few prayers on my walk to take them killers into custody. Thanked a merciful God the chase turned out so good for our side. Course being jerked up short didn't keep the murdering survivors from damn near yammering us to death, soon as we got within earshot.

Runyon quaked like a leaf in a thunderstorm and yelped, "You didn't have to go and kill Leo, for Christ's sake. Man was almost sixty year old. Had a bunch of grandkids. Led a hard life. Wouldn't hurt a fly."

Boz pitched me his rifle, and started searching Runyon for more weapons. He snapped, "If this back-shooting weasel moves without my permission, Lucius, show him how it feels to be his brain-busted friend over there."

Tatum took three pistols and a seven-inch bowie off Snake River Tom. Then, when I thought the dance was all over, Boz found a lethal, palm-sized derringer in one of the outlaw's boots. Dangled it in Tom's face like it was a piece of deadly jewelry on a braided gold chain. "Never can be too cautious, Lucius. Just imagine what might have happened on the way back to Sweetwater, if I hadn't found this miniature popper."

Runyon sounded almost pathetic when he said, "Well, you cain't be too cautious out here in the wild places, Ranger. Only carried that'un for snakes, and such."

Moses Hand laughed out loud. He had already searched Latigo and put the man under the gun, but couldn't help himself. "You must be a-runnin' up on some damned small snakes, Mr. Runyon. Mayhap they be Arkansas snakes, or some kind of midget Louisiana wigglers. Or, mayhap one 'dem northern Montana snakes. Belly crawlers don't get very big up there in the cold. Sho' nuff ain't no full-bore Texas diamondbacks. Seen one 'dem beasts out west of Fort Worth, a spell back, what could stand up like a man, take that little pistol away from you, and spank yo' butt with it."

Well, that one set all us lawmen to giggling. Runyon obviously didn't like being the object of our humor. Murderous brigand got right indignant. "I'll tell you sons of bitches somethin'. Damned good thing you boys managed to sneak up on us so's we didn't have no chance to give you what fer. Hadn't surprised us so bad, we'd of made you wish you'd never seen me, Latigo, and Kershaw."

All Runyon's rant did was make Boz laugh that much harder. "Hell's fire, Tom, you had plenty of chance to fight. Gave up mighty damned fast after Deputy Sheriff Hand put that one in Leo's brain bucket. Gets me to wonderin' just where that reputation you're carrying around came from. Cain't count on both hands how many tales I've heard 'bout your lethal nature. Man of your reputed deadly skill, with pistols and knives, shouldn't have thrown his hand in with no more fight than you showed."

Latigo toed at a bloody spot on the ground and popped off with, "We didn't know who'n the hell you fellers was. Here we went a-ridin' along, a-mindin' our own business, same as deacons on the way to Sunday meeting. All of a sudden we got three men shootin' at us like we're criminals, or somethin'. Scared the bejabbers out'n us. Ain't prayed so much in twenty year." God Almighty, but he sounded real pitiful. "Soon's we realized you boys was Rangers, we give it up. Ain't got nothin' to hide. Law and order all along the line. That's what I always tell everyone I done ever knowed."

Stunning audacity of the heartless killer just god-damned infuriated me. I said, "You mean you're gonna deny butchering the Jacksboro stage driver and his express agent? Surely you don't have *cojones* that big and brassy."

Latigo looked all wretched and ignorant. He held his hands out, palms up. "What the hell are you a-talkin' about, Ranger? We doan be knowin' nothin' 'bout no dead stage driver and shotgun guard. Be totally innocent of any such unfounded charges. Show us who seen us commit that dreadful and bloodcurdling act. Why, the thought of such shocking behavior is enough to curl my toenails. Most awful kind of wickedness I done ever heard tell of. Makes me shiver all over, right here in the sunshine."

Boz jumped in Snake River Tom's face with the notepad in his hand. "One of the Nightshades give you up, Tom. According to her, you tried to blame the murders on her family, and she didn't like it much. Then we tracked you sons of bitches from the scene of the killings. Found your friend Jesse Dodd, less than two hours behind us. Guess you must have thought he'd already give up the ghost. But he hung on long enough to tell a lethal tale that's gonna turn you into worm meat, ole son."

Runyon's bluster showed some sizable cracks. "Don't matter what Jesse mighta said. He's probably out'n his head. Delirious, I'd bet. Crazed from being shot by renegades just after we crossed the Red."

Boz let out a demented cackle. "Bullshit. I've got his statement right here in my book. These other two lawmen witnessed poor gut-shot Jesse's dying declaration. Words on this paper's gonna ensure you boys swing. We'll take you back to Sweetwater and, first chance we get, over to Weatherford or Fort Worth. You'll be tried, found guilty, and hung by the neck till you're dead, dead, dead. Law's gonna make you about six inches taller 'fore it's all over and done, ole hoss."

Mighty sobering stuff when you're confronted with the absolute certain prospect of hanging. Snake River Tom and Latigo Cooley got real quiet. We slapped them in wrist shackles and trussed them up so they couldn't go far if either man tried to get away afoot. Threw Kershaw over the back of his horse and headed for the spot where they'd left Jesse Dodd. Boz made Tom and Latigo dig the hole for their friends. God, but they hated that piece of work.

Didn't have any shovels along on the trip, so them bellyaching crybabies had to scratch out a shallow depression with broken limbs from the tree where parts of poor Jesse still lay. By the time we made it back, some kind of animal had been at the corpse—looked like the work of a coyote, maybe more than one. Grisly business no matter how you whittled on the subject. Took almost an hour to find his head. Eventually, we came across enough of him to throw in the thin hole with his friend, Kershaw. Covered them with any kind of rock we could scrounge up.

Runyon wanted someone to say words over his dead amigos. Got right put out when none of us stepped up and assumed the responsibility. "Why, you cain't just ride away
and leave a man without offerin' up somethin' to smooth his
path to glory. Goddammit, it ain't Christian. Civilized folk
don't do such as this. Mighty sorry thang when you see a
man off to his maker and don't at least send a prayer along to
help him navigate that dark path to the Pearly Gates."

Well, that just about ripped the rag off the bush for me.
I said, "Shut your sorry mouth, Runyon. Likes of you've
got a lot of nerve lecturing anyone on how *Christian* folk
are supposed to act. You murdered two unarmed men you'd
put on their knees in a ditch for an express box full of air.
Bet both of 'em were praying when you pushed a pistol
muzzle to their skulls and blew their brains into the mud.
So don't get all pious and concerned about the spiritual
well-being of the poor devils that followed you. Hadn't
been for your leadership, they'd probably still be alive."

Suppose Snake River Tom had some residual bit of conscience. His head dropped, and he looked shocked by my
spit-slinging outburst. But I wasn't about to let him off that
easy. Didn't matter to me whether the two-tailed rattler re-
gretted his actions or not.

Pushed him even further down with, "Besides, I just
cannot bring myself to believe there's a coon dog's chance
in hell for any of you miserable skunks to spend more'n a
few seconds in front of the Pearly Gates. Bet everything I
own you're gonna get turned around real quick, and sent
the other direction. Fact is, when I hit my knees tonight,
that's exactly what I'll be praying for."

Took considerable wind out of their sails with that
speech. Don't think either man said more than a dozen
words all the way back to Sweetwater. Caused quite a stir
when we rode into town. Everything seemed as peaceful
as Granny's flowerbed in the sunshine, at first. But as soon as
we rode across the bridge over Walnut Creek, all the saloons

emptied out. Street filled up with rowdy drunks, cowboys, and town folk so fast I couldn't believe my eyes. Heard several men mumbling in the background about "getting a rope and taking care of the murderin' scum right here and now."

By the time we drew up in front of the jail, the continually growing swarm had surrounded us and worked itself into a chest-thumping rage. Surprising thing was that most of those good people wouldn't have been caught dead making such a commotion in the company of a bunch of red-eyed, drunken rowdies. Faces, I noticed, belonged to some of Sweetwater's leading citizens. God-fearing, righteous, churchgoing individuals you wouldn't have believed could act so obviously angry in public.

Crow Foot must have heard the noise. He jumped through the door to the sheriff's office and onto the boardwalk carrying a shotgun. Surprised the hell out of me when he pulled the hammers back and fired two ear-shattering blasts over the crowd's heads. He reloaded like greased lightning. Flipped the empties over his shoulder, cocked the hammers again, and yelled, "Go home. Ain't nothin' here for you today. Law's gonna take care of these men."

Good many of the raucous throng hit the street running for the safety of hearth and home. Some ducked behind the nearest tree, horse, or corner. But a surprising number didn't even budge. We hauled our captives down, and pointed them toward the jail. Once afoot, people ganged up around us, and went to yelling, shoving, and swinging at Runyon and Cooley. Jostling got pretty rough, then some in the back of the crowd, who couldn't get a lick in, went to throwing all manner of loose objects. I didn't mind the dirt clods and rocks, but some son of a bitch hit me in the back with a big, wet cow flop the size of a Mexican sombrero. Caught me in a kind of ricochet, and sprayed half-a-dozen other people too.

Good God, but I swear you'd find it hard to believe churchgoing people could curse like that. My tender young ears had never heard such language from men and women

I'd grown to respect. Sounded worse than a bunkhouse during a fistfight. A blind, seething anger came pouring off that crowd, and for the first time since we'd met, I saw genuine concern on Boz Tatum's face. Became glaringly obvious to me that my friends and I might be in just as much danger as our prisoners.

Crow Foot snapped off another blast and waded through a knot of those who'd managed to get between our party and the jailhouse entrance. We bunched up tight as we could and pushed our way inside. Boz brought up the rear, slammed the heavy door soon as he could, and threw the bar. Runyon and Cooley dropped to their knees and went to praying. Every one of us was wound tighter than fiddle strings at a barn dance, and sucking air like we'd just run a footrace.

Slumped against the door, Boz said, "Hell, Crow Foot, the whole town might have been slightly pissed when we left, but I don't remember 'em being this mad. Something happen while we were gone?"

Crow Foot grabbed Snake River Tom under the arm, hoisted him to his feet, and pushed him into the cell. Moses ran Cooley in and banged the door closed. My old friend from Lampasas dropped his shotgun on top of the desk and flopped into his chair. "Well, Boz, you could say that. I do believe you can truthfully say something happened while you were away."

A second or so of silence followed. Boz dragged a cane-bottomed instrument of torture over from the stove and twirled it around so he could lean on the back when seated. "Well, Sheriff Stickles, you gonna tell us or what?"

Crow Foot pushed his hat to the back of his head and massaged his temples. "You ready to hear about another killing, Ranger Tatum? Worst one so far?"

16

"Who Would Commit Such a Monstrous Act?"

I'M CONVINCED THE tiny world of the Sweetwater, Texas, sheriff's office could not have got any quieter, unless Death himself had walked in, pulled up his own chair, propped a cloven hoof on the stove, and said, "Howdy, boys."

Boz looked like someone had slapped his face. He popped upright in his seat, ran a shaking hand from wrinkled forehead to stubble-covered chin, and flicked sweat from his fingers to the floor. Shook his head from side to side, then slapped his knees with open palms.

Sounded distant, as if he spoke from the bottom of an empty rain barrel, when he finally said, "Who? Who done went and got kilt now?"

Crow Foot snatched his hat off. Threw it on the desk atop the still-warm-barreled shotgun. Gave the mop of hair on his head a vigorous scratching. Glanced around at all of us, then stopped on Boz. He said, "Ezra McKee."

Honest to God, I felt like something sucked the breath

of life right out of my lungs. All around me the room closed in tight. Got all flusyfied, and beads of surprise popped out on my forehead. Had to bend over and grab my knees to keep from falling. Odors of tired, fearful men overwhelmed my senses, and sent my mind to spinning like a kid's top.

Barely heard him speak when Boz said, "Who would commit such a monstrous act?"

Crow Foot let out a raspy snort. "Who the hell do you think did the killing, Boz? We've played the same hand before. Think Nightshade, and you'll be real close to an answer."

Regained enough of my composure to look into my friend's eyes and say, "Which one? Jack or Nance?"

Crow Foot wallowed himself deeper into his chair cushion and rolled a smoke. "Good boy, Lucius. You done went and hit that bull in the butt with the first shot."

Moses Hand leaned against the cell door and looked bewildered. "You mean both of 'em kilt Mr. McKee?"

"Naw, naw, naw. Don't mean to say exactly that. Jack done it, but Nance was with him when it happened."

Ranger Randall Bozworth Tatum slumped all over. The lines in his face deepened, and dark moon-shaped patches appeared under his eyes. He rested a bristled chin on crossed arms, and his shoulders sagged as if someone had walked up behind and loaded him down with a burden too heavy to carry. Great sadness in his voice when he said, "You gonna tell us what happened, Crow Foot, or do we have to sit here and guess at the thing till we get somewheres close?"

Stickles fired his hand-rolled cigarette. The flame died in a shaken hand. He puffed twice, and flicked the still-smoldering wooden stem onto the floor. Clouds of blue-gray smoke swirled into his nostrils and around his face. A piece of errant tobacco was pinched from a chapped lip and thumped to a spot near the doused match.

He said, "Two days after you sent me back to town, took

my chair outside and set up for the morning shake-and-howdy session with them folks as happened by. Ezra and that oldest gal of his come to town. They nodded, howdied, and headed on over to Hickerson's. Didn't think anything special 'bout our 'How're you doin?' ritual at the time. Pulled my hat down over my eyes and proceeded to take myself a before noon siesta—same as you'n Lucius been doing ever since y'all got here."

Must have sounded a bit on the panicked side when I blurted, "Martye? Martye came in with Ezra?"

"Yep. Knew the McKee girl 'cause she rode that paint horse I seen her on before. Anyhow, while I snoozed, guess they went into the store for some staples, or whatever. Barely got into my nap, when I heard more animals comin' across the bridge. Sound from all them hooves growled its way up the street and covered the town in a blanket of yellow-toothed, slobberin' fear faster'n anything I ever seen or heard tell of. Street emptied like oily water runnin' off a pane of glass. Everyone backed up against the wall of his choice, and watched as Jack and Nance Nightshade, and another joker I'd never seen afore, come riding in and pulled up in front of Shorty Small's place. Kilt my need for a snooze and sharpened me up so sudden I vibrated like ringing steel. Didn't take my eyes off'n them from the time they hit Main Street."

Boz said, "They appear to be looking for trouble?"

"Not as you'd notice, not right off anyways." Crow Foot paused and glanced at each of us in turn. "But when I think back on the thing, comes to me that all of them was armed to the teeth. Musta been wearin', or carryin', every piece of equalizin' iron they owned. Should have known. Hell, if I'd paid better attention, probably could have heard the Devil chuckle. Swear to Jesus, boys, was like the entire town sucked in a single lung of air and held its collective breath to the verge of explosion. So quiet you could hear flies breathin'. Everyone told us 'bout these visits. But this 'un was the first I'd witnessed."

Moses said, "They get drunk and start somethin' like they usually does? Go out lookin' for some poor soul to kick the bejabbers out of, just for the fun of it?"

"Never even got inside Shorty's place. One of 'em musta spotted McKee and his daughter comin' out of Hickerson's. Someone in the Nightshade bunch pointed fingers that direction. 'Fore I knew what fer, Jack, Nance, and that other gunny headed Ezra's direction fast as they could leg it. Caught him tying a bag of victuals behind the saddle on his mule."

"Couldn't you have stopped them, Crow Foot?" For some reason the entire ugly scene played out on the backs of my eyes like a vision in a gypsy fortune-teller's crystal ball. I instinctively knew how the story worked, before he could tell us all the brutal details. "Nothing you could have done, old friend?"

His chin dropped to a spot on his chest. "Knew you were right tender toward the girl, Lucius. So, I hopped up and hustled over that way myself. Arrived on the scene of all the jawin' and commotion in time to hear most everything said. Suppose me and about six or seven others, from inside Hickerson's, seen the whole dance, up close. Nightshade gang lined up behind McKee and went to raggin' on him right off. Jack said, 'Owe me for a pig, you clod-kicking bastard. Figure that sow you had the Rangers steal right out of my hungry family's mouth was worth at least ten dollars. I want my money. Gold coin will work just fine.' Jack's new friend laughed. Startled farmer turned to confront his tormentor. 'Bout then all of 'em realized they'd miscalculated ole Ezra's willingness to put up with any more abuse. See, McKee was a-holdin' a shotgun when he faced 'em. Don't know how he came up with it the way he did, but he had both barrels cocked and ready."

"What about Nance?" I asked.

"Funny thing, you know. She kinda laid out of all the struttin' and smart mouth. Can't say for certain sure as how I ever even heard her say a word. Didn't back away or anything. Stood behind her brother, and that other'n, and let them do all the blusteratin' and mouthin'. Anyhow, Ezra made it real plain as how Jack and his friends might be on the way to lightin' a shuck for Heaven's front door. Seem to remember something about shit-eating dogs from Hell. Have to give the gutsy farmer credit, no flinch in the man when the chips went down."

"You try, at any point, to put a stop to the dance?" Boz sounded a bit impatient, like he expected *Sheriff* Crow Foot Stickles to have stepped up and asserted his freshly appointed authority.

Crow Foot snapped a challenging glance at Boz before he replied. "'Bout the time I'd decided to wade in on the discussion, felt the cold steel of a pistol muzzle against the back of my neck, Ranger Tatum. Another friend of the Nightshades had managed to sneak up from behind. Hell, boys, they had it all planned. Had to. Lifted my weapons and put me on my knees right there in the middle of the street. Said not to move, or I'd be shakin' hands with Jesus in a heartbeat, and he wasn't by God kiddin'."

Storytelling stopped for a few seconds. Gave Boz, Moses, and me time to visualize the ugly tableau in front of Hickerson's store. Crow Foot took the last hit from the smoke he'd let burn down to his fingers, dropped the butt on the floor, and ground it out with his heel.

"Didn't know who that ole boy wuz at the time, but I gotta tell you fellers, thought my travels in this world had come to an end. Remember at one point, I looked at the dust on the knees of my pants, a horse fritter a few feet away, and thought sure I'd be covered with the same dirt and manure faster'n God could get there to save me."

"Get on with it. What happened then?" You could tell from his voice, Boz had hit the end of his tether.

"More jawin' back and forth. McKee girl pulled at her father's sleeve and tried to get him to head for home. He wasn't havin' none. Said he'd leave soon's the Nightshades got out of the street and made way. That's when Jack said McKee might oughta get on back home to his ugly whore of a wife 'fore he got shamed in public."

Heard Moses mumble, "Sweet Merciful Jesus."

"Exactly how I felt, Mose. Guess the slur must have pulled Martye McKee's cork as well. Girl jumped over in Jack's face and slapped him so hard his ancestors in Hell must have felt the palm of her hand. That's when the shooting commenced. Can't say, for sure, as who started the ball rolling. Blasting from both sides got right intense. So much spent powder in the air the shooters disappeared on me. Took the opportunity to pull the bowie in my boot and slip it into the man behind me. Got him in the leg, just below the crotch of his pants. When he yelped and bent over, punched a nice-sized hole in his neck just under his chin. Knife went in all the way to the hilt. Got him going in so many directions at once he didn't know which end was up. Grabbed my pistols and tried to stand. Someone whacked me on the head, or maybe a bullet nicked me, can't be clear which.

"When I come around again, Ezra'd already passed, along with his mule, and Martye's mustang. Girl hovered over her father. Never heard such weeping. Town's been a-workin' on its anger, like fire stokers in Satan's kitchen, since the day they buried that man. Whole bunch is all horns and rattles. They're madder'n a herd of red-eyed cows and looking for any reason available to kill somebody. If'n my name was Nightshade, I'd stay out of Sweetwater fer a spell."

Probably sounded just a bit too concerned when I blurted, "What about Martye, Crow Foot? She all right?"

Could tell by the way he looked at me the news couldn't be real good. "She's staying with the Hickersons, son. Got pricked a couple of times by flying lead. One creased her arm, and, as she went down, noggin got a little scratch. Nothin' life-threatenin'. But she bled so much from the head wound it might well have saved her life. Witnesses on the boardwalk in front of the mercantile said Jack went to shoot her again. Stood over the girl and cocked his pistol, but Nance stopped him. Maybe Nance thought Martye was already dead. Can't testify to seein' Nance stop the thing myself, but that's what others told me."

Boz looked surprised. "Neither of the Nightshades got hit?"

"Not so much as a single scratch, as near as I've been able to determine. But Ezra got the new boy what came to town with 'em. One load of 10-gauge shot. Kilt him deader'n John Wilkes Booth. He'd crowded Ezra to the point where that's all it took. Cut the poor idgit in half, right at his suspender buttons."

Boz said, "Been able to find out who he was?"

"Yeah. Had the town look 'im over. Three different people identified the chewed-up mess as a thief and killer from the Round Rock vicinity named Roscoe Slidell. Usually ran with Chalky Snow's gang of cutthroats. Had to bury 'im that day. Don't suppose we'll ever know now for certain, lest we can get it out of Jack when, and if, we bring him in. But I gotta tell you, Boz, if'n Chalky Snow gets involved in the chaos we've got brewin' here, things could get considerable nastier 'fore it all shakes out."

Boz ignored unforeseeable possibilities and stayed with the problem at hand. "Say you couldn't tell who fired first?" Sounded like he hated asking the question.

Crow Foot looked sneaky. "Well, no, cain't say as how I seen who opened the box with that particular one."

Boz scratched his neck and looked thoughtful. "Jack and Nance Nightshade will just naturally claim Ezra caused the killings when he started the dance. Be willing to bet my next month's Ranger pay on it. Know that's what I'd do, if'n the law came after me. Swear to self-defense. Hell, Crow Foot, his lawyers would probably call you as a witness for the defense."

Mose said, "What about the one you went and stabbed, Sheriff Stickles?"

"Oh, he crawled to his horse, got mounted somehow, and made it to the creek. Unfortunate drygulcher bled to death. We found him just this side of the bridge. Had a letter in his saddlebags addressed to a Jeff Proctor. Bunch of them Proctors from over in Comanche County. Maybe this is one of 'em what went bad."

By that point in the bloody tale, I'd made it halfway through the front door and yelled over my shoulder, "Gonna go check on Martye, Boz. See you boys later."

Angry swarm of citizens on the street had thinned out some. One or two, fortified with plenty of liquid nerve, shouted insults at me as I made my way over to our friend's store. Loudmouthed bastards acted right foolish. Would have gladly attended their rude behavior had it not been for my single-minded desire to make sure of Martye McKee's well-being.

Soon as my foot crossed the threshold, Marie Hickerson spotted me. Concerned lady came flying over, grabbed my arm, and pushed me toward her and Burton's quarters in the back. My other visits had restricted themselves to the kitchen and dining areas of their residence. For some reason I never realized, or imagined, they had bedrooms available once you passed through a doorway behind, and to the right, of her Excelsior cook stove. Barely large enough for the bed, nightstand, chair, and chest, the space had but a small window for ventilation. Smelled stuffy and close. I stood in the doorway and looked at the wild, beautiful girl asleep there.

Tiptoed my way to the chair and eased into it. Straight-backed and cane-bottomed, it groaned under my weight. Three-inch wound in the hair above her right eye must've scored the bone. Shade deeper and I would've surely spent that bit of time staring at a grave.

Martye stirred and woke to find me seated next to her. She smiled and reached for me. Held her hot fingers squeezed in mine for several minutes before she spoke.

"They killed my father, Lucius. Bullied up, picked a

fight, and shot him like a dog. All for a pig he'd raised from a shoat." A tear appeared in the corner of her eye, and she turned away, but went on talking. "Got to admit, we had a bushel of fun getting ole Maggie back from those thieves. But, oh, my God, the final tally on our effort was mighty dear."

I wanted to reassure her. Show off my manly side. Step up and brag on how the law, and the Texas Rangers, would see to her comfort and revenge, but I couldn't. Crow Foot's rendition of the shooting left too many holes to fill. Given the history of such proceedings in the courts, I knew Boz was dead-on accurate with his assessment of how such an effort would likely resolve itself. At that moment, my frustration and confusion with the situation at hand existed on a level more profound than any I'd ever felt.

Sat with Martye for most of an hour. As I got up to leave, she pulled me down and kissed my cheek. Whispered in my ear, "I've missed you, Lucius. Try not to stay away so long again."

"I'll keep myself nearby," I said. "Get some rest. Heal up. Want you well as soon as possible."

She tried to grin. "Don't worry. Now that you're back in town I plan on being up and around by tomorrow noon at the latest." Gently pulled the door closed, and headed back for the office.

Boz caught me climbing on Grizz and said, "Where you goin', Lucius?"

"Gonna pay the Nightshades a friendly visit." No mockery in my voice, but he didn't take to the idea.

"Now wait just a damned minute. You might want to think that 'un over for a spell. No need to go out there all half-cocked yet. Give me a day or so to mull this situation over, and then we'll all stroll out together. Let 'em know how the cow ate the cabbage."

Held my animal in place and said, "Don't worry, Boz. I'm just gonna mosey by the ranch and talk with Nance.

Maybe I can keep this killing spree from turning into any worse bloodbath than we've already got. Seems like we're working our way up to a dozen dead. From the looks of what's going on here in town, someone needs to warn the Nightshade band and their friends not to come back for a spell. Any of 'em show their faces tomorrow, or the next day, and there's gonna be more lifeless folks on the street. Sure as hell can't imagine we need that."

He thought over my rant for a few seconds. Crow Foot and Mose strolled out on the boardwalk and listened in. Finally he said, "Actually, you ain't got a bad idea there, son. Fact is Nance likes you. Yes. Yes indeed. Probably better if you make the visit alone, than all of us running in on 'em at the same time this soon after the shootings. Go on out and see what you can do. Think such a visit will be good for our side, no matter how you slice it. If you're not back by dark, we'll come a-looking."

Didn't necessarily like the rather ominous sound of his final words on the matter. Wheeled Grizz around in a tight circle. "Sounds good to me, Boz," I said, and kicked for Little Agnes Creek.

Made no effort to conceal my movements that time out. Rode right to the front of the main house, the same way Boz and me had on our first visit with the rowdy family. Youngest of the kids started yelling and running for home as soon as they spotted me wading the creek.

Pulled the Henry. Laid the iron-framed weapon across my saddle while Grizz was still knee-deep in water. Snapped the hammer thongs on all my pistols and cocked each one. By the time I reined up, the whole clan had assembled on the porch, armed to the teeth. Appeared my intent for a private conversation with Nance would have to wait.

Noticed several new faces in the congregation. Sweetwater gossip had more than a little basis in truth, as near as I could tell. Nightshade ranch tended to host a new bunch of cutthroats about every other day or so. Three newcomers had the hard-eyed look of living on the run, eating from campfires, and sleeping on the ground.

Jack went surly on me as soon as I pulled up. "Lord Almighty, please save the Nightshade family from the god-damned law. What the hell you want this time, Dodge? Come out here to brag on how you killed my friends up in the Nations? Want me to slap you on the back for dragging Tom and Latigo in for a certain hanging? Want to gloat over how Ezra McKee and that ole bastard of a deputy butchered my compadres like dogs? Well, you come to the wrong place. Ain't nobody on Little Agnes Creek gonna sing any of you do-rights' praises for murdering Jesse and Leo, or Chalky's boys."

No point getting involved in a spit-slinging debate with a man convinced he's right. Jack's addled, wide-of-the-mark reasoning didn't leave any room for discussion, and I figured the rest of his poorly informed family felt the same way. So I went ahead and dropped the whole load on him first jump out of the box.

Forced my voice as low as I could. Dozen or so people on the Nightshades' porch had to lean forward to hear me. "Jack, you folks have backed yourselves into the only corner of a burning building. The good people of Sweetwater won't put up with any new call-out shootings on Main Street where a well-liked man is killed and his daughter wounded. Won't abide another stage robbery, especially one that ends in double murder—even if none of you Nightshades had anything *directly* to do with it. Those folks feel they've been put upon for the last time, and all indications point to a community that won't stand for anymore disappearing livestock, or abuse of its citizens in the saloons, mercantile stores, or on the streets. You've hit the end of your bullying string."

Being out front made Jack bold. He stopped me with a raised hand and snapped, "Cain't prove none of that. Just a bunch of Rebel lies told on us 'cause my family sided with the Union during the Rebellion."

Wanted them to hear it all, so I kept moving soon as I could get a word in edgewise. "For all your protests to the contrary and assertions of innocence, you've made so many enemies in these parts that I genuinely fear for your family's safety—especially the women and kids. Those of us who carry the weight of the law on our chests will do what we can to avoid more murderous confrontation. But, I'm truly fearful that the next time you, and yours, ride into town looking for trouble, you'll get way more than you bargained for. You keep messin' 'round and oak-tree justice seems like an absolute certainty."

Thought there for a second Jack Nightshade's head might explode. "Damn you and all those like you," he yelled. I'm certain he meant it, but his words didn't fall on me with the force I expected. Wish I could say as much for his mother.

Dusky stood between her oldest son and daughter while I spoke. Soon as Jack got finished snapping back, the belligerent woman tore into me like a wounded mama bear. She shook a knotted finger in my face and screeched, "We're God-fearing country folk here, Ranger. Ain't done nothin' to nobody. Just tryin' to get along. And I'm damned if I'll tell my children to hide from the likes of those yammerin' gossips from hell in Sweetwater. We done put up with their brand of tall-tale-carrying and sanctimonious nattering muck since the day we got here. Vacated Alabama to get away from the same sort. Nightshades go where we damn well please. Enjoy the company of our friends. Do as we please, and don't need the likes of you to show up on our property and tell any of us a goddamned thing. You best put yourself on the road back to town, boy. Lest I turn my pack of dogs loose on you right this instant. One word from me, and you'll be crow bait."

Thought the old lady might snatch me off Grizz's back and set to kicking bloody hell out of me her very own self. But guess she satisfied any need for venom, and retired behind the shelter of her sullen, itchy-fingered brood.

The most vicious-looking of the three newcomers stepped up to fill Dusky's place. Heavy silver spurs chinked against the plank boards. Could barely see his leather breeches for all the pistols hanging around his narrow waist. Wine-colored silk vest covered a homespun pullover shirt, and the whole shebang got topped off with a short-brimmed black felt gambler's hat festooned with a turkey feather. Every piece of flesh available to the eye had a lumpy pink scar or pockmark on it. Bandanna, poorly tied around his neck, did little to hide a ragged chunk of flesh that someone left after what appeared to me as an attempt to cut his head off.

Left-handed, he removed the half-finished hand-rolled smoke dangling from his lips. "Name's Chalky Snow, Ranger. Sure you've heard of me." His rough, grating voice clawed its way across my eardrums. Coarse sound that emanated from a tobacco-stained, snaggle-toothed mouth led me to hope he didn't have much to say. He winked like we might be friends, or something. Ruffian obviously felt he was the most dangerous man around, and wanted as much fear introduced into the conversation as possible.

Didn't feel inclined to go giving the evil snake any credit, if I could help it. "No. Can't say as I have. Your name supposed to mean something, Snow?"

One eye closed, then the lid fluttered like a wounded bird. Appeared as though a pain hit him somewhere on the back of his head. "Well," he growled, "if'n you'd ever been down Round Rock way, you would, for damn sure, have heard my name. Chalky Snow's known as a pretty bad sort, from Waco all the way to the border."

Kind of liked the idea I'd managed to put a burr in his drawers, and decided to see just how far I could push it. "That a fact. My family ranches near Lampasas. Lived in the area most of my life. Usually when there's a skunk out and about word gets around, but like I said, never heard of you."

He bulled up and snorted, "Could be I might have to see to your education on the subject down the trail a piece, Ranger."

Didn't give him any slack when I shot back, "Little doubt, if you work a bit harder on your reputation, the law will see to your comfort and security at some point in the near future. As past events now stand, followers of yours have done enough damage in Parker County. I'd advise you to stay out of this problem henceforth, or I'll personally settle your hash myself." Mighty bold talk from a tenderfoot in the Ranger business, but I figured the badge on my chest gave more than enough official weight for the move.

Don't think ole Chalky had ever been challenged outright like that in front of those he counted as friends. He swelled his scrawny chest even more, got right bullfroggy, and eased a hand toward one of his weapons.

I brought the Henry around and kind of quiet and slow said, "You touch that pistol, Snow, and it'll be the last thing you ever lay a hand on in this life."

Nance jumped between us and shouted, "Stop it. Stop this right now." She glanced over her shoulder at the quivering gunman and snapped, "You're a guest in my family's home, Chalky. There's kids standin' behind you this morning. Put your anger aside. Don't make any moves that might get more than you dead."

Jack grinned. "Hell, Nance, let Chalky have Ranger Lucius By-God Dodge. Could be he'll kill this arrogant do-right and save me the trouble. Personally don't have no problem with such an outcome myself."

Being as how I'd jumped in feet-first and fully dressed, went ahead and really bored in on all of them. "Won't say but one other thing before I take my leave, Nightshade. You, family members, or any of your friends, even look like the killers responsible for the death of a Texas Ranger, and a force of Biblical proportions will fall on this place the likes of which can't be imagined in midnight's most fearful reveries. Company B will erase your peckerwood-sized ranch from the face of the earth." Finished with Jack and turned to Chalky Snow again. "Best saddle up and get on back to Round Rock, Snow. Ain't healthy for the likes of you in these parts. Make one bad move around here and your friends down south will be attending a funeral."

Backed Grizz all the way to the creek, then slanted my way across so I could keep them in view till I'd put some distance, and a few trees, between us. Didn't get in any hurry and couldn't have managed more than a mile or so when Nance caught up with me. She fogged up the trail fast as her animal could run. Came to a jumping stop so close, she was able to reach out and grab me by the arm.

"Please stop. I need to talk."

Altogether the most courtesy I'd heard from any of the unruly bunch that morning, so I sheathed the Henry and waited.

"Jack's gone crazy, Lucius. My brother's had a bent axel since the day Ma birthed him. But after Euless White-cotton killed Pa, he's gotten worse by a ox-drawn wag-onload. The towheads can't see it, and Ma won't admit it." Then she almost whispered, "Sometimes I think she's crazier than Jack."

Her chin dropped to her chest, and she shook her head back and forth like a weary dog. "I'm tired of this life, Lucius. My family's fought everyone we've ever met, anywhere we've lived. Been going on my entire life. Hell, we learned it from Pa. I loved the man because he was my father, but anger, quarrelsome behavior, and isolation from decent folk can prove a heavy burden once you've carried it long enough."

"Less than a month ago, you would have fought me yourself. Probably gone down shootin', Nance."

"True enough. But the day we buried Titus something came over me. Jack, and the rest of 'em, drank, ranted and raved about how Pa'd been foully murdered. But I knew the truth. Cap'n Whitecotton wouldn't have hurt a fly—lest he was pushed into it. Stood beside Pa's grave and, for the first time in my life, realized how desolate I really felt. Worst of it was when I finally recognized that the man I shoveled dirt on carried full responsibility for my family's disastrous behavior. I want out of this state of affairs alive, Lucius. Want to take the two youngest with me. But I can't do that right now."

No way not to be touched by the girl's wobbly dilemma. "Nance, do your best to keep Jack and Chalky out of town. They show up unbidden anytime soon, and there's no way to predict what'll happen. Can tell you certain that if you folks rode in for a visit today, wouldn't be any riding out. Lot of fair-minded, decent people looking for blood over Ezra McKee's killing. One more dumb mistake, no matter how trifling, could spark a fuse Boz, Crow Foot, Moses, and me couldn't keep from running to powder."

She pushed her hat to the back of her head and wiped a beaded lip with a faded bandanna. "Can't promise anything, but I'll do what I'm able. Jack gets the smallest notion into his head to visit Shorty Small's and there won't be any stopping him. God only knows what might happen. He's always been a hothead. And, if you put a thimble of any kind of coffin paint in the man, he can get out of control in a heartbeat."

"Handle your situation here however you can, Nance. I'll do as much as possible for you in town." Took my leave at that point. Looked back several times. She didn't move as long as I could still see her. Couldn't put a finger to it, but an uneasy sense of approaching calamity settled on me during my ride to Sweetwater. Just one of those things where you feel the hairs on the back of your neck stand up, and you don't understand why, till a spell later.

Next morning, over biscuits and bacon, Boz kind of surprised us when he said, "Think I'll take a ride to Weatherford and roundup a justice of the peace. Convene us an inquest into the murders we've had around here lately. Need to get all this down official and properlike. Want you boys to keep a tight lid on this bubbling jug till I get back. Shouldn't take more'n two or three days."

He headed out before noon. Must admit I didn't feel

comfortable without him around. Still considered my level of experience and ability to cope with more tragedy as sorely lacking, no matter how Boz felt.

His absence didn't seem to bother Crow Foot and Mose, though. They got along well for men of such dissimilar backgrounds, and obviously enjoyed their newly established relationship. Our greenhorn sheriff and his even newer deputy spent most of the next three days at a battered checkerboard Mose dredged up from somewhere. Left me to sit in the shade and contemplate nightly dreams of a lethal future.

Visited with Martye several times. She recovered well and, on the third day, I took her home in Mr. Hickerson's buggy. Poor girl's mother looked about as desperate as any living person I'd ever seen. No way to comfort her. Life on the frontier was hell on women, no matter how you cut it. Even worse for one burdened with three kids who'd just buried her husband. Couldn't picture how she would manage to survive.

Moon disappeared, and a storm blew through the night before Boz got back. Pitchfork lightning stabbed at the tortured earth for hours. Vague, unsettling nightmares woke me twice. The kind of visions you can't describe, but jerk you to a sitting position in your bed, while chicken flesh ripples up and down your back. No way to know then, but I'm fairly certain now what I felt was Satan's fiery breath.

For some unsettling reason Marie Hickerson's words came back to me, over and over. The day we arrived she'd said, "The Devil is coming to Sweetwater and won't be satisfied until he's collected many an unsuspecting soul. Take my word on this, there's a bloody time ahead." Woman should have been a mystic seer in a traveling carnival. But "bloody" don't come close to describing what happened next.

17

"... KILLED EACH OTHER IN AN ACT OF MUTUAL BELLIGERENCE."

CROW FOOT, MOSE, and me kept the lid screwed down tight as we could. Visited the saloons and talked with those willing to pause and listen. Told the angriest and most vocal where Boz went, and what he had planned. We thought our forthrightness about the matter had a calming effect on most of Sweetwater's openly belligerent citizens. Fooled me into believing they'd given up their anger for a spell, and perhaps some did.

Four days after we'd watched him amble off for Weatherford, Boz moseyed back across Walnut Creek in the company of a black-draped, stern-faced, runtified wart of a man riding the tallest dun horse I'd ever seen. Hideous little troll appeared a shade on the elderly side, and gave me reason to think he might need a ladder to get his creaking bones off that oversized beast.

As they made their way up the street toward us, I heard Mose mutter, "Looks like a dead rabbit riding an old ugly elephant, if'n anyone should ask me."

After he lit, shook hands all around, and stretched a bit, Boz turned to his pint-sized ferret of a companion, placed a familiar hand on the man's shoulder, and said, "Got lucky. Chief justice of the peace for Parker County had a full plate and couldn't make it. But I found us an honest-to-goodness former member of the bar. Like you boys to meet retired, but still active, Judge Solomon Pitts. He agreed to stroll over and conduct a full, and legally binding, inquest into Sweetwater's recent series of unfortunate killings."

The scrawny judge didn't offer to shake any of our hands. Clawlike fingers jerked a spotless hankie from his sleeve, and he went to dabbing at a soggy nose. Watery eyes scrunched up, and our Biblically named adjudicator sneezed like a ten-year-old girl. He nervously fidgeted with every button on his vest, toyed with a gold chain across his gaunt belly, and, in a high-pitched, tinkling, sissified voice squeaked, "Give 'em the summonses, Tatum, and let's get on with this. I want to be back in civilization 'fore the end of next week."

Over a scrawny shoulder, Pitts cast a sneering glance at the Texas Star. "We'll set up in that place over yonder. Tell the owner I want the use of his establishment beginning three days from now. That should give you and your men sufficient time to serve everyone on the witness list I had you compose, Tatum. Better for me if you boys can get the deed done by tomorrow afternoon. No bigger than this cow patty of a town is, shouldn't take that long."

He glared a path past us and carried his bedroll into the jail. Picked a spot in the only clean corner, then confiscated the table and one of our chairs. Solomon Pitts had everything set out like a visiting potentate in less than ten minutes.

Boz put us to hustling. For the next day and a half, we rode all over hell and half of Parker County. Most folks just nodded when we slapped them with a summons. Fact is, the only objection I heard came from Jack Nightshade.

We threw so much paper at Nance's brother, and his family, it must have looked like a blue norther of printed law blowing across Little Agnes Creek. One of those storms that come on so fast the front half of your horse is covered in sweat and the back half is frozen.

Titus's oldest son stood on his porch with a fistful of the writs in his hand and snapped, "This is bullshit. You can't make us show up for no damned inquest. We ain't done nothing illegal."

Crowfoot, Mose, and me sat on our animals, behind Boz, with rifles and shotguns cocked. Boz said, "That's for the court, in the person of Judge Solomon Pitts, to decide, Jack. And yes, I can make you appear. You ignore that document, and I'll have every Ranger in north Texas here in a week to pull this house down—plank by plank. Then, we'll drag you to town by the scruff of the neck, along with your dear ole white-haired momma, all the rest of your family, and any friends around as well. By the way, where's Chalky and them gun hounds of his?"

Jack got surly again and went to lying. "They left after that last visit Dodge paid us. Ain't seen 'em around in two or three days. Maybe they'll be back. Maybe they won't."

"Don't have no paper for him or his questionable sidekicks, not right now anyways. But if he shows up, bring him to town with you tomorrow. Tell him if he don't come in, I'll have the judge issue a warrant. We'll arrest him and drag him back."

Dusky Nightshade snatched the court order from her son's hand. Nance tried to stop her, but couldn't. The old lady jerked the pipe from her crusty lip and growled, "Getting mighty damned high-handed here, ain't you, Ranger Tatum? Feeling right powerful, I'd guess. Probably spread tales around town this afternoon as how you done got the Nightshades buffaloed with bona-fide legalities and such."

Sounded to me like Boz'd hit the end of his string with the Nightshade tribe's antagonism when he snapped, "No longer'n I've been in Sweetwater, this family has had some involvement in at least two killings. While there's probably not much way to prove any of the sordid rumors about what you do out here in your own home, or regulate who you folks associate with, we can control your behavior when you're in town. Now, you've got the o-fficial word from Judge Pitts. Near as I can tell, he's not the forgiving, forgetting type. You ain't in town tomorrow at one o'clock, and I can personally guarantee you'll regret that mistake till Hell freezes over."

Well, they came all right, in force—the whole ornery bunch. Roared over Walnut Creek, stormed up to the Texas Star, and elbowed their way to the best seats in Nate Macray's packed booze emporium. Forced everyone else off the front row and set up camp right in Judge Pitts's prunnified, pinched face. One of the most blatant acts of defiance I've ever witnessed before—or since. Got to thinking and figured their aggressive appearance was the first time I'd seen the whole clan lined up in a single row. Looked like a pew full of angry, heavily armed Baptist deacons and their kids.

Boz had Mose and me posted up front so we could eyeball the crowd. Mose pointed out, and named off, the whole bunch. "Course you know Titus's missus, Dusky. Then, by age, they's Jack, Nance, and Arch. They's the three oldest. Of them younger ones, Caroline and Martha is fourteen and fifteen, I 'spect. Judith's maybe thirteen. Jesse and his twin sister Analisa, they's the youngest. Cain't have managed but ten or eleven so far. Rumor's been goin' around for years of an older brother. But I ain't never seen 'im. Youngest of 'em ain't been caught stealin' or nothin' yet. They does go about carrying weapons, and I've seen 'em in Shorty Small's place with Titus 'fore he passed."

Chalky Snow and his boys came in as well, but kept to a corner as far away from the action as possible. The packed saloon might've held a hundred people, if everyone stood nose to nose and didn't move much. Chairs were arranged so the cow-country tavern took on the look of something like a courtroom. But they reduced the dusty bar's capacity to a body or two over forty. Really aggressive souls, who could elbow their way into leftover space, scrunched up, gawked, and filled the room to sweaty, wringing wet capacity.

Outside, the host of staring louts gaped through the Star's beveled glass window. Heated debates over violated "rights" resulted when belligerent yahoos in the street couldn't obtain an adequate point of observation. Several scraps broke out between them as had the choice viewing spots and others who wanted one so they could bear witness to the historical proceedings and brag on the episode afterward.

Didn't take but about ten minutes for the smells of sweat, tobacco, whiskey, and dung-covered boots to damn near overpower everyone inside. Judge hadn't been hammering at the problem but little over an hour, when several men had to carry their womenfolk out. Vacated chairs didn't stay empty more than a few seconds.

Pitts whipped through witnesses like a sharp scythe through dry buffalo grass. Stunned everyone with how rapidly the proceedings progressed. He suffered absolutely no foolishness, and could question, and dismiss, those testifying so fast the seat of the witness chair never had a chance to cool off. Started the proceedings at one in the afternoon. By five, he was finished.

Martye McKee testified last. Girl wept through most of the description of her father's brutal murder. Soon as she'd vacated the witness stand, the judge took a twenty-minute break, wrote everything up, then reconvened. Gaveled the room into somber-faced silence and announced his authoritative findings.

"As to the matter of the shooting of Titus Nightshade, it is my judgment that Captain Euless Whitecotten acted in defense of his own person and is held blameless in the matter."

Whole Nightshade tribe, except for Nance, jumped to its collective feet and set to screaming and cussing at the top of their lungs. Dusky Nightshade used the kind of language I'd never heard come out of a woman's mouth.

Judge Pitts rapped on his table so hard people in Fort Worth must have heard him. All us lawmen surrounded the irate family and forced them back into their chairs. Nance's chin rested on her chest. Girl appeared worn to a frazzle, and wearily shook her head.

Pitts yelled, "Any other such outburst and I'll clear this courtroom like a bolt of double-geared lightning." He pointed at Jack with his gavel and snorted, "You Night-shades park your butts in a chair—and stay there. Jump in my face again, and I'll have the whole damned bunch of you jailed." Threw a snarling glare around the room, jerked a pistol from his belt, dropped the six-shot author-ity on the table, and went back to reading. "As to the mur-der of the Baynes Company's driver and Wells Fargo agent, I find sufficient evidence for Thomas Alfred Run-yon and Ernest Poorman, alias Latigo Cooley, to be bound over for trial. I hereby instruct the sheriff of Sweetwater to deliver them to the jail in Weatherford for judgment and sentencing at the county court's earliest conve-nience."

No one much cared what happened to Snake River Tom and Latigo, not even the Nightshades. Rumble of nodded agreement swept through the crowd. Pitts waited for the yammering to quiet again before he continued. Everyone in attendance knew the most important announcement of the day waited a few gulping breaths away.

"In the matter of the death of Mr. Ezra McKee, I find that while Jack Nightshade should have known better, his actions were not sufficient grounds for Mr. McKee to react in the manner he did. Appears to me, from all available tes-timony, that Ezra Mckee and Roscoe Slidell killed each other in an act of mutual belligerence. And, further, that

Sheriff Stickles killed one Jeff Proctor in an act of self-defense. This hearing stands adjourned."

Everyone in the room, except the Nightshades, was stunned. Martye McKee and her mother looked like someone had slapped their faces with a wet cow flop. Solomon Pitts hopped up, hastily shuffled all his papers into a single pile, and stuffed them inside a battered leather case.

During the aftermath of anger, noise, and confusion, guess I was the only one who noticed something important. Jack Nightshade stepped to the judge's table, held out his hand, and pressed a small bag into Pitts' talonlike fingers. Didn't take more that a fleeting second. Ole Solomon flashed a thin-lipped grin, then dashed for the door, while the hoots and jeers of Sweetwater's most vocal citizens peppered the snaky bastard's bony backside.

Jack, and his still-fuming family and friends, pushed their way to the street and hustled over to Shorty Small's joint. Boz watched them go, shook his head, and mumbled, "Guess they're gonna celebrate. Don't see how this could've come out any better for 'em. Damnation. I thought sure Judge Pitts would hold their feet to the fire over Ezra McKee. Just cain't fathom it."

We stood on the Texas Star's step and watched as the packed town gathered into various vocal groups to discuss the events of the day. Some shouted curses as the Nightshades hustled past.

I leaned over and whispered in Boz's ear, "How tough you think it'd be to bribe a judge?"

He winked, grinned, and said, "Oh, not very. Long as you have the money, and nerve enough to broach the subject. Why do you ask?"

"No reason. Just wondered. But I'll tell you this, Boz, bet Judge Solomon Pitts is going back to Weatherford with more money in his pocket than he had when he arrived."

Tatum scratched his chin and mumbled, "Could be, Lucius, could very likely be."

All four of us lawmen armed up with everything we had, and took posts on the boardwalk outside Shorty Small's place. Crowds of locals milled around in the streets and acted like they wanted to take some action on their own, but didn't. The Nightshades kept their drinking to a minimum, then headed back for Little Agnes Creek around eight, but not before Jack had one final word with Boz on the matter. With the entire clan behind him, he pulled up in front of us and drunkenly leaned over his saddle horn.

"Law says this is over, Tatum. You, and the rest of your badge-totin' bastards, ain't got no more business on Little Agnes Creek, as far as I'm concerned. You come out our way actin' all high-and-mighty again, and the Nightshades will be talking back with lead. You can take that promise to the Texas State Bank in Fort Worth, Ranger."

He wheeled his mount around in a tight circle, and the whole band plowed through town leading a pack of barking dogs and squealing kids. Tribe thundered across Walnut Creek Bridge like bloody-eyed Comanches on a raid. Last face I saw was Nance's. She looked tired, confused, and angry.

Next morning, Boz pulled me aside and said, "The judge wants to head back to the county seat today. Insists I accompany him, and that Crow Foot bring Snake River Tom and Latigo along. Tried to get him to reconsider my presence, but he's afraid of retaliation from unknown Sweetwater citizens displeased with his findings. Looks like I'm gonna have to leave you and Mose alone for a few days, Lucius. Reckon you can take care of things hereabouts?"

I didn't like the sound of the proposition one little bit, but could tell Boz had no choice in the matter. "We'll be fine. Way I've got it figured, once Judge Pitts' ruling settles in on everyone for a day or so, they'll just accept the decision and get on with life."

Tatum stared up and down the street, shook his head, and said, "Maybe. But something deep down tells me there's more to come. Hope I'm wrong. Prisoners gonna slow us down. May take a day or so longer than the first trip, but I'll be back soon as I can."

Mose and me waved the judge, the jailbirds, and our friends away about two hours later. Then, we took a meadering, leisurely tour of town, just to let everyone know the law was still about and looking to their interests. Rest of the day passed, and nothing of any note occurred.

Hour or so before noon the following morning, Jack, Dusky, and Nance, along with Chalky and his two thuggish friends, charged in and headed for Shorty Small's. All of them, except Nance, tried to glare us down as they rode past.

Mose said, "Sweet Jesus, this don't look good a'tall, Lucius."

We decided it best to split up. Mose watched from our regular spot in front of the jail. I commandeered a well-worn corner on the bench just outside the Texas Star's batwing doors. My petrified perch gave me a good view of Shorty's, and most of the still-congested street. Good many of the country folk had traveled some distance for the hearing. A sizable number had decided to stay over, being as how their entertainment ended so abruptly. Unknowing visitor would've mistaken the crowded thoroughfare for a busy month end, or regular Saturday night meet-and-visit session of people, horses, wagons, and kids.

Got hungry 'bout two o'clock. Nate Macray brought me a sandwich and glass of warm beer. I'd barely choked the first swallow of a mighty good chunk of country ham down when I saw one of Chalky's boys stumble drunkenly out of Shorty's and into Hickerson's store. Would bet no more than two minutes passed when Lenny Milsap came hoofing my direction. Poor boy was so excited he could barely talk.

Broom in hand, he jumped to a fidgety stop in front of my chair, went to sweeping, and said, "Mu-mu-mister Dodge. Mu-mu-mister Hickerson be needing you ri-ri-right now. This v-v-very minute. Cain't wait."

Snatched up my Henry and won the footrace back to Hickerson's. Marie caught me on the boardwalk. "Burton's just inside the door, Lucius. Be careful."

Eased into the sunlit doorway. My friend had a shotgun leveled in the direction of Chalky's cornered man. "What's the problem, Burton?"

"This son of a bitch tried to walk out of the store with that thirty-dollar pair of boots he's holding. Didn't feel it necessary to pay for them."

Scraggly-bearded would-be thief swayed on his unsteady feet and yelped, "Thassh a black lie. Tole thish sanctimomioush thread pusher I'd come back wish the money. Jus' ain't got nairry'n on me right thish minute. I can git it. Maybe tomorrer . . . or the nesh day. Bastard pulled at 'ere big man-popper on me. Won't let me move. Said he'd kill me if'n I even thunk about such."

Low and steady, I almost whispered, "You can put the shotgun down, Burton. No need to blast him to Kingdom over a pair of boots." Turned back to the drunken thief. "What's your name, mister?"

Arrogantlike, he popped off with, "Jimbo Pine. Me and my brother Hubert rode in wish our friends, the Night-shades, for a few dippers of giggle juice. Needed me some boots. Thish here storekeepin' son of a bitch won't let me have 'em."

"No money, no boots," Hickerson snapped.

"Store's his, Pine," I said. "His store, his rules. No money, no boots."

Drunken lout threw the goods across the room and shouted, "Well, goddamn both of yew to Satan's fiery pit. I'll git the money and come back later." He stumbled to the door and pushed past us. Ran into Marie Hickerson and almost knocked her down. Over his shoulder, as he unsteadily wobbled back to the Nightshades' favorite watering hole, heard him mumble, "Or maybe I'll jush come back wish some friends."

Burton sighed. "I'd appreciate the gesture if you'd stay around for a spell, Lucius. Bet he's good for his word. But if he shows up with money, I'll be amazed."

Marie dragged a rocker out for me. Had a nice cushion in the seat. Got right comfortable. Almost napped off watching Lenny move his favorite piles of grime from one end of the boardwalk to the other. Less than an hour had passed when Sweetwater's favorite family, and their friends, poured out into the street like a nest of angry wasps. Jack, Chalky, Jimbo Pine, and his brother whipped their mounts my direction. Nance and her mother laid back and waited at Shorty's.

Lenny swept his way up next to me and smiled at all the noise and dust in the air when the horses came to a jumping stop in front of us. I went to stand. Never made my feet.

Hailstorm of bullets swept over us like a cloud of buzzing hornets. Somehow Lenny landed on top of me. Everything got wet and sticky. My ears rang so loud I thought my head would explode.

Then, the blackest night I've ever seen wrapped itself around me like a funeral shroud.

18

"... SURE AS HELL'S HOT
AND SNOWBALLS ARE COLD."

MUDDY-MINDED AWARENESS GRAD-
ually chewed its way back into my brain. Confusion and
darkness came and went. Faces, twisted by a blistering
ache behind my eyes, bobbled above me. Heard people
talk, but couldn't make any sense out of it. Their words
hummed inside my throbbing head. Down in the deepest
part of my ears, screams bounced about. Sounded like someone's innards were being removed with hot horseshoe tongs.
By and by, I came around seated in Marie Hickerson's
rocker. Couldn't figure out how I got there. Caked blood
covered the front of my shirt.

Moses Hand wiped at my face with a wet rag and said,
"You be all right, I think. Just got a nice grove in the noggin over here by your right ear. Take a spell to grow the hair
back, but you're gonna look just fine in a few days." Then
he dabbed at a spot on my right side. "This here crease
done bled a lot, but I don't think she caused much real

damage. Pistol ball bounced off all the muscle under there. Furrow looks nastier than it really is."

I tried to speak. Nothing came out for several seconds. Finally mumbled, "All this blood mine?" Screams from inside the store answered me. Agonized, horrid, pitiful sounds that caused dogs in the street to howl. Sent chicken flesh crawling along my spine.

Mose snatched a nervous glance behind me and said, "Naw. Most belongs to Lenny Milsap. He caught two in the stomach, and another in the spine, Lucius. Terrible wounds. Boy's gonna die an unspeakable death. Doc Bryles been working on him near'bouts an hour now. Guess they've poured a bucket of whiskey down the boy's throat. 'Pears like they ain't enough liquor in the world to stop his hurtin', though."

My senses kept spinning, but I noticed only women and kids milled around in the street. Pulled at Mose's sleeve and said, "Where are all the men?"

"They done possied up and beat hell out to the Nightshades' place. Near'bouts every able body in town went. Mr. Hickerson, Mr. Bashwell, Shorty Small, the Bruce brothers, and anyone from the country what could carry a gun. Musta been nigh on fifty of 'em. Even Cap'n Whitecotten had some of 'em lash him to a horse. Most folk herebouts loved Lenny, and had no cause not to like you. Seein' you boys get shot down like Jack and his friends done sho' nuff snatched the cork outta the jug. Town's murderous angry, Lucius."

"Why didn't you go with 'em?"

"Mr. Hickerson said he thought it best if I stayed here with you. Wanted somethin' like law around should the shooters come back. Besides, I wouldn't have gone anyways."

"Why not?"

He pressed a fresh bandage to the gash in my side, shot a worried look toward the bridge, and said, "Looked to me like every other cracker in the posse was braidin' up rope for a dose of oak-tree justice, or revenge, whichever you prefer. Don't do to be a black feller when white folks get lynchin' on they minds. This here pissant deputy sheriff's badge won't mean a wagonload of postholes to men as mad as that bunch. They hit the briars and brambles, and git enough liquor choked down, no tellin' who might end up danglin' from a tree limb."

Doc Bryles took a break from working on Lenny and did what he could for me. He poured whiskey over anything of mine that was still bleeding. Looked right grim behind his thick spectacles and said, "Douse the hole in your side about every two hours. Keep the bandage loose where some air can get to it. You should be fine. One on your head might not allow you to tolerate a hat for a spell, but I can't see either of these scratches killing you."

"How's Lenny, Doc?" I said.

The sweaty, bloodstained sawbones wearily removed his glasses, and used his shirtsleeve on a clenched brow. "He'll die—sure as Hell's hot and snowballs are cold. My wife, Melinda, and I'll stay with him till his time comes. Ain't nothing else to be done."

Couple of hours later, Mose helped me limp over to the jail and the prospect of the modest comfort it allowed. Just outside the door, we stopped and watched as the posse straggled back into town. Tired, dirty, and looking whipped, most of them headed for the saloons. Burton Hickerson appeared right gloomy as he peeled away from the others and reined up at our hitch rail. With some difficulty, the weary grocer dismounted and loosened the girth on his horse. He motioned us inside, threw his hat on the sheriff's desk, and slumped into a chair.

After almost a minute, I got tired of waiting for him to speak. Image of a cross-eyed, purple-tongued Nance Nightshade flashed across my brain and I blurted, "Well, what the hell happened? Did you catch 'em? Kill the whole family, or what?"

Hickerson looked sad when he said, "Got to their house. Couldn't find a soul. Rode up and down Little Agnes Creek. Beating the bushes for most of an hour. Somebody spotted sign that led over toward Denton Creek. Lost whatever they claimed to see 'bout ten miles into Wise County. Course you couldn't have formed up one good tracker out of every drunken nimrod in the party today. Not finding the shooters made all them that was already intoxicated even madder. They charged back to the Nightshades' ranch and burnt the whole shebang to the ground. Nothing left but ashes. Even burnt the outhouse and that old wagon Titus and his bunch first came to town in. I tried to stop 'em. Didn't have no luck with my efforts, though."

I said, "You think the Nightshades got away?"

"Couldn't say, Lucius, but I can tell you one thing for certain. If Lenny Milsap dies, the mob will press Mose into service and go after 'em again. Everyone knows our deputy sheriff for the best tracker in the county. Lord help that benighted family, and their friends, if the town's broom-lovin' saint of a boy passes."

Sweetwater's gut-shot "saint" held on for quite a spell. Didn't stop screaming till nearly ten o'clock that night. Gave up the ghost so abruptly, when the silence finally came, it felt as though a great weight had been lifted from the town's collective broken heart. About a minute later, red-eyed unreasoning anger boiled out of the saloons and into the streets. Men rogued about, yelling and hollering almost all night.

Burton woke us at first light. Sounded like the voice of doom when he said, "They want Mose, and they want him right now." I glanced out the window. The enraged town's seething fury rippled up and down Main Street like waves on windblown water. Looked to be near'bouts half-a-hundred men in the street. Never seen such resolute rage on the faces of that many people at once.

For the first time since we'd met, deep lines of concern creased Moses Hand's ebony countenance. A twitch gnawed at the corner of his mouth, and his hands trembled. He held his hat in supplication. "I'd rather not do this, Mr. Burton, sir. If it's all the same to you."

Hickerson shook his head. "We ain't got no choice in the matter, Mose. You're the only one can find the people who killed Lenny."

I could tell there was no profit to be had in arguing the point. So I pulled at my friend's sleeve and said, "I'll go along. See to it you're safe."

He balked again. "You don't know these things like I does, Lucius. This is a bad 'un. No good gonna come from anything done today—a tale of horror and bad dyin' just waiting to happen. Besides, you're hurt and don't need to be out ridin' around all over the countryside on no horse."

I leaned closer and whispered, "You can't refuse this time, Mose. All you have to do is look outside. I'll go along. Should anything out of the way occur, they'll have to take my life before they come for yours."

Don't ever let anyone tell you it doesn't hurt to get shot. The holes and furrows Jack and his friends put in my hide ached, burned, and stabbed at me with every fall of Grizz's big ole feet. Time or two, I got so dizzy I almost passed out. But the promise I'd made, and concern for my friend's safety, kept me going.

Got about an hour's respite when we pulled up at what remained of the Nightshade ranch. Ashes still smoldered. Mose made Burton, and the rest of the party, stay put while he scoured the surrounding countryside for sign. Seemed as though I'd barely laid myself out under a big gnarly cottonwood when the whooping and hollering went up again.

Original posse'd been on the right track when they started searching around Little Agnes Creek the day before. Took him a spell to sort out the jumble of various prints, but

Mose proved his amazing hunter's skill, and followed the desperate family's trail north along the shallow stream for about five miles. Then, the route turned into the sea of prairie grass and headed south and west.

'Bout half past noon, the leading edge of our still-fuming band of whiskey-saturated avengers came upon a low hill situated beside a sluggish, unnamed brook lined with blackjack oak and walnut trees. As we got closer, I remember thinking as how, from the top, you could probably see near everything that moved in any direction. Jack and Chalky couldn't have found a better spot for an ambush if they'd drawn up plans.

No one had really expected the fleeing killers to stop. Early on, Shorty Small had even expressed the opinion that we'd most likely have to chase them all the way to Mexico.

A torrent of hot lead, from the rocky hill, renedered his self-assured presumption into nothingness. Struck down four of our party in the first barrage. Two of them died before their limp corpses hit the ground. Nearly half of those who survived the initial hailstorm of bullets panicked, tucked their cowardly tails, and ran like scalded dogs. Any doubt in the minds of those who stayed as to the deadliness of our situation vanished when the first man died.

Waist-high grass doesn't offer much by way of shelter, when bullets are zipping around your ears like angry bees and all you can hear is screaming and dying. But I got lucky beyond words that deadly day. Landed in a sheltering depression in the hard ground. Pulled Grizz down on his side next to me. Took months to teach him that trick. First time I'd ever had any real, life-saving need of it. Wouldn't be the last.

Return fire erupted from our resolute band of liquor-brave leftovers. A rippling line of rifle and pistol balls nibbled its way up the hillside like some kind of invisible, meadow-eating monster. Dust, rock shards, dirt clods, wood chips, and grass blasted into the air. I'd still bet today that inside half an hour Sweetwater's avengers fired near a thousand rounds into the Nightshade gang's sheltering mound of dirt. So much lead filled the air, it's a wonder anyone in front of the scorching onslaught could breathe. Muzzle flashes set several spots of grass afire. Spent black powder added to the confusion and overall insanity of the situation.

Now and again, I'd raise up on my elbow to try and see whatever I could. Bolder members of our crew inched their way forward behind a blazing shield of gun work. The drifting smoke stung my eyes and looked like blue-gray thunderclouds shifting on the breeze.

Then, as suddenly as it started, the yelling, screaming, and bombardment ceased. Heard my name called. Stood to see Mr. Hickerson, and several of the town's other *leading* citizens, use rifle and pistol barrels to push three men my direction.

Jack Nightshade, Chalky Snow, and Hubert Pine must have had a cupful of shot in their gory hides. Pine caught the worst of it. Man sported so many holes, I don't know how he stood and walked. All three dropped to their knees in a wallowed-out spot where some of our men had tried to take cover.

Pine went to carping and moaning. He said, "If'n you're gonna hang us, get it over with and done. Ye've already kilt brother Jimbo on yonder bloody hill. I ain't got no reason left to live. I'm shot to hell and in right smart of intolerable pain, Ranger."

Chalky's ashen face cracked into a smile. He looked me straight in the eye and sneered. "Thought I'd kilt you in Sweetwater, you lucky son of a bitch. Give back one of my pistols, and I'll finish the job." Blood trickled from his twisted mouth. I counted three terrible, life-oozing wounds on his person.

Someone shouted, "You ain't gonna get another chance, you murderin' skunk." Half a dozen lengths of hemp fell over the kneeling men's heads like rainwater. Before I could catch my breath, all three were dragged, kicking and yelping, to a twisted, gnarly piece of oak tree located hard by the stagnant steam's edge.

Pulled my pistol but, before I could make a move to prevent what I knew was coming, a knot of red-eyed drunks pressed in around me and waved their weapons. Mose caught my hand and urgently whispered, "Let it go, Lucius. You try and stop 'em, could get us both killed. These folks ain't the same as you knew 'em. They's a mob now."

In less than a minute, men I'd once thought reasonable and law-abiding hog-tied their wounded captives and had the terrified killers mounted under the hanging limb— ready for God and Glory. Burton Hickerson offered each of the bullet-riddled trio an opportunity to speak. Hubert Pine couldn't do anything but make noises like a wounded animal. Someone whipped the horse from under him, and put an end to his ramblings. Chalky's face turned into a mask of fear and resolution. Jack didn't even bat an eye.

Hickerson asked Snow if he had anything to say. The south Texas bad man blinked away sweat and grime and snapped, "Hell, no. I ain't got nothing for you bastards. No way I'm gonna make this any easier for you. Go on and do your—" He never finished his sentence. A rump-slapped horse set him to swinging.

You go and hang two men, and I can guarantee the act gets people's attention, sobers them up pretty damned quick, no matter how much coffin varnish they've consumed. Got mighty quiet under that tree limb for a spell.

I pushed my way to a spot near Jack and said, "Where's Nance and the rest of your family?" Don't think he heard me. "Tell me where she is, Jack. Maybe I can still save her."

Mose elbowed up to my side. "He be gone, Lucius. Already be in another place."

I spotted the hand holding the quirt as it drew back and whistled forward. But that blink of time lasted long enough

for Nance's brother to look down at me with glassy eyes
and say, "You're too late, Dodge. It's all over." Heaven's
judgment snatched him out of the saddle. His boot brushed
against my cheek like a lover's kiss.

Lynch party held Mose and me at gunpoint for near an
hour. As one of our guards put it, "Just to make certain them
as we've done went and hung is good and dead." Once the
rabble seemed satisfied with the outcome, I tried to get them
to cut Jack and his friends down, so we could take the bodies
back to town for burial. The mob wasn't having any of it.
They even dragged Jimbo Pine's corpse out of the rocks and
strung him up too. Someone scratched the misspelled mes-
sage "Theaves and Merdurers" on pieces of rough butcher
paper and attached them to the hanged men's vests.

Posse finally gathered up its wounded or dead, and
headed back for town. A pretty solemn lot by then. Mose kept
saying, "We'll come back later, Lucius. Let it go for now."

Two or three miles down Little Agnes Creek from the
Nightshades' place, we ran upon a scene so horrific, it still
fills my nightmares. In a sheltered hollow near the slow-
moving stream, fifteen to twenty of the yellow-bellies
who'd crawfished from the gunfight with Jack and Chalky
lounged about on saddle blankets like they were on some
kind of solemn-faced picnic.

Drunken oaf named Baxter Toomes, who owned a ranch
near Reno, staggered forward and bragged on their handi-
work. "We caught 'em doublin' back toward their house.
Guess they didn't realize we'd done went and burnt 'em
out. No need for you law-bringing sons of bitches now.
Took care of the thang ourselves."

Dusky, Nance, Caroline, and Martha swung, broken-
necked, from the limb of an enormous live oak. Brother
Arch, trussed like a slaughtered animal, knelt beneath the
lifeless women. Someone had shot him in the back of the
head—execution style.

Of a sudden, time turned into syrup and the day got so

quiet I could hear violent thoughts swarming around inside my brain. Behind me someone muttered, "Good God almighty." Mose grabbed my arm and said, "Take care, my good friend. Take care."

One of the liquor-soaked yobs I couldn't see said, "Ain't gonna be no more fiddle-playin' and belly-rubbin' out here on Little Agnes Creek, by God. Guess these ole gals done lifted their dresses and danced their last dance round these parts. Dancin' with the devil now. Right where they should have been all along. Yessir, dancin' with the devil."

Guess I must have gone crazier than a sunstroked lizard. Jumped off Grizz, pulled my big bowie, and went to hacking at the rope holding Nance's body. Something whistled by my ear, and the world went black on me again. Didn't wake up till late the next afternoon, stretched out in one of the Sweetwater jail's bunks. For a few seconds, my mind played tricks on me, and I went to thinking as how maybe the whole business was nothing more than a monstrous nightmare. Then I felt the pain in my head, the ache in my side, and knew the truth.

Crow Foot sat in a chair he'd dragged into the cell, and fought to keep his eyes open. Through rubbery lips I mumbled, "When did you get back, old man?"

Startled, he snapped upright, scratched his chin and said, "Early this morning. Been keepin' you company ever since."

I tried to sit up, but stagecoach-sized drums pounded inside my skull, and invisible hands pulled me back to the pillow. My old compadre lifted a damp rag from my brow and replaced it with a fresh one.

"Got quite a lump on your already abused noggin there, Lucius. Way Mose told it, you was tryin' to cut the oldest Nightshade gal down when your former running buddy, Judas Tierney, darted out of that pack of rope-swinging dogs and whacked you from behind."

"Thought I ran his sorry ass out of town sometime ago."

"Well, he musta been lurkin' around in the shadows all

along. Guess he seen his chance to get a dose of retribution and took it. Mose said Bob Horton jumped on Tierney and damn near beat the poor chucklehead to death, right on the spot. Ain't nobody seen ole Judas since."

"Where's Boz?"

"Mose took him out to the hanging trees. They've been gone all morning. Them bodies still out there swinging, I suppose. Seems once the deed got done, no one had grit enough to cut 'em down and bury 'em. Now the whole town's too scared to do anything. 'Fraid they might be next, I expect. Boz wanted to settle on anything we could do to kinda make what happened right by them poor dead folks. Man was madder'n seven kinds of hell when he rode out. Sure would hate to see what's left of anyone brave enough to cross him today."

Of a sudden, through the fog of pain clouding my tortured brain, a thought came to me that I couldn't account for some of the Nightshades. "Anyone know what became of the three youngest of Nance's brothers and sisters—Judith, Jesse, and Analisa?"

As Crow Foot pulled a pocketknife and picked at his fingernails, he said, "Posse found 'em hiding in the mes-keet not far from the home place out on Little Agnes Creek. Some of those blood-crazed bullyboys musta not seen enough death for one day. Wanted to string them kids up too. Heard Mose, Burton, Nate Macray, and a few more good folk who still had their saddles cinched down nice and tight, wouldn't allow the deed. Hear tell Marie Hickerson has the kids now. Rumormongers are sayin' she's made arrangements for some of her relations up in Chico to take all three of 'em."

I'd heard all I wanted for a spell. Napped off again for another hour or so. About the time I got able to stand and move around, Martye Mckee showed up. She flew into the office and grabbed me like a drowning swimmer on the way down for the third time.

Shimmering green eyes floated in pools of tears when, with forced formality, she said, "I have to leave, Lucius. There's no way we can make the ranch go without Pa. Texas is mighty hard on women, especially those with no man in their house. We have kin in Shreveport. One of our neighbors, Mr. Amos Tolar, along with his three sons, has offered to deliver us to the bosom of our relations. I fear if we don't go, Mother might loose her mind. She's not acted right in the head since Pa's death, and I can't take care of her, and the kids, alone."

Something in her eyes begged for help I couldn't give. Certain she wanted me to offer marriage, or anything that would keep the inevitable upheaval confronting her from happening. All I could say was, "Guess I'll never get to see what a barefoot girl riding a pony Comanche-style promised to show me out behind the church house. Will I?"

Disappointment and resignation crept into her voice. "No, I don't guess you will." She flashed me a clenched, bitter smile, kissed my cheek, and added, "If God's willing, maybe we'll meet again someday. In the meantime, I'll pray for a future of more favorable circumstances, and that you won't forget the kisses you stole off a barefoot girl from Sweetwater."

Nothing much left to say. The uncomplicated assessment of her familiy's situation, and our budding, but doomed, relationship, didn't leave me anything in the way of room to wiggle. Clung to each other for as long as we could. Then, less than five minutes after she'd blown into the room, I stood in the dust-laden street, out front of the jail, and waved good-bye as two wagonloads of kids and belongings rumbled across Walnut Creek Bridge, and disappeared. Just like that, she was gone. Never saw her again.

Boz and Mose came dragging in an hour or so after beautiful Martye vanished from my life forever. Stricken look on Tatum's face told the whole story. Tried to speak with him, but he waved me off and hustled over to Hickerson's. Took several more days before we could round up three spring wagons and a like number of wooden crates, large enough for whatever might be left of nine corpses.

Boz tried to make me stay behind the day he, Crow Foot, and Mose went out to collect the bodies. And, while my wounds still had me stove up and limping around like I was born ten years before Methuselah, I made it as clear as rainwater he'd have to shoot me in the foot to keep me from making the trip.

But Sweet Weeping Jesus, I'd give anything I have today if I hadn't forced that particular issue. Worst piece of work I'd ever done, up till then, or for most of my life afterward. Poor folks were pretty much nothing but festering gobs of worm-riddled rot. We got them down anyway. Pulled a wagon beneath each limb, chopped the ropes, and let them drop. Put three in each box.

Nailed the last lid down and Boz said, "No point taking this gruesome cargo back to Sweetwater. I've been told, in no uncertain terms, not to try and plant 'em in the town's cemetery." So, we spent most of the next day on Little Agnes Creek, near what was left of the Nightshade house, digging a hole big enough for those uncommon coffins.

That night, after we'd all bathed and scrubbed ourselves raw in an attempt to rub away the sickly smell of death, we sat in the jail and polished off two bottles of bonded-in-the-barn tornado juice. Talk commenced hot and heavy as how we should arrest everybody in the county who might've had anything to do with the lynchings.

But sometime around the darkest part of midnight Boz said, "Naw, we're just gonna have to lay back on this one, boys. Messages comin' my way indicate nobody's gonna testify against nobody about nothing to do with the 'Nightshade incident.' Folks are petrified scared. Don't know whether you've noticed or not, but lips round here are clamped together like the lids on seal-tights. Only three survivors have vanished. Heard they got sent to Chico, but

I cain't get a straight answer on the question when I nerve up enough to ask."

After a few seconds of stunned silence Mose said, "Mighty sour pill to choke down for you fellers. But I've seen as much before—lots of times. Mob done had its way, and that's the end of this story."

Well, not exactly. Boz and me worked like field hands, for almost three weeks, in an effort at getting someone to step forward and offer to testify as to what occurred that lethal day. Overwhelming opinion expressed by everyone we talked with went something along the lines of, "Well, we don't know anything about those killings. Weren't there when they happened, if such horrors took place at all. Besides, sounds like Old Testament justice prevailed, by God. People who killed Lenny Milsap deserved to die."

Pointed out to some of them as how I'd been present for the event, and seen them in attendance myself. To a man, everyone I accused said, "Well, that's nothin' more'n your word agin' mine, ain't it, Ranger. Besides, I've got lots of witnesses as'll testify just the opposite. Say I was in Shorty Small's all day." Boz just shook his head and finally gave up trying.

In the end, Crow Foot handed his sheriff's badge to Moses Hand, and we saddled up and headed back to Fort Worth. No one came out to say good-bye, or wish us well. Not even Burton and Marie Hickerson. Pretty sure everyone in Sweetwater was gladder'n hell to see us go.

EPILOGUE

DON'T KNOW WHAT Boz told Captain Cul-
pepper. Whatever he said must've worked. I didn't hear another word about the matter from either of them—leastways,
nothing official or informed. As the years passed and piled
up, gruesome rumors, labled as legends, filtered around
about those lynchings. But that's all it ever amounted to—
rumors and legends.

Within a few days of our return to Company B's head-
quarters, Grizz and me struck out for the Indian Nations.
Reports from over Fort Smith way had it that One-Eyed
Whitey Krebbs and Erasmus Delaquoix were headquar-
tered in the Winding Stair Mountains. The Light Horse police believed Whitey and Raz had robbed and murdered a
schoolteacher named Richard Gill from Tuskahoma. Mr.
Gill sometimes worked as an amateur biologist who studied cotton boll weevils, or some such nonsense.

Seems Gill wandered out in the big cold and lonely, hunting for bugs in the wrong place. Whitey and Raz caught him

up short. Killed the poor man, deader'n Julius Caesar, for his saddle and a pair of boots. Tried to hide the body under a log, but left the feet sticking out. Whiskey-drinking sport named Tuney Bailey happened along and spotted the corpse.

I scoured the area around Tuskahoma for a month, and never did discover hide or hair of Whitey and his murderous partner. Eventually came to the conclusion that maybe the locals were mistaken when they identified the same men who'd murdered my father as the killers of Richard Gill.

Wag put Boz and me on the trail to San Augustine, upon my return from the Nations. Life-long disputes, between the Wilbarger and Duckworth factions in the east Texas area known as the Redlands, had bubbled up into some of the worst feuding anyone had seen in years. Didn't take long for the urgencies of the present to push the past into a dark, sheltered corner of my heart and mind. Never forgot what happened to the Nightshades, but found any reason I could not to think on it much.

Bumped into Moses Hand in Fort Worth some years after those awful events. We sat down in the Delaware Hotel's bar to pass the time and have a drink. He said, "Stayed on as sheriff, you know. But Sweetwater never recovered. Somehow, seemed most like the town done kilt itself with all them hangings. Folks drifted away. Never came back. Mr. Hickerson and Shorty Small closed up they places the same week. Packed my belongings and left, right after that. Heard tell Mr. Hickerson's conscience beset him something awful. Some told around as how he put a pistol in his mouth and ended the misery not long after he and his missus scampered out."

"Ever go by the Nightshade place?" I said.

He twirled his glass in the wet circle on the table. "'Fore I left town, checked on the graves we dug over on Little Agnes Creek. Couldn't really find them, for certain sure. Truth is, you'd never know anyone had ever set foot on the place. Kids all 'round town started calling the spot where the women wuz strung up Hangman's Holler. Said it were haunted. Talked to several young'uns what swear they seen a fair-haired girl, dressed like a man and wearin' pistols. Said she looked right pitiful, and lost. But you know how kids is. Could just be their 'maginations working at 'em. Ain't been back in years. Hear tell nothing but empty buildings, and windblown dust, left of the place these days."

We stood outside the Delaware's main entrance, shook hands, and said good-bye. Mose turned and started away, but stopped and said, "I know you and that gal Nance had almost become somethin' like friends, Lucius. Not a day goes by I don't think on her and them other poor women. And how we might have been able to save them. Plagues my dreams, you know. Plagues my dreams." He lurched away like a man lost in thoughts of dreadful nightly reveries.

Well, now you know the dreadful tale. Lucius By God Dodge's deepest, darkest, most carefully guarded secret. Never breathed a word to anyone before this. Never even mentioned the gruesome episode to my wife, and, hell, I told that woman damned near everything—from my wild days in San Augustine, to the Salt Wars over in El Paso, and a lot more.

I've scribbled my last pencil to a stubby nub. Big ole chunk of gum eraser's almost gone, done rubbed out so many misspellings and such. But I've still got three or four of them Big Chief tablets left. Noticed something odd lately. Once I started this process, nightmares of my own, that'd pestered me for over fifty years, disappeared. Guess maybe I'll have to write out some more of my adventures. 'Cause like Tilden said, "You never know but what somebody just might publish one of these tales."

More important, to me anyway, the ghost of Nance Nightshade stopped coming to the foot of my bed every night. Could be the poor girl's spirit has finally found some much-needed peace just by knowing her tragic story got told.

The Reverend Ellis P. Thunderation Jones preached a mouthful on how confession is good for the soul. If I can put a few more of the apparitions that parade through my slumbers to rest by telling their stories too, guess my initial stab at writing will be worth it, don't you think?

ABOUT THE AUTHOR

J. Lee Butts left the teaching profession in 1981 to seek a career with IBM in Los Angeles, California. After six years with Big Blue managing customer relations for MGM, 20th Century Fox, Orion, William Morris Agency, and other large entertainment accounts, he left the company and worked for a time in the public sector.

Jimmy faithfully attends weekly meetings of the DFW Writer's Workshop in an ongoing effort to hone the skills required of accomplished authors. His previous Berkley novels are *Lawdog, Hell in the Nations,* and *Brotherhood of Blood.* Other works include nonfiction titles and short pieces for various magazines and reviews. Butts now makes his home in Dallas, Texas.